THE GIRL IN THE DARK

DEIRDRE PALMER

Storm
PUBLISHING

To request permissions, contact the publisher at rights@stormpublishing.co

Ebook ISBN: 978-1-80508-072-5
Paperback ISBN: 978-1-80508-074-9

Cover design: Lisa Horton
Cover images: Trevillion, Shutterstock

Published by Storm Publishing.
For further information, visit:
www.stormpublishing.co

For my amazing Monday writers' group friends: Merryn Allingham, Sue Griffin, Wendy Clarke, Liz Eeles, Margaret Mounsdon, Emma Jackson, and Suzanne Merchant

PROLOGUE

ELLEN

It was my first day back at work after Christmas and New Year. A day of catch-up office chat and leisurely tackling of routine tasks, interspersed with constant trips to the coffee machine. I left bang on five, the freezing air like a smack to the face as the revolving glass doors ejected me into the winter dark.

As I was swept up in the crowd moving along Victoria Street towards the underground and mainline stations, I noticed a black-and-white checked baker-boy cap bobbing up ahead. I was fairly sure it belonged to Georgie, who worked in our staff restaurant. I didn't bother catching up with her. It wasn't that sort of situation. In any case, Georgie didn't like me. She talked to me like she talked to everyone else – an endless stream of chitchat – but there was always an edge to it when we were face to face, almost as if she resented me. Which is ridiculous, as I've never given her any reason.

I'd already lost sight of Georgie by the time I reached the entrance to the Tube. I scanned my Oyster card, stepped onto the escalator and descended.

It was his scarf I noticed first. Red and cream, in a large

checked pattern. It was wound loosely around his neck, one of the fringed ends thrown over his shoulder, the way a child might wear it, or a model in a fashion magazine.

He wasn't the only person to own a scarf like that – it was by a popular, mid-range designer and available in every good department store – but as it caught my eye, I immediately thought *Rosanna*, and then *Matt*.

My sister had given her lover a scarf like that for his birthday. He'd liked the Rupert Bear books as a child, and it was the closest she could get to Rupert's red and yellow scarf. She never did tell me how Matt reacted to the gift: whether he laughed about the Rupert thing, or found the whole present idea alarming and intensely awkward. What did he tell his wife? That he'd bought it for himself? Depending on what kind of man he was, and the kind of woman she was, this might have sounded plausible. Whatever, he was wearing the scarf, because as I looked more closely, I realised I was looking at Matthew Leyton.

The crowd surged through the tunnels. I almost lost sight of him, and then I saw him enter the tunnel for the northbound line, and I followed.

He reached the platform before me, and I shuffled through the crush, keeping him in sight. I'd met him once, briefly, and Rosanna had shown me photos, mostly unclear, neither of which were much to go on. But his height – around six-two – and his facial features, from what I could see, showed enough of a resemblance for me to be ninety-nine per cent certain it was him. And ninety-nine per cent was good enough.

He was wearing a long, dark-coloured Crombie overcoat, unbuttoned. He was standing still, close to the platform edge, not looking along the track but straight ahead. The resigned stance of the regular commuter.

The train was due any minute. There were people in front

of me on the platform. I threaded my way between them, tracing a diagonal path to the left and arriving next to Matt without much difficulty. I put a hand on his arm. He must have thought he was being jostled by the crowd because he didn't respond immediately. And then, as my hand didn't move, he turned. His face showed puzzlement, and then it cleared, zipping my ninety-nine per cent up to a hundred.

Whether he remembered me from our one brief meeting is debatable, but I have a look of my sister, so I imagine he knew who I was.

My hand gripping his arm through the thick material of his coat, I launched into a tirade. 'Lying, cheating bastard! Selfish, egotistical dickhead! Blokes like you deserve to burn in hell! That's it, go home to your poor wife and make out you're the perfect husband. If she doesn't already know what a scumbag you are, Matt Leyton!'

Even as the words spewed out of my mouth, I knew I had no power over him; that he'd laugh in my face. But even if my little performance had no impact, it would make me feel better. In fact, I already did.

Heads turned in our direction. There was muttering. Matt himself stayed silent, pulling his arm to free himself, shrugging at bystanders: *Who is this madwoman?*

And then, as I carried on lambasting him, he spoke, his tone aggressive, his voice a violent hiss.

'Stop this! What d'you think you're doing? You're making a show of yourself.'

I went to pull at his arm again and he swung around and laid a firm hand on my shoulder. He was breathing heavily. I think he was about to try and calm me down but I wasn't having any of that. My hand on his forearm, his gripping my shoulder, we tussled on the platform edge. The train approached, filling the tunnel void with dusty paintwork and lights.

More lights flashed before me as my anger flared and caught fire, a red wall of brilliance across my vision.

I let go of his arm, moved my hand to the middle of his back and pushed, hard. The train rocked alongside the platform.

Matt was gone.

Somehow, I reached the exit tunnel, leaving behind the echo of a single shout from somebody in the crowd and a collective gasp that had risen to the arched roof like a reprise of the air-rush in the tunnel. Unless I'd imagined both of those: I couldn't be sure. Why had nobody stopped me leaving? Too many people, too much confusion?

At the top of the escalator, I dared to turn and glance over my shoulder, expecting to see a posse of guards pelting towards me, people shouting *Stop!* But no. I was free to leave, it seemed.

The wail of sirens met me as I surfaced, and continued all through the taxi ride home, skewering the buzzing in my head. Breathless and sweating, I'd half run, half walked, back along Victoria Street before hailing a black cab and stuttering out my address to the driver, not daring to risk joining the taxi queue outside the train station. My veins were singing with shock and fear, and the horror of what I had done. The overload of sensation took over my mind, held it captive, leaving no room for anything else, and as we crossed Vauxhall Bridge there was a moment when I forgot where I was going, forgot I was going home. Even where home was.

Luckily, the driver had no such memory lapse and duly delivered me to my block of flats in Brixton. As the cab plunged into the night with a wink of orange lights, I stood outside the main door, gulping in air and letting my heartbeat settle before letting myself in and taking the lift to the second floor.

. . .

'Did you get a taxi home?' Rosanna twisted around on the sofa to look at me. 'I was looking out and saw you get out of one.'

My sister wasn't due back at work until the following Monday. Nothing better to do than gawp out of the window, apparently. That wasn't fair. I didn't retract the thought.

'Well, then, you know I did,' I said, then tempered my snappy response with the offer of tea.

I was suddenly desperately thirsty, and downed a tumbler of tap water while the kettle boiled. The kitchen, arranged on a dais at one end of our long living room, was quite tidy for once. The day's washing-up stood in the draining rack. There were even signs that Rosanna had made a start on dinner. Sausages flopped on the grill pan, oven chips on a baking tray.

'I didn't start cooking,' she said, turning down the sound on the TV. 'I wasn't sure when you'd be in. Why didn't you get the Tube, anyway?'

My hands were shaking as I switched the oven and grill on to heat up and reached into the cupboard for a tin of sweetcorn. 'It's perishing out. First day back and everything.'

'Okay.' Rosanna had already lost interest in my travel arrangements and was gazing at the phone in her hand.

Ice pooled in the pit of my stomach. This was how it had been these past few weeks. Rosanna, her phone glued to her palm, waiting for Matt to get in touch, in no doubt whatsoever that he would. Never giving up on that certainty – and it was certainty for her, never just plain old hope. And me, trotting out well-worn sympathetic phrases and agreeing with every excuse my sister came up with as to why she hadn't heard from her lover, in order to keep the fragile peace: he'd broken his phone, or lost it. The family had gone away for a post-Christmas break, his wife's idea, somewhere countryfied and remote, with no signal. He'd been struck down by the flu bug that was doing the rounds. Or there'd been some sort of family crisis, et cetera, et cetera.

And anyway, she and Matt had agreed that a break over the festive season would be sensible. A ploy to avoid suspicion at a time of year when emotions run high. This, according to Rosanna, was how they'd left things at the end of the special night that had not been special after all.

Matt had loved the dress, though. Adored her in it. Promised he would take her somewhere better, somewhere wonderful, where she could wear it again, soon. Which was obviously why the dress was still hanging in Rosanna's wardrobe and hadn't been returned to the shop, as she'd said she was going to do.

Matt's promise had carried Rosanna through Christmas, and we'd had a pleasant enough time, even though it was just the two of us. Aunt Margaret had invited us to spend it with her and Uncle Derek, but I could tell by the tone of the message she was only asking out of duty, and I politely declined on behalf of Rosanna and myself, wishing them all the joys of the season. My sister's exact words had been: 'If they think I'm spending Christmas holed up in a titchy cottage in the Lake District, drinking sherry, playing Scrabble and eating her godawful cooking, she can bloody well think again.'

I was inclined to agree, apart from the cooking thing. Aunt Margaret's food was plentiful and tasty, if lacking in imagination. But the journey to Cumbria in the depths of winter didn't bear thinking about.

We'd invited a few people to the flat on Christmas Eve. A random collection of work colleagues, casual friends who lived close by, and neighbours we were on chatting terms with. The buffet was minimal, the alcohol extravagant. Consequently, Rosanna and I had raging hangovers on Christmas Day and stayed in bed until 1 p.m. Still in our pyjamas, downing copious amounts of juice, we exchanged presents. I gave Rosanna a silver necklace and matching bracelet. She gave me pale grey cashmere trackies and a matching hooded top, soft as clouds, the kind of thing I'd be afraid to wear in case I got chocolate down the front. We didn't bother cooking Christmas dinner but ate pizza and ice cream from the freezer, then crashed out in front of the box with more wine.

But as Christmas slipped by and New Year approached, Rosanna's laugh went up an octave and her phone checking grew more obsessive.

Rosanna and I had a prickly relationship. Petty jealousies on her side, sheer aggravation at her thoughtlessness on mine. Plus, she could be hellish annoying at times – most of the time, actually. I'm sure she felt the same about me. But she was my sister; I wanted her to be happy, I really did – and pinning her hopes and dreams on a man who was playing a game as old as time was never going to make that happen.

Stubborn she might be, but I'd never known Rosanna to be so naïve, so short-sighted, as she became when she got involved with Matthew Leyton. She said it was love. I'd call it addiction. I used to listen to her going on about him as she thrust her phone under my nose with the latest photos of him. Photos she seemed to be taking without his knowledge, as far as I could tell from the lack of pose. But Matt was married, and unlikely to be overjoyed about being snapped, so it made a kind of sense.

I'd stopped trying to reason with her long ago, given up pointing out the age difference – he was thirty-nine, or so he said, my sister twenty-five – as well as the obvious fact of his unavailability. She never listened anyway.

Rosanna needed protecting from herself, and I'd shouldered the task because there was nobody else. Our parents were gone. They died in a plane crash when I was eight and my sister ten, on their way home from one of our father's business trips to Zurich – he did something in insurance, I was never sure exactly what. Our mother had gone along for the trip, leaving my sister and me with the family next door.

After the accident, Aunt Margaret and Uncle Derek, childless themselves, had taken us in and raised us in their modest semi in Bexleyheath, and while I've never doubted that they cared for us, as far as they were concerned, their job was done.

Now, Rosanna threw her phone down on the sofa and came to stand beside me as I started cooking, although I didn't know how I was going to eat anything.

'You okay to do this?' She balanced on one foot, a hand on the countertop to steady herself.

'Yes, I'll do it.'

Rosanna wandered out of the room, and I felt relief at the temporary respite as my mind scrolled backwards to the Tube station.

The sheer horror of what I'd done was gnawing at me like a plague of hungry rats. When I'd seen Matt walking towards his homebound train without a care in the world, I'd only intended to confront him, give him the full benefit of my opinion. What he was doing was a common enough crime; even so, nobody was allowed to hurt my sister and get away with it, not while I was around. He may have already ended the affair by the time I encountered him, even if my sister didn't know it – his silence certainly pointed in that direction – but that made it worse, somehow.

Then, as he laid a hand on me, trying to stop me yelling at him, I wanted to kill him. I really did. It may have only been for a few seconds, but it was long enough. Long enough for me to give way to the red-hot burst of uncontrollable anger that consumed me.

How was I to live now? If I deserved to live at all, after what I'd done. Visions of CCTV footage assaulted my mind, the indisputable, filmic evidence of my crime. Arrest surely wasn't far off; I didn't understand why it was taking so long. The waiting only increased my terror, if that was possible.

Meanwhile, I would just have to carry on as before, acting

the part of the concerned sister – which I was, but in an entirely different way from how Rosanna imagined it – whilst knowing that the man she claimed was the love of her life was dead.

ONE

ELLEN, THREE WEEKS LATER

'Shall we go shopping? Over Oxford Street? There are still sales on.'

I'm not really in the mood for shopping. I only suggest it in desperation, and to stop myself checking online for the hundredth time to see if Matt's death has been reported – strangely, it hasn't as far as I can see.

It's a cold, bright day and the rooftops are silvered with frost. Razor-sharp light floods the flat, giving me a headache. I feel claustrophobic, but don't want to go out on my own and leave Rosanna.

She has seemed fairly normal lately, even cheerful, in a brittle kind of way. No longer is her phone checked every half-hour, at least, not in my presence, although I suspect she still does it in private. But the cheerfulness is all on the surface. It makes me fear for her and want to protect her more than if she was mired in despair.

The irony of this doesn't escape me.

I've thought long and hard about what happened that day – what I *made* happen. There has hardly been a moment when I haven't thought about it on some level. I try and kid myself that it wasn't me, that I was merely a witness to the horror. It doesn't work; my brain refuses to be fooled.

Sometimes, I allow Matt's wife and children to enter my head, and the poor train driver, too. But they appear as shadowy figures from another point in time. I try to imagine his wife, flanked by caring relatives, in the courtroom during my trial, but I see only a cardboard cut-out figure on the bench. Not real. But of course she is real. Her name is Laura, Rosanna said. Did she know about her husband's affair with my sister? Rosanna said not – *of course not!* – but Matt may have lied about that. I've never understood how Rosanna could believe every word he said whilst knowing what an inveterate liar he was. And she used to accuse me of being naïve.

Now, Rosanna swings her feet up onto the sofa and picks up a paperback she is only pretending to read – the bookmark hasn't moved in ages. 'No, you go shopping if you like. I'll stay here.'

I cross to the window and look out. 'It's a beautiful day. It'll be nippy but the air will do us good,' I say, as if I haven't heard her.

After a while, Rosanna decides she will go out after all, but not to the West End. We wrap up in fur-lined parkas, drag on boots, then walk down to Brixton Village and jostle amongst the crowd, browsing the stalls in the covered market. We root through vintage jewellery, hold bright cotton skirts against ourselves, and try on multi-coloured knitted hats with pompoms and ear flaps, laughing at ourselves in the mirror, and at each other. Rosanna tries on stripy woollen gloves, lifting one pair after the other off the stand before she settles on a navy, yellow and pink pair.

'Haven't you already got some like that?' I say, as she hands over the cash.

'Did have. I lost them. Left them on the Tube, I think.'

I roll my eyes and laugh again. For a time, we're just two

sisters perfectly in tune with each other, out for some Saturday morning fun with not a worry in sight. I feel good inside, settled, but it's only a brief respite. I try to hang on to the feeling but it's like trying to grab handfuls of morning mist as it rolls along the river.

We choose a coffee shop and sit at a delphinium-blue table with flat whites and a plate of churros to share. Strings of brightly coloured bunting loop above our heads. We sit opposite one another in silence as the bustle goes on around us and the throng passes by outside. My sister seems deep in thought, not with me at all, and I feel unaccountably lonely and cut off from the world, as if I'm on the outside, looking in.

Rosanna dips a churro into the ramekin of dark chocolate sauce. 'He still loves me, you do realise that? We are still together, Matt and me. This is just a hiatus.' She sighs theatrically, and bites the end off the strip of sugary dough.

I'm used to these sudden mentions of her lover, out of the blue, with no context, as if we've already been talking about him.

There is another angle at play here. My sister has always enjoyed a drama, especially where her love life is concerned. She seems to take a perverse pleasure in these things, not something she would ever admit.

I remember a summer's evening in Bexleyheath. I was hulling strawberries and Aunt Margaret was rolling out the pastry for a strawberry tart when the front door banged open. We watched, open-mouthed, from the kitchen, as Rosanna flounced into the hall, her face tear-stained but her chin set in fearsome determination. She saw us looking.

'I'm having a massive row with Steve! He's being *horrible!*'

'Come in and shut the door, dear,' Aunt Margaret said, levelly. 'Go and watch TV with your uncle. That'll calm you down.'

'Oh, I'm not stopping,' Rosanna flung at us. 'I've only come to get a cardigan.'

Moments later, she banged out again, presumably to pick up the argument with Steve while the fire was still stoked, only with less chilly arms.

Aunt Margaret and I just looked at each other and carried on with our tasks.

I watch my sister now as she demolishes the last churro and licks chocolate sauce from her fingers. 'Rosie, don't you think there could be another reason you haven't heard from Matt? Maybe he's had a rush of guilt and decided it's time to stop. Have you thought of that?'

My heart hammers as the untruths fall out of my mouth. But what else am I supposed to do? If Rosanna can forget Matt Leyton and the fantasy she's built up around him, she'll be free to find happiness elsewhere. It's my job to lead her in that direction, at whatever cost to my sanity.

'You've never been on my side.' Her eyes are accusing. 'You've always tried to stop me doing the things I wanted.'

Not everything, Rosie. Just the things that will hurt you.

'That's a bit overdramatic. And not true, as it goes.'

I'm wondering what new excuse Rosanna has invented to explain Matt's silence because, sure as you like, there is one. She answers my unspoken question.

'It's obvious to me what's happened. His wife's found out. Maybe not about me, as such, but she suspects him of having an affair and he's having to lie low, and not take any unnecessary risks.'

I give her a small smile. 'Even if that were true, he would have found a way of getting a message to you by now. You haven't heard from him since your date before Christmas, have you? When you wore the pink dress.'

The dress Rosanna bought for her date with Matt was a strappy affair with sparkles across the bodice and a calf-length skirt comprising artfully overlapping layers which would swish when she walked. I can picture it now, hanging on her wardrobe door – I'd gone into her room for a closer look while she was in the bath. The dress was pale pink, although in the gloom of the dimly lit bedroom it looked almost white, ghostly. The three-figure price tag bore the name of a Knightsbridge boutique, the kind of place where the minute you walk through the door your voice becomes a whisper.

The dress had set alarm bells clanging in my mind. Either her date with Matt was a special one, or – and I was more inclined to this version – my sister intended to make it so. Matt, she would announce triumphantly when she came home at some ungodly hour, was ending his dead marriage and now belonged to her, lock, stock and bloody barrel.

Okay, maybe things wouldn't have progressed that far, but she'd have made sure the seed was planted and watered so that it was only a matter of time before the shoot broke through into the light. Rosanna, I had the impression as soon as I saw that dress, had waited long enough.

I was more afraid for my sister that night than at any other time. There was so much about her so-called love affair that didn't align with her story. Did she not find it strange that Matt had never been to the flat, not once? I certainly did. Since I already knew about him, it made no sense that he had never once called for her or popped in for coffee. I wasn't a hermit, I did go out in the evenings, but there'd never been any sugges-tion of the two of them enjoying a cosy night in.

Some of the things he told her about his background, too, and home life, seemed sketchy and prosaic. If he was seriously interested in my sister, in love with her, as he claimed – or rather, she did – wouldn't there be a deeper connection between them? Instead, the relationship was all fluff and no substance, like candyfloss.

If I could see that, why couldn't she? The idea of that man

ever leaving his wife for my sister was so ludicrous I almost laughed. Almost. Instead, I had felt inordinately sad for Rosanna and her misplaced confidence and her wasted dreams. And angry at the bastard who encouraged them.

'Rub it in, why don't you?' Rosanna says now. 'He's staying away to protect me, don't you get it? He knows I'll realise what's going on. We're on the same wavelength, Matt and me. He knows I'll wait for him until things have settled down again.' She smiles, a secret smile with a stubborn edge, telling me I know nothing about her relationship and that I should keep my opinions to myself.

My heart reaches out to her. She isn't giving up easily. Apart from the phone checking, I wonder if she's been actively trying to reach Matt. Perhaps I should find out. I'll be less likely to trip myself up if I'm up to speed with her activities.

'Did... does Matt use his normal phone with you, or does he have a separate one?'

Rosanna sighs impatiently. 'Ell, I told you before. No, he doesn't have a separate phone. He said it would be more risky if his wife should find it than if he used his normal one. He keeps it close to him all the time, and she never looks at it.' Rosanna looks thoughtful. 'Or she never used to. Why are you asking me that, anyway?'

'No reason. I just wondered. So, have you messaged him, or tried to ring?'

'Of course not. He made me promise right at the start that I'd never ring him. Anyway, I'm not that stupid.' Rosanna's gaze leaves mine for a moment, then returns. 'Well, okay, once I messaged him, that was all. Just once. I did it during the day, a week or so back, when I knew he'd be at work, not at home.'

'And?'

'The message wasn't delivered.' Her mouth twists, as it does when she's puzzled about something. 'But as I said, if his wife's suspicious, maybe he's blocked me, temporarily. It would be sensible, wouldn't it?'

'I guess so.'

Where is Matt's phone? Under the dark shelf of the platform edge, smashed to bits? In a sealed plastic bag in a police locker? An icy shiver passes through me.

I press on, although the conversation is becoming increasingly uncomfortable. Which is nobody's fault but mine, I realise that. 'Okay, so have you looked for him in any other way? Messaged him through Facebook, or the company website?'

'He's not on social media. That's not Matt. And the company website doesn't allow contact with individual staff.'

She has looked then, I think.

'I wouldn't do those things anyway,' Rosanna says, raising her chin. 'I'm not a stalker.'

I sigh. 'I didn't say you were. So, what about his office? Have you tried there?'

'You want to know a lot, don't you?'

'Only out of concern, that's all.'

And because it feels best that I know these things, though for what purpose I have no idea, other than keeping some semblance of normality, however fake.

'If you must know, I went there last week. I sat on the wall opposite his building, around lunchtime. And then I remembered he usually has lunch at his desk – his architect's drawing board, I mean. He told me that when I suggested meeting for lunch one day. But I got a bit panicky after a while in case his wife was around, keeping an eye out, so I left. It made me feel even more stalkerish. I didn't like that.'

I nod. 'Where exactly is his office?' I ask, as if I'm not that bothered.

'Not far from yours. A few streets back. It's a tall building, coloured mint green. Trubridge and Jensen – that's the name of the company – has floors at the top.'

I know the building she means. I've seen the company name on the plaque outside. Funny how it's only a stone's throw from Printabilly. I never knew that before. But, of course, he uses the same Tube station as me. *Used*... Thinking about Matt in the past tense doesn't come naturally, and just as well.

'Anyway, Ell, you don't need to be concerned about me any longer. I've decided it's best I get out of London as soon as possible. It won't make any difference to Matt and me. As long as I've got my phone, he can reach me. I'm going to Cornwall to stay with Sarah and Jay. I'm not sure how long for. I haven't decided. They said they'll be pleased to have me.'

I rock back on my chair. The legs screech on the unforgiving tiled floor. 'You're leaving? Leaving London?' *Leaving me.*

My brain locks onto practicalities, forcing back the wall of emotion that threatens to come crashing down. 'But what about work? Will you take extended leave or something?'

Rosanna works for a recruitment agency in Bond Street; a 'people' job, perfectly suited to her personality.

She waves a vague hand. 'Oh no, I'm packing it in. That way there'll be no pressure. I'll take all the holiday I'm owed and that'll almost cover my notice period. I can always get another job, if and when I need to.'

My throat tightens. Despite what Rosanna said about not knowing how long she'll be away, it's obviously going to be more than a couple of weeks. I decide to press her on this; I need some clarity as to what's happening here.

'So, when d'you think you'll be back?'

'I just *said*, I don't know,' Rosie says, with a touch of impatience. 'It depends how I feel.'

So much for clarity.

'You didn't tell me you were planning to go away. You never said a word!'

Rosanna's eyes soften. 'I know. I'm sorry. I've been thinking about it, but I only finally decided yesterday. I was going to talk to you about it. Of course I was.' She smiles. 'You don't mind, do you? You'll be okay. You'll have the flat all to yourself. Think about that.'

I am thinking, and I don't like it one bit. I'm scared. Scared to be left on my own with nothing to dilute my terrifying thoughts.

Sarah and Jay are friends of Rosanna's from her college days – Sarah taught on the business course Rosanna took. I've met them a few times and liked them. They married, moved to Cornwall, and renovated an old farmhouse. It sounded idyllic, the way my sister described it when she went there for a holiday. It will do her good to get away, I can see that. And isn't this exactly what I want for her? A diversion, a signpost pointing the way to a future that doesn't involve Matt Leyton?

I sigh. We were going to embrace the future together, Rosie and I, not separately. *Unless I'm banged up in a prison cell.* But I've stopped factoring that into my vision. I just can't deal with it.

Rosanna and I might have our differences, but we've never been apart. After our parents died and we fell under the stilted care of our aunt and uncle, a kind of unspoken pact grew between us. It was always going to be us against the world, and I need it to stay that way, at least for a little longer. Apart from Aunt Margaret and Uncle Derek, who are so far off the scene as not to count, I have nobody else.

My hands cradling the coffee mug are shaking. I'm losing my anchor; that's how I think of my sister. She is, after all, nearly three years older than me, although mostly we act as if it's the other way around.

An image comes into my head. I'm floating out to sea in a tiny boat, being carried helplessly towards the horizon, and over it, to vanish off the edge of the world. Since I turned into a killer, my head has been full of such vivid imaginings. It's a miracle I manage to put one foot in front of the other, let alone function as a normal human being.

As if this is anywhere close to normal.

I finish my coffee, put the mug down and clasp my hands tightly together below the table edge. 'Okay. Well, it sounds as if you've got it all worked out.'

'It was love at first sight, for both of us. Eyes meeting across a crowded bar, that old cliché.'

Rosanna clearly hasn't heard what I said, but perhaps I didn't speak aloud.

She gives a little laugh. 'I didn't believe in love at first sight until it happened. Well, you don't, do you?' She looks at me, her gaze intense, willing me to understand, as if this is the first time she's said it. 'He *is* the one, Ellen. I just have to be patient and hold my nerve, as Matt will be doing, right now. You'll see.'

TWO

ROSANNA

Ellen didn't want her to go, Rosanna could tell, despite the brave face. And although Rosanna didn't show it – at least, she doesn't think she did – it actually took some courage to leave London, even for a short break. Or a longer one, depending on how she feels once she's in Cornwall. She has to do this, though, she really does.

Okay, it's a tad late to start playing hard to get with Matt – understatement! – but he has to know she has a life, too. If – no, *when* – he gets in touch, she'll make him wait a while before she hotfoots it back to London. Not *too* long, just enough time for him to miss her, and worry a bit, and appreciate her more when they are together again.

This is how it will pan out, because it *has* to. The alternative is too painful, too hard, to even contemplate; although at times during these past weeks, it's been all too easy to believe Matt has disappeared off the face of the earth.

The train isn't full to capacity, and Rosanna has two front-facing seats to herself. In the window seat opposite her, a kind-faced woman, late sixties or so, turns the pages of her newspaper before folding it into a solid square and starting on the crossword. The seat next to her is empty.

Rosanna takes out a paperback and puts it on the table but doesn't open it. It's a long way to Exeter, the first leg of her journey to Cornwall. There's plenty of time to fill. And plenty of time to think. Is this a good thing? She doesn't know.

A family occupies the four seats across the aisle. At least, she assumes they're a family. Mum and dad, two sons. The boys are facing Rosanna. She guesses they're around ten and thirteen, give or take a year, the ten-year-old a smaller edition of his brother. They're playing games on tablets; she can hear the beeps and pings, faintly. Although the train is only now gathering speed, crisps already spill out of packets on the table in front of them, and bottles of juice sprout paper straws. The older boy reminds her of somebody. She looks without seeming to stare, and then it comes to her. *Theo*. He looks like a boy she used to know at school. Same dark, brooding looks that will kill the girls when he's older. Or maybe already does.

Rosanna's mind backtracks through the years. When she was thirteen, Theo asked her out on a date. Like that was ever going to happen. Aunt Margaret and Uncle Derek imposed a ludicrous curfew of 7 p.m. with the generous concession of an extra half-hour on Fridays and Saturdays. As for having a boyfriend at her age, that was way off the scale of permissible socialising. An absolute non-starter.

Theo was in the year above, and it was a miracle he'd noticed her at all, let alone asked her out. Lots of girls fancied him. A mere sighting of Theo in his rugby kit could cause a ripple of giggles to pass along the dinner queue. He could have gone out with any number of girls, but Rosanna was the chosen one and she wasn't going to let a little thing like a curfew get in the way.

And so she did the obvious thing, and lied. She said she'd been invited to supper at Martha's house, and Martha's family didn't eat until half past seven. Her aunt pronounced this habit as 'slovenly' and 'downright unhealthy' but agreed it would seem rude to refuse, and as it was a Friday, it wouldn't hurt to be a little later 'just this once'.

Aunt Margaret's words bounced off and rolled away. All Rosanna heard was a big fat 'yes'. What would happen when it reached the sort of time she might be expected home she hadn't yet figured out. Something would come to her, she had no doubt about that. But probably by that time, she wouldn't care.

The date with Theo had never happened. She'd been in a huddle with Martha outside the science block, lining up her willing alibi and running through the *what ifs* and *supposings*, shoring up the bank of lies in case something went wrong, when Martha glanced over Rosanna's shoulder and made a face. Rosanna turned to find her sister standing nearby. Near enough to have heard every word, which her stony face and folded arm stance confirmed.

The news reached home before Rosanna did. Aunt Margaret and Uncle Derek could be heard discussing it behind the closed kitchen door, her aunt stating in a voice that brooked no argument that Rosanna must be punished for her deceit, her uncle mildly excusing it on account of the plane that crashed into the Swiss Alps and made orphans of the girls. Ellen had been sitting on the stairs looking guilty but smug at the same time.

The punishment – grounded for a week and no TV – wasn't too hard to take. Her sister's treachery hurt the most. But according to Saint Ellen, she'd acted entirely for Rosanna's own good. Hadn't they agreed they would stick together, always? Look out for one another? Ellen had made up her mind that Rosanna was too young to be going out with boys, especially an older one like Theo, and that was why she'd given away her secret. It was for her own protection, she said – as if that was ever going to wash with Rosanna.

She'd overreacted, of course – yelled at Ellen and accused her of trying to ruin her life. And, worse, she'd told her sister she had an evil streak in her that went all the way through, 'like the writing in a stick of rock'.

She shouldn't have said that; she'd known immediately the words were out of her mouth. Ellen had looked so crestfallen she'd nearly taken it back and said sorry. Then again, Ellen hadn't apologised for squealing to their aunt and uncle, and anyway, it was none of her business who Rosanna went out with.

The bedroom door had closed with a bang, and her sister's feet were heard attacking the stair treads as if they, too, had caused offence.

The Theo thing had been smoothed over in time and consigned to the junk-pile of forgotten sisterly spats. Funny how these things come back into your mind when you're least expecting them, Rosanna thinks, as she surreptitiously watches the Theo lookalike tapping at his tablet with one hand while steadily posting crisps into his mouth with the other.

The landscape streams past the window, a blur of green and brown, and blue-and-white sky. Rosanna opens the paperback at the bookmark but doesn't feel like reading. The pancakes she ate for breakfast are heavy in her stomach. The cream was probably a mistake, but she couldn't disappoint Ellen when she'd gone to so much trouble. She reads half a page, then gives it up to a little daydream about Matt instead. Or, actually, Ellen is on her mind again to begin with, because what she's remembering now is coming home after her last date with Matt back in December – the last for now.

She'd got home annoyingly earlier than expected, and flopped onto the sofa in a manner which, she realised too late, had given too much away. Ellen hadn't asked how her evening had been, and where Matt had taken her, as she usually did, even if she was only pretending to be interested. She hadn't said a single thing, except to warn Rosanna not to drop tea down the dress if she was returning it to the shop. Had she said she was returning it or had Ellen made that up? Anyway, her sister's silence had felt judgemental, but at the same time Rosanna had been grateful for a reprieve from the questioning.

The date hadn't been entirely successful. She'd tried too hard, firstly by wearing the pink dress, which had cost a whole chunk of her salary but suited her so well. Secondly, by planning too far in advance, and getting it wrong. Well, a little bit wrong. She could never be *completely* wrong with Matt, that was a given. She knew him too well.

Mentioning Christmas Eve had been a test to see how far she could push things. Not far enough, as it turned out. Of course he wouldn't be free on Christmas Eve, as he'd patiently explained, leaving her feeling just a tiny bit foolish. At least she hadn't got as far as actually inviting him to the party in the flat, and then had to listen while he smooth-talked his way out of it.

But her suggestion that they hold their own celebration after Christmas provoked a different reaction. Matt had looked at her with such longing she could tell immediately that his vision matched hers. Champagne in the bar of an expensive hotel, a delicious lunch trolleyed to their room by a discreet waiter. Then more champagne which they wouldn't finish because by then they'd be in each other's arms and giving way to the sweetest, almost unbearably exquisite passion. Similar scenarios had occurred during their time together, the choice of hotel dictated by convenience, a sandwich and a tumbler of vodka-tonic as a prelude to sex, if she was lucky.

It would have been their first Christmas. She'd wanted it to be special.

And then he'd gone and spoilt it with his talk of ending it.

Rosanna physically flinches now and shuffles her feet beneath the table as she recalls, almost word for painful word, the scene she made in the restaurant. The woman opposite lifts her eyes from her crossword, gives her a slightly questioning look and turns it into a small smile. Rosanna tucks her feet in neatly and pushes away the latent embarrassment. So what? It was only a tiny little scene, over in a flash. Looking back now, it was nothing at all. It was just the shock and panic that had made her overemotional and, for a moment, out of control.

He'd been panicking, too; she realised that, afterwards. It wasn't easy for Matt, leading a double life, knowing what lay ahead. She could tell that was the only reason he'd said those hurtful things. Matt loved her. They were *in love*. Hadn't it been said often enough? Falling in love when you least expected it, especially for somebody in his situation, had the power to unsettle and splinter the world into fragments that could never be fitted back together in the same way. She was one of those fragments. She belonged in Matt's world. There was a place for her, she knew that, and so did he. They might only have known each other for a matter of months, but when you knew, you just knew, didn't you?

Rosanna finds her phone in her bag and checks for messages, then puts it away. She's not allowed to look again until Exeter. She makes these rules for herself, all the time. And breaks them.

Do not think about kissing Matt until the Love Island *credits have rolled.*

Do not check messages until first tea break at work.

Do not look at photos of Matt until five more buses have gone by.

Do not pass Go. Do not collect two hundred pounds.

Rosanna suppresses a sigh, gazes out of the train window and wishes that being good at waiting was one talent that had not passed her by.

THREE
ELLEN

My sister left yesterday. While she crammed her rucksack and wheeled suitcase with as much stuff as she could fit in without the zips bursting, I made us a special breakfast of pancakes with blueberries and raspberries, drizzled with maple syrup and swirled with cream. I'd bought a bottle of Buck's Fizz, but Rosanna said she'd rather have tea, which suited me, too. It wasn't a celebration.

Over breakfast, we talked about the flat and other practicalities raised by Rosanna's departure. Not that there was much to discuss, given my sister's vagueness as to how long she'll be in Cornwall for. If it turns out to be an extended stay – or even a permanent one – money won't be a problem. Rosanna said she'll keep up her share of the regular bills, for now, and there's no rent or mortgage to pay. We own the flat outright, bought with money inherited from the sale of our family home, a substantial mock-Tudor in Epping.

While we were growing up, we didn't give any thought to our inheritance, and how the money side of things had been handled. It wasn't our new guardians' way to discuss such matters with us, and in any case, our lives were taken up with school and friends, and inventing ploys to escape the claustrophobic confines of our somewhat regimented upbringing.

It wasn't until I was eighteen and my sister almost twenty that we were hustled into the dining room to sit at the table, like wrongdoers about to be read the Riot Act, and enlightened as to our financial status. Our parents hadn't got round to making wills, and a firm of solicitors, along with Aunt Margaret and Uncle Derek, had laid down the arrangements for our future. Our parents' assets, apart from the house, had been put into a fund to cover our care and expenses while we were growing up. The house itself was sold, the proceeds to be passed on to us at our guardians' discretion, but no later than our twenty-first birthdays.

Far from being pleased to discover she was relatively well off, my sister had flown into a rage. Why had they waited until I, Ellen, was eighteen to pass on this news? Why hadn't she been told when she was eighteen herself? I remember sitting in silence while Rosanna banged on about how unfair it was, and how she and I were never treated the same, blah blah blah, while Margaret, Derek and I exchanged knowing glances, like conspirators.

It made little difference when we knew about the money. It was there, and it was ours, whatever. Rosanna never did learn how to pick her battles.

When the designated time arrived and we bought the Brixton flat, we were hugely excited to be striking out on our own but afraid, too. At least I was afraid – if my sister was, she hid it well.

A few months later, Aunt Margaret and Uncle Derek sold the Bexleyheath house and decamped to a small stone cottage in Ambleside. Their dream of half a lifetime, apparently, although Rosie and I failed to see the appeal at the time.

I made my sister promise to let our aunt and uncle know she was in Cornwall. They'll want to be told, I said. She frowned over the contents of her handbag, swapped a comb for a hair-brush, and stuffed in a packet of tissues and a tube of fruit sweets. Satisfied, she hooked it over her shoulder. 'I'm not moving to the other side of the world, Ell. It's only an extended holiday.'

'I know, but you will ring them, won't you? As soon as you get there.'

'Yes. Yes! If it keeps you happy.' She grinned, punched me in the arm and passed me the rucksack. 'Here, take this one, will you, till we get downstairs?'

My stomach switch-backed as the reality of my sister's leaving slammed home. Before, it was simply a plan, one I coped with reasonably well. The actual event felt like something else entirely. She said I didn't need to go and see her off, but I wanted to, and I think she was pleased, really.

We took a taxi to Paddington Station and hugged briefly on the platform, as the train was already in.

'I love you,' I said, and within those three little words was so much more, so much more, that my brain felt like it would explode with the enormity of it.

Rosanna laughed. 'Me, too. Stay safe, little sis. Have fun. I'll be in touch.'

The following morning, I wake to grey clouds tumbling across the skies, holding the threat of snow. I've made up my mind to keep busy and try not to miss Rosanna too much, but already the flat has a desolate vibe, as if she was the only one who brought it to life. I switch the radio on while I shower and dress, but the DJ's breezy babble intensifies the emptiness and I switch it off.

I leave home earlier than usual, thinking I'll feel better once I'm at work. I was right about the snow. As I step off the bus in Victoria Street – I haven't used the underground since that day – icy flakes swirl around me and gather in the dirty gutters like shreds of used tissue paper. My face stings with the cold and I hurry through the streets, eager to reach the familiar safe haven of the Printabilly building.

Sitting at my desk amid the usual tired Monday morning chorus of hellos, I try to kid myself into believing this is an ordinary day at the office. It's not easy, given my fragile state of mind and my sister's departure, but I manage it – up to a point. I feel as if everyone's looking at me. They're not, of course; it's just my imagination which, at the moment, is doing me no favours at all. Nobody comments, or looks at me strangely, or anything like that, so I suppose I must look normal.

The mirror in the ladies' tells a different story. I look, and I see a gamut of emotions etched on my face, as surely as if they had been drawn on with indelible ink. Fear and loathing because of the kind of person I apparently am. Sadness for my sister, and for the man who didn't have to die. And guilt – mountains of it. I've committed a terrible crime, sent my sister away in the process, and now I don't know how to live any more.

I move through the following days in a zombie-like state. I go to work, do what is required of me, and go home again, in the wintry dark. Rosanna messages one evening to say she's fine, and Sarah and Jay are spoiling her. She hopes I'm getting out and seeing people, and not moping around the flat. This is followed by a teary, laughing emoticon. As it happens, I text back, I'm in a pub right now, with friends from work. We might go on to a club later. I add my love, press 'Send', then throw the phone down on the floor next to the sofa. I was actually invited out that night, so there's a smidgeon of truth there. But all I wanted was to get home and hunker down in the flat, alone with my thoughts.

It's Friday, and I'm still at the office.

We had cake and non-alcoholic fizz at four o'clock for Jake's birthday, resulting in crumbs on desks, a sticky patch on the floor where somebody spilled a drink, and paper plates and plastic beakers on every surface.

I volunteered to stay behind and clear up. I was in no hurry to face the empty flat and the equally empty weekend ahead, whilst knowing I lacked the energy to do anything about it.

Once everyone's gone, I sit down at my desk and the weirdest sensation steals over me. It feels as if everything in the world around me is somehow impossible. This moment, with me sitting at my desk, is impossible. *I* am impossible. It's as if my brain and body are flashing up a gigantic, neon-lit *NO!*

Weird? Yes, as I said. Unexplainable? I don't think so. I have, after all, existed for weeks now in a state of delayed shock, which manifests itself in various, equally distressing, ways.

I try to stand up from the desk but all the energy has drained from my body. After what seems like hours but is probably only a minute or two, the feeling passes, and I get up and begin the clearing up, letting the mechanical tasks soothe my nerves.

I've almost finished when I spot the cake knife on Paula's desk, on a paper napkin. I cross the office to fetch it and find that the top drawer of her desk is partly open, its silver key on a pink pompom keyring poking from the lock. Paula obviously forgot to lock up before she went.

As I slide the drawer closed, I notice the tartan-patterned shortbread tin inside, the one we use as a collection tin for the various charities and worthy causes we support – Printabilly is that kind of company.

Paula usually takes charge of these activities because nobody else can be bothered – our altruistic efforts are usually instigated by her. The last, back in December, was a collection in aid of an animal shelter in Finsbury Park, or somewhere like that. Those who donated were given a paper sticker with a dog on it – mine is stuck to the corner of my computer stand.

I have no idea why, unless it's to delay going home a little longer, but I find myself pulling the drawer fully open and lifting the lid off the tin.

Inside is an oversized neon-yellow paperclip gripping a wad of notes, on top of a slurry of coins. Paula is enthusiastic and persuasive in her collecting. She particularly enjoys visiting the design floor – there's a guy up there she fancies, we think. Anyway, the tin holds quite a bit of cash, by the look of it. A list of those who donated – just names, no amounts – spiders across a lined sheet torn from a notepad. It isn't like Paula not to have passed the money on to its destination – she's usually quick off the mark – but then I remember she was off sick for a week in December, and I suppose that after that she was busy catching up, and then it was Christmas.

Fair enough, I think.

The lid of the tin is in my hand, ready to replace it, when an echo of the strange feeling I experienced earlier comes over me, and I freeze. My eyes fix themselves on the neon-yellow paper-clip. It seems to rise out of the tin, and for a moment I think I might be going to faint.

I drop onto Paula's pink chair and take slow, deep breaths until the feeling passes. Then I stand up, fold the cake knife into the paper napkin and take it back to my own desk – I'll wash it on Monday and return it to the kitchen. Back at Paula's desk, I close the drawer and lock it, dropping the key in the pen pot on the desk.

But not before four of the notes – three tens and a twenty – have found their way into my trouser pocket.

When I get home, I stare disbelievingly at the cash. I don't need money. I've no idea why I took it. But clearly I did, and now I'm a thief as well as a murderer.

FOUR
ELLEN

The past week has been hellish, the weather on my journeys to and from work at its worst with snow, rain and biting winds. I hate the cold. Aunt Margaret once said I'd been born in the wrong country and by some quirk of fate was popped out in England instead of somewhere more suited to me, like Morocco or Australia. *Popped out.* I remember laughing at that. It didn't seem very like her.

At work I've been constantly distracted by the sight of the pen pot on Paula's desk containing the key to the drawer. Paula herself has been away on a training course.

I couldn't make up my mind whether I welcomed this reprieve or not. Of course, nobody knew I was the thief, but in my head, it was only a matter of time before the finger was pointed at me, or I did the honourable thing and owned up: an option I considered seriously, many times. Until I decided I had enough to deal with without being sacked from my job in disgrace.

The obvious solution was to wait until everyone had left and then replace the cash. I tried a few times, but as soon as I went anywhere near Paula's desk, I sensed movement in the corridor outside the office as people working late passed the double glass doors through which the whole office is visible.

Oddly, I hadn't given it a thought when I did the deed in the first place.

I tried telling myself that nobody would think anything of it if they saw me putting the money back. But you never know who's watching, or who knows who in this building, and eventually I lost my nerve and gave up.

Monday again, and Paula duly returns. As she pushes in through the glass doors, laughing and joking with one of the guys, my stomach sinks like a stone and my eyes follow her progress across the office. My anxiety ratchets up several notches as she searches for the key to her desk, first in her handbag, then all around, until finally she locates it with a frown and a shrug, and unlocks the drawer.

I watch, and I wait, but nothing happens. Presumably, dealing with the charity collection isn't high on her agenda.

It was stealing, yes, but it wasn't Paula's money. I haven't harmed her in any way. I could donate the money to another charity. That would give me some absolution – if I deserve any. I decide to stop working myself up into a state and put the incident behind me. After all, it's nothing compared with my real crime.

Rosanna phones, and I tell her, truthfully this time, that I've been out for dinner with a couple of girls we both know, and also to a live music night at the pub. I actually managed to enjoy myself both times. Last Sunday, I left the confines of the flat and caught the bus to Covent Garden where I browsed the shops and market stalls and treated myself to lunch, listening to the opera singers performing in the piazza.

Doing these ordinary things, proving I can do them, tells me my world hasn't crumbled completely. I go to work, I shop, I cook, I eat, I clean the flat and do the laundry, I talk to people. This is how to live with a secret: ignore the nightmares, and pretend the deep ache inside me isn't there. Nothing feels marvellous, nothing feels truly fine, but nothing feels truly awful, either. I can do this. I *am* doing it.

And then, something happens to bring me crashing down again.

It's almost midnight on Saturday. I've not long been in bed when my phone pings an email notification. I reach for it, click on the message, and sit bolt upright in bed.

'I know what you did. You might think you've got away with it, but think again.'

No name of sender, and I've never seen the email address before: *catcreep@marvelmail*.

I drop the phone onto the bed as if it's red-hot. My heart thunders. I can't find my breath. The roar of the approaching Tube train fills my head and I press my hands over my ears, but it only makes the noise louder.

His shocked face appears before my eyes, and I feel the pressure of his fingers hard against my shoulder. I hear my own rasping breath as I shoulder my way through the crowd, my rapid feet echoing on the tiled floor of the exit tunnel, and the wail of sirens, proclaiming disaster to the darkening skies. Sights and sounds and sensations that are never far beneath the surface, no matter what else I do, or where else my mind travels.

It isn't over. It will never be over.

How did I become so complacent, so... *deluded*? How did that happen? Stupidly, I'd convinced myself that too much time had passed, that nobody was coming for me. That I had, unbelievably, got away with murder.

I make it through Sunday, I don't know how. I can't bear to stay in the flat, but at the same time I'm too scared to go out. I stay by the window, scanning the street, watching the heads of people passing by and the traffic streaming through Brixton. Waiting for... what? The white, yellow and blue of a police vehicle? Uniformed officers marching across the car park?

I drink the best part of a bottle of wine, eat little, and wait for the day to pass. Finally, exhausted by stress and pure emotion, I switch off my phone and climb into bed. I wake in a sweaty panic at 3 a.m. and switch it on again, in case.

But nothing comes.

By the time Monday morning comes around and I set off for work, I've begun to believe the message was a mistake, not intended for me. Or it's some idiot's idea of a joke. *Some joke.*

I've made a little headway with this positive mindset when another email arrives as I'm walking to the bus stop at the end of the day.

'That was a wicked thing to do. You deserve to be locked up!'

I let two buses go by while I sit in the bus shelter, fiddling with the buttons on my phone. I want to reply, ask who this is, but I'm too frightened in case it triggers more vitriol and leads me into a trap.

When, finally, I make it home, I'm shaking all over, and not only with the cold. I turn up the temperature on the radiators and switch on the electric fire in the living room, sinking down on the carpet in front of it. And still I can't get warm or stop the tremor in my hands.

I don't cook dinner – I can't eat. I don't do anything other than sit there until, eventually, I force myself to shower and put on pyjamas.

Another email arrives at 9 p.m.

'Confess to your crime or I will do it for you. Be warned.'

An hour later, another:

'Remember, your time is running out.'

In the morning, I phone work and tell them I'm sick. I *feel* sick. It isn't a lie.

Two more days pass, or three; I've lost count. I keep my phone by me all the time and jump every time it beeps, but no more messages come from *catcreep*.

I can't sleep, I can't eat, I can't leave the flat – the outdoors is a threatening place. I lurk beneath the duvet, my heart leaping at every bump and knock inside the building, every purr and click of the lift, every siren that scores the London streets, however distant.

At times, when I'm able to summon some kind of rational thought, I think perhaps I should tell somebody I'm being threatened. A friend, a neighbour, a work colleague? But there is nobody I can tell; nobody I can turn to to make this go away. I'm on my own, in a way I never have been before.

I am falling apart, mentally and physically – I'm sufficiently self-aware to recognise that.

On the third day, or the fourth, I shower, wash my hair and dress properly for the first time in days. I make myself eat some scrambled eggs on toast, then resume my vigil at the window while I try to think logically, and realistically.

I have to do this; I have to find a way out of this waking nightmare. Nobody is going to do it for me.

The flat is no longer a sanctuary. Being trapped within its walls feels as dangerous as going outside. I can't stay here, that's obvious. I must get out as soon as possible, go where nobody can find me, at least until the danger had passed – if ever there is such a time.

I could go to the Lake District to stay with Aunt Margaret and Uncle Derek. They'd be happy to have me, as long as I didn't disrupt their peaceful lives for too long. I'm supposed to be an adult now, capable of sorting out my own life. Besides, it's hardly fair to expect them to harbour somebody wanted for murder, even if they aren't aware of it. If whoever *catcreep* is knows what I've done and has tracked me down, then it's only a matter of time before the police come knocking, wherever I am.

As I stare out of the window at the pigeons fluttering across a thick white sky, time folds back on itself and I'm at the pub, on a night out. It's October, I think. I'm wearing my new yellow dress. Rosanna is with me, and we've got chatting to some guys we only knew by sight before. Two of them are urban explorers, it turns out, and they're regaling us with stories of their exploits, some of which are clearly embellished for dramatic effect as the drink flows.

One of the guys – he's called Leo, I think – tells us to follow him and he'll show us a special place, a secret place. A place nobody knows exists – except, presumably, a whole tranche of urban explorers and no doubt a lot of other people. But we agree, just for the hell of it.

I can't see Rosanna in my head now – maybe she ducked out – or anyone else. I can only see Leo and myself, trekking through the night streets. I'm wearing my black teddy coat over the dress, and heels. My feet are beginning to ache. Eventually, we stop before a rust-coloured wooden door, set deep into a wall. It has no handle on the outside and takes some effort to open. Leo tells me to watch my footing on the steps.

I see all this, reeling in front of me like a film, or the memory of a film, and I know I've found my hiding place.

FIVE

GEORGIE

The first thing Georgie notices that morning is the evil draught that finds its way under the back door to lash her already chilly feet with an icy blast. Enough to cut your toes off. The second thing she notices is her reflection in the mirror above the kitchen table, the mirror with a cat as the frame, its striped tail coiling around the lower part of the glass, its orange eyes dimmed from years of wiping with a damp cloth.

The draught from the door isn't new. She's been meaning to get a carpenter in to whack a bit of four-by-two onto the bottom of the door. Except carpenters don't come cheap, and a sixty-year-old woman living alone would no doubt be asked to cough up a lot more than the fair price. Their first mistake – Georgette Smith is nobody's fool, as any fly-by-night chippy would soon find out.

All the same, it would be quicker and easier to stuff the leg of an old pair of tights to make a sausage draught excluder, like those her mum laid at every damn doorway in the house. Georgie warned her they were trip hazards but she took no notice. In the end, the only person who constantly tripped over the sausages was Georgie herself.

'You're such a great clod, Georgette!'

Her reflection in the mirror *is* new. Not the reflection itself – she always looks at it while she waits for the kettle to boil for her early morning cuppa in case any new wrinkles have manifested themselves overnight, or her roots need touching up. But that look in her eye, and the subtle lift of her chin, weren't there the last time she checked. The wrinkle and root inspection draws a merciful blank, but the steely expression, sharp as you like, is evidence that seven hours of dreamless sleep have not altered the decision she reached last night.

The kettle boils. Georgie makes tea in the *Coronation Street* mug and takes it through to the living room at the front of the flat. The flat is in the basement of a once-handsome stucco house in Pimlico. There are two more flats above hers and, under the eaves, a studio – which not so long ago would have been called a bedsitter.

Georgie doesn't mind being in the basement. The filtered light from the street above gives the room a warm, intimate feel, and the Ikea floor lamp has a good strong bulb to read by. The rear of the flat, where the bedroom and kitchen are, is flooded with sunlight on a good day. Plus, she owns the best part of the garden: a square of soft grass and shrubs, right outside the back door. The remaining strip of garden, reached by an iron gate at the side, belongs to the flat above hers. The other flat and the studio do without.

The basement flat has been Georgie's home since her divorce in 1998. She bought it on a small mortgage with a sizeable deposit, using her half of the proceeds of the marital home, plus the money she'd squirrelled away over the years, which she'd called her escape fund. Getting shot of Raymond – so old for his years, so pernickety over bloody everything – and buying a tiny bit of London that was all hers were major victories in Georgie's life, no argument about that.

Now she might be about to achieve another. Not major, as

in life-changing, like the divorce. Nothing to get too excited about. Just a little something to spice things up, show a certain person what was what and put that person back on the straight and narrow. If she was ever on it in the first place.

Pulling the mohair throw off the end of the velvet sofa and arranging it over her bare feet, Georgie sips her tea, lifting the mug to admire the wraparound picture of The Rovers Return. Her mind wanders back to the working week, and work it was, too – not like sitting at a desk all day. On your feet from breakfast till half four when the staff restaurant shuts. Or doesn't if they're holding one of their endless meetings or some such, requiring somebody – usually Georgie – to hang on and serve pots of tea and posh biscuits.

Of course, it was nobody's fault but her own that she hadn't got off her backside and got herself an education; followed a career instead of just getting jobs. Jobs that would do, at the time. She'd let herself be dragged down, that was the trouble. And how easy it was to fall into that trap.

She enjoys working at Printabilly, though. Can't pretend otherwise. The building is conveniently situated, just off Victoria Street; a hop, skip and a jump from Pimlico if the Tube isn't playing up. The pay isn't a fortune, but who needs one of those? And you can talk to people all day, if you're so inclined. Which mostly Georgie is. How else do you find out what goes on in other people's lives if you don't strike up a conversation?

Georgie has her favourites among the staff. Well, why not? It's only natural to take to some people more than you do others. Most of the young men are a treat, with their snappy dressing and their charm and pretend-flirting. Pretend or not, it raises a smile. The more standoffish ones, who say *please* and *thank you* and not much else, probably think of her as somebody's gran, if they think anything at all.

Chance would be a fine thing.

The girls are like a flock of colourful birds, twittering away to one another as they queue at the counter in their Miss Selfridge fashions, all glossy manes and Mac make-up. Most of them are all right. She's especially fond of the girls who go out of their way to chat and ask how she is that day. Others, for some reason, she doesn't take to at all. Just because they tap away in the offices upstairs, with neon-coloured butterflies suspended from wires, bubblegum-coloured chairs, and silver desks with more screens than the multiplex, they think they're better than the likes of those who serve below stairs, as it were.

They'll find out one day, Georgie thinks, *once life has knocked the corners off*.

And then there's Ellen Randall, the girl with the watchful eyes and shoulder-length hair the colour of acorns. According to what Georgie's sharp ears have captured, she lost her parents in a plane crash when she was a kiddie, which is tragic, but only if it's true. It sounded to Georgie when she heard it as if *somebody* had embellished that story, if not downright invented it for the drama and sympathy.

Whichever it is, and for no reason Georgie cares to examine, it is a point against. The girl carries an air of secrecy about her. If she smiles, it's like she's smiling from behind glass. Another point against, although Georgie would be hard-pressed to explain why. But there, sometimes you just have to go with your gut.

The main crux of the thing, though, the deep-down, admittedly shameful, reason why Georgie dislikes the Randall girl is because of the sister.

Ellen smuggled her in for lunch one wet day at the back end of last year. Georgie shovelled sweet-potato fries onto square white china and looked at this other girl, so similar to Ellen for the relationship to be noticeable, only with hair a shade darker and her build slighter, and thought of her own sister. The older sister whom Georgie had stupidly believed would be her friend for life, her ally, her protector, her saviour. Especially when Dad went all funny and frightened her half to death.

Only it wasn't to be, because Charlotte, at the age of seventeen, and after two earlier cracks at it, managed to kill herself with pills and goodness knows what else. Georgie has never relied on a single living soul since.

Every time Georgie looks at Ellen and sees the smile that hides a thousand secrets, she thinks, *That could have been me*. Everything about her is right; everything fits with Georgie's idea of herself in another lifetime – or a parallel universe. Even the dubious orphan aspect can't shift this perspective. It might even have been a blessing in her own case.

It was only ever a fantasy, the idea of bringing the girl down in some way and giving her a scare. A secret punishment for stealing Georgie's life.

And then, by pure chance, Georgie found out that sweet-faced Ellen was not so perfect as she appeared. So far from perfect it shook Georgie to the core. She wouldn't have believed it had she not seen it with her own eyes. She couldn't be allowed to get away with it. It was a miracle – a travesty – that she seemed to have done just that.

Something had to be done, and it was up to Georgie to do it – she'd finally realised that last night. Something that wouldn't drag her into anything nasty, of course. She couldn't be doing with that.

A rattle and bang comes from up above as next door's front door slams shut. Georgie goes to the window and, sure enough, the lower portion of little Sonny comes into view, leaping down the steps, enormous feet landing slap onto the pavement. He isn't actually little; he's sixteen and built like a rugby scrum half, but still only a kid.

How fortuitous, Georgie thinks. Just when she could use a

little help, it turns up. Isn't that often the way? Feet stuffed into slippers, she's out of her front door and up the basement steps before Sonny's chewing gum is out of the packet.

'Oh, hi,' he says. 'Nice morning.'

Really? Georgie, minus a coat, shivers. The soles of her slippers are as useless as wet cardboard against the damp chill from the pavement.

Sonny slings a long leg over his bike and hops it from the railings to the kerb.

'Look, I could do with a bit of help,' Georgie says. 'When you've got a minute.'

'What's that, then?' Sonny unwraps a bit of gum and pops it into his mouth.

'With the computer. I'm doing emails when I need to, no problem there. And the internet thing, got the hang of that. But I want to try something out. Another email thingy. With a different name.' She makes herself sound a bit daft, prehistoric, on purpose. She needs this lad and his expertise.

'A different name? You mean, you want to change the name on your email account. It's quite simple. I can write the steps down for you, if you like.' Sonny puts a foot on the pedal, preparing to push off.

'No, I don't want to change that one. Not now I've got the gist of it, Heaven help me. No, I want a new one, another one altogether. To use as well as the first one.'

Sonny switches the gum from one side of his mouth to the other and looks ahead, along the street, then back at Georgie. 'A new email account?' The bike wheels grind impatiently forward, back, forward.

'Yes, that's it,' Georgie says hurriedly. 'Could you show me, properly? I don't want to break the thing.'

'Yep, suppose I could. What, like, soon?'

'Soon as you like.'

'Okay. I'll pop in later, when I get back from the sports centre. That do you?'

Georgie smiles. 'That'll do very nicely, thank you, Sonny.' Then she adds, 'Give my regards to your mother.' We're on nodding terms, that's all, but I like to be polite.

Sonny is already whizzing away with a scrunch of tyres.

SIX

CARL

Carl has little use for the Tube during the day. It's a method of transport that harks back to a time when the number of commuters was a mere fraction of what it is today. In other words, the whole damn system has become unfit for purpose. Unless he's short of time, he swerves the overheated crush of humanity in favour of walking or taking the bus. But when the shutters come down on the pubs and restaurants, late-night revellers gather in braying groups on street corners and night buses rumble across the city, he enters the subterranean world, where reality crosses over with imagination, the slow drip-drip from the tunnel roof becomes his own heartbeat, the rush of air his own breath.

There are many possibilities for his night-time forays, mapped out in a pattern as familiar to him as the landscape above ground. Sometimes he'll meet up with the crew; at other times, depending on his mood, he'll go solo.

He's alone tonight as he nudges the rust-coloured door with his shoulder until it grinds open, then descends the two-section concrete stairway to the platform.

This is where he finds the girl, on a bench set into an alcove.

Knees drawn up, back pressed hard against the tiles, shrouded in some sort of padded material.

At first, he sees only a humped shape that might be a bag of rubbish or bundle of old clothes. It moves as he passes, just discernibly. A trick of the eye, perhaps. He carries on walking, slowly, then something makes him stop and turn back. He always carries a torch but prefers not to use it. It's never quite pitch black; the shape and width of the platform is familiar, and it's a good test of his night vision. Now, he takes the torch from his pocket and switches it on. The beam finds first the padded material, the hem of it drooping down over the edge of the bench. He raises the torch and recognises a sleeping bag. It's occupied.

He's puzzled. Rough sleepers don't come down here. They wouldn't know how to get in. Clearly, this one does, though.

'Hey, do you mind?' The female voice is young, well modulated, and cross.

'Sorry.' Carl angles the torch to the left of her face. 'Are you all right? Only this isn't the best place to sleep, you know.'

'I'm well aware of that, thank you,' she says.

Carl's eyes adjust further. Her head is no longer hooded by the sleeping bag, which has slipped down to shoulder level. She's wearing a hat, a beanie. Beneath the bench is a rucksack with a water bottle, or perhaps a flask, sticking out of the front pocket. Next to the rucksack is an empty food wrapper, from a sandwich, perhaps.

'Are you hungry?'

The sleeping bag shimmies. 'I can fend for myself. I'm not a beggar, or destitute or anything. And will you stop waving that light about?'

'Fine. Well, if you're sure you're okay, I'll leave you to it.'

He switches off the torch and puts it away, but stays where he is. He doesn't want to leave her without knowing why she's set up camp in an abandoned Tube station. She may not be in need, not in the way he'd assumed, but obviously there's something wrong.

Through the gloom, he sees the sleeping bag being pulled back over her head as she shrinks back further into the alcove.

He takes the hint, and walks on.

The tunnel curves, and there's another straight stretch of platform, which collides with a brick wall. The wall dates back to September 1968, when Maystone Road station was closed and left to rot like a corpse in a sarcophagus. Those with inside information know that the wall doesn't quite meet the tunnel wall on the left, and although the darkness renders it invisible, there is a gap, wide enough for a thinnish person to squeeze through. Carl knows this from coming here with the crew, and it's mentioned on the forums often enough. Beyond the false wall, it's possible to walk on for several hundred yards until the disused track – a former spur of the main line – intersects pointlessly with the Victoria line and a second brick wall seals off the tunnel completely.

Maystone Road is a ghost station, the scores of tramping feet and hiss of pneumatic doors a distant memory. For those who care to remember.

He doesn't feel like walking beyond the false wall tonight. The buzz he usually gets from being in this hidden city beneath a city has deserted him, and he turns around and walks back the way he came. This backtracking, of course, isn't really anything to do with his mood.

But when he reaches the bench, she's gone. There's only the sandwich wrapper being pulled across the platform by a back-draught.

SEVEN

ELLEN

I'm not scared, not of this place, anyway. I wasn't when Leo brought me here, either. Just intrigued, then. Which might have been the drink talking. Anyway, there's nothing to be scared of. I've never minded the dark. It's not even that cold. I've come prepared, though. Plenty of warm layers, and the sleeping bag. I've got a torch, and a handful of paperbacks to pass the time. The bench is a bonus. I don't remember seeing it, the first time. I brought some food with me, and little boxes of juice. Some clothes, wipes to clean myself with, that sort of thing. I brought my phone, too. I'm thinking it's safer down here, where there's no signal, rather than in the flat. It's switched off, of course.

The 24/7 minimart is only a few minutes' walk away. I'm careful when I go in and out of here. It's a risk, but only a miniscule one. Same as the toilet – the public ones in the corner of a scrubby square of green too small to be called a park. I go when I need to, but try not to leave here in full daylight if I can help it. The short days of winter can be a blessing.

I feel safe, that's the main thing – the only thing. I have no plan, no end game. I have a feeling I'll know when it's safe to go home, when my stalker or persecutor – both, yes – has given up.

Okay, I can't truly know how long it will be until the danger has passed. *How long is a piece of string?* Uncle Derek used to say that a lot. Still does, probably. I shall rely on gut instinct.

That guy who came by last night frightened me at first. I hadn't thought there'd be other people. I know about the urban explorers from Leo, but for some reason I never thought I'd actually see one, nor anyone at all. He shone a torch on me. I was terrified then. But he wasn't in uniform, so not Transport Police, nor any other kind, as far as I could gather. He was just being curious. He assumed I was sleeping rough, which I am, I suppose, but not in the way he must have imagined. He spoke kindly to me, though, which made me sorry afterwards that I'd been sharp with him. But I wasn't going to take any risks, and as soon as he'd walked on, I gathered up all my stuff, went back to the steps and hunkered down on the floor on the other side of them.

I was relieved when he left. I held my breath as his feet trod the stairs, and when I heard the grind and clunk of the door being closed – faintly, as it's quite a way up to the surface – I almost cried, I'm not sure why. A whole mixture of things, I expect.

I check my watch – the little Timex with the luminous hands my aunt and uncle gave me for my thirteenth birthday. It's only nine o'clock. I'll need the loo before long, but I can hang on for another hour or so. I'll pick up a sandwich and some chocolate while I'm out.

Footsteps send my pulse racing. I huddle into the sleeping bag, head well down.

'Hey, you're still here,' he says. No torch this time, but the pale oval of his face looms above me.

'Full marks for observation.' I turn my face to the wall, a hint in anybody's language. Not his, apparently. He stays right where he is. I relent. 'Look, what d'you want? I'm fine, as I said last night.'

'I'm sorry, but you're not fine, obviously, otherwise you wouldn't be sleeping on an abandoned Tube station platform. How long have you been doing this?'

'Long enough.' I sigh. He isn't going to be fobbed off that easily. 'Since Tuesday. The Tuesday just gone. It's a short-term thing – a project, sort of.'

'A project.'

'Yes, so if you want to help, jog on or whatever it is you lot do.'

He laughs softly. 'No jogging involved. Just walking. Just being down here. It's what we do. Or I do.'

I don't reply. I figure that if I keep quiet he will go away and mind his own business. Except that some part of me doesn't want him to go.

He brings out his torch, switches it on but keeps it pointing downwards. The beam lights up the space between us and casts ghostly shadows across his face, and presumably across mine. Panic wells up inside me. Who is he? Does he know who I am, what I did? I force the panic back. He has kind eyes that find my face then leave it, as if he doesn't want to be caught staring.

For some unaccountable reason, I trust him. Or perhaps I just *decide* to trust him, which is not the same thing at all, but I'm already fearful, and any more reasons to be scared would push me even further to the edge.

'Please tell me why you're hiding down here. And before you say you're not hiding, you're doing a pretty good impression of it. I'm not leaving until you talk to me.'

I see a smile begin. He's not being threatening in any way, this guy. He genuinely wants to help, it seems. I hate to disappoint him.

I play for time. 'Did you come back tonight to check up on me?'

'Can't pretend I didn't. I was concerned.'

'Well, that's...' I run out of words.

My chest is tight with emotion, as if there's no room for any more feeling. The bench feels hard beneath me, and despite the padding of the sleeping bag, the tiled wall is ice-cold. The tunnel seems blacker than before, the rail leading to nowhere but despair. A shiver runs right through me, as if someone walked over my grave. That's what they say, isn't it?

'What's your name?' he asks.

'Ellen. Ellen Randall.'

'I'm Carl Teviot. Pleased to make your acquaintance.' He gives a little mock bow, and I laugh, despite myself. 'So now,' he says, squatting down to be at my level, 'are you going to tell me what you're doing here?'

EIGHT

CARL

Carl thinks how difficult it must be for her, spilling out her problems to a complete stranger. He doesn't hurry her, but encourages her to talk about general things at first, easing her into what is really on her mind. She tells him she works at a company called Printabilly, where they design and produce personalised greetings cards and add-on gifts like personalised mugs. He's heard of it, of course. Who hasn't? It's a very successful outfit. Ellen is part of the team that handles the orders. She describes her working environment: vibrant colours, crazy posters, mobiles, lifts papered inside with examples of the funniest cards, the rudest ones in the loos, that sort of thing. She makes it sound like a setting from a Disney cartoon. A fun place to work. But her face is sad.

'I've messaged in sick,' she says. 'But I won't be going back. Not ever.'

He doesn't pursue this. Instead, he tells her he works in fashion, which is another way of saying he's a sales assistant in a clothes shop. She smiles at that; he doesn't know why.

He tells her about the crew, and the places they've hacked their way into: abandoned hospitals, derelict warehouses, empty office blocks, an old asylum, and the ghost stations of the underground. He keeps it low-key, leaving out their rooftop exploits and the most dangerous elements of urban exploration. Besides, he doesn't hang out with the crew so much now. He prefers his own company for his night-time meanders.

She tells him about a guy called Leo she met in a pub who had brought her to Maystone Road and shown her the main entrance to the former station, locked and sealed behind a heavy metal grill. Its name, in Johnston typeface – the same one used for all the underground signage – is still attached to the ox-blood coloured brickwork with the roundel sign jutting out, so much a part of the streetscape that nobody notices it any more.

'Leo said it's impossible to get in that way,' Ellen explains.

Carl nods in agreement.

'Then he showed me the secret door,' Ellen says, 'and we came inside.'

The door is a short way along the street from the main station entrance, scruffy and mostly unnoticeable to passers-by. It was one of two emergency escape routes for passengers if the main Tube exit was blocked, and was rarely used, if ever. Leo apparently told Ellen this, too.

They chat about jobs, and where they live now, and where they used to live – the sort of things you say to someone you've met in a pub. There they are, making small-talk in a silent, forgotten tunnel. It should feel bizarre. Strangely, it doesn't.

They exchange ages: Carl is twenty-seven, Ellen twenty-three. She looks younger, he thinks. He tells her his parents were divorced years ago. His father lives on Guernsey. He has no idea where his mother is. Ellen's parents, she tells him in one rushed sentence, died when she was eight years old. She doesn't go into detail and he doesn't ask. She has a sister, who has gone to stay in Cornwall for a while. And then she stops talking, lowers her eyes and bites her bottom lip, as if she's said something she shouldn't.

Eventually, they arrive at the crux of the matter.

'I do crazy things, stupid things,' she says suddenly. 'You don't want to know. Believe me, you don't. In fact, why don't you go now? Then you won't know and you won't have to think about it afterwards. That's what I'd do, if I were you.'

'Oh, you would, would you?'

He's sitting next to her on the bench. She'd moved her rucksack to the floor. Now she lifts it back up and places it between them, forming a barrier.

'I would, yes,' she says firmly.

She waits. He doesn't get up.

'I'm a good listener,' he says. 'I'm not easily shocked, either. Why don't you give me a try?'

She shuffles inside the sleeping bag, which is pulled up to chest level. She looks cold, hungry and, despite the confident talk, very frightened. 'It's late. Don't you have to be somewhere?' she asks. 'Like... home?'

'There's nobody waiting for me. I flat-share, with a mate.' He imagines this is what she's asking.

She nods.

A pause, then Carl asks: 'Who's frightened you, Ellen? Has somebody hurt you?'

She laughs, without humour; a ripple of sound that rises to the arched roof and joins the ghosts of the tunnel's echoes. 'If you knew...' She pulls off her hat, shaking out a tumble of brown hair.

'If I knew what, Ellen?' he says gently.

The lowered eyes again. 'I killed somebody. I murdered my sister's boyfriend. Pushed him in front of a Tube train. And yes, before you ask, I meant to do it. In that moment, that one crazy little moment, I wanted him dead.' She looks up sharply. 'There. Satisfied?'

He wipes the shock from his face, fast. But she's seen it.

'Told you.' Her voice carries a note of triumph. 'I said you wouldn't want to know.'

He doesn't speak. He looks at her, this girl called Ellen. Looks at her intently, studying her, reading what he sees in her face. Translating her private language into one of his own. Eventually, as he keeps looking, her eyes are drawn to his. Their gazes lock, and whatever she knows, or thinks she knows, about herself, Carl knows to be untrue. He knows it in his heart, and in the deepest, darkest part of his mind, like tapping into a sixth sense.

'You're hiding down here in case somebody's after you?' he says.

'There's no *in case* about it. I've been getting emails, messages from someone who says they know what I've done and they'll tell if I don't confess. I could go to the police and hand myself in. It's what I should have done in the first place but I was scared and in shock, so I ran. And nothing happened. Nobody came for me, and I thought... well, never mind what I thought. It's different now. Everything's changed.'

Carl's mind leaps on, hurdling over a multitude of unasked questions to land on firmer ground. 'You have to get out of here. It's not safe, and it's illegal, as it happens.'

'I know it's illegal. But you're here, too.'

'That's different. But if you're determined to hide, let me help.' The idea forms in his brain, getting clearer by the second. More than an idea. A plan. He just needs her to go along with it. After that, well... one step at a time.

'I have a house,' he tells her, 'in Sussex, in the countryside. Technically, it belongs to my father but that kind of makes it mine, too. It's empty. No one goes there now. I could take you there. I'll look after you, I promise.'

She double-takes, then frowns. 'You're serious. You really mean that, don't you?'

'Of course. I wouldn't lie to you.'

She stays quiet for a moment, her expression thoughtful. Then she seems to make a decision. 'Okay. But if you don't come back here tomorrow, I'll know you were making it up.'

He shakes his head, tells her this isn't how this is going to work. He wants her to feel safe, and protected, and to do that he needs to get her out of this tunnel, tonight. She has no one, it seems. Except now she has him.

NINE
ELLEN

It seems strange, being back in the flat, as if I don't belong. It's less than four days since I left, yet it feels as if I've been away for a very long time. We talked for so long in the tunnel that it was well past midnight by the time we got here. Carl came up in the lift with me. He insisted on seeing me to the door, and although I told him it wasn't necessary, I was glad of his company.

He said he would come and collect me around two this afternoon, but now I'm back here, I keep wondering if I imagined the whole encounter, and there is no Carl. And did I really spend three nights in an abandoned Tube station, or was that a hallucination as well? I wouldn't be surprised.

Before I went to bed last night, I screwed up my courage, switched on my phone and, using the little power that was left, checked my messages and emails. There were no more emails from *catcreep*, but the original ones sat there, taunting me, their message as strong as before, yet I can't bring myself to delete them.

There was a text from Rosanna asking me how I was, telling me that leaving London had been the right decision, and that she still hasn't heard from Matt. At the end was a row of red hearts – not for me, I assumed – and two emoji faces, one with a resigned look, the other, kind of hopeful. I wish she'd told me she wasn't bothered about him any more; it would have been slightly easier to take.

I sent a short reply – I was fine, and I was glad she was enjoying Cornwall – and left it at that. Then I let the battery die completely.

I slept surprisingly soundly, then woke up at half past nine in a sweat, panicking in case Carl had been and gone while I was asleep. Panicking in case he didn't come at all. Once I was fully awake, I remembered he wasn't due until this afternoon, and all I could do was wait and hope.

It's almost midday now. Since breakfast, I've done nothing but wander around the flat, the silence following me from room to room like the ghost of a faithful dog. I should start packing, but the doubts flood back, stronger than before. Even if I didn't dream up this Carl guy, is he really taking me to Sussex, or did he make the whole thing up for the hell of it? Maybe he's mentally unstable, or on drugs or something. I didn't have the impression of either, but my impressions are hardly to be trusted.

All the same, I can't bring myself to make any preparations other than to haul out my biggest rucksack, one I used to go camping, and sift vaguely through some stuff I might take. Half my mind still insists I won't be going to Sussex, or anywhere else. Unless it's to prison...

Oh God! I collapse onto the sofa, pulling a cushion onto my lap, as the full horror of what I've done, my fear of being hauled in by the police and my guilt over my sister hits me afresh. I want to cry, sob my heart out, but I'm beyond tears now.

The door buzzer sounds, filling me with sudden dread. I tiptoe to the entry phone panel. It's Carl. At least, the voice says it is.

The lift purrs upwards. I open the flat door cautiously and

when I see him standing there I want to fling myself into his arms with relief, but I hold back. If he's really come to rescue me – *Why would he do that?* – the last thing he needs is hysteria.

I find a steady voice. 'You're earlier than you said. Sorry, I'm not quite ready.'

I make it sound as if I'm going on holiday with a friend, as if this is an entirely normal situation. Instead, I'm about to head out of London with a guy I know nothing about except what he's told me, which could be pack of lies, only at this moment I'm too exhausted and desperate to care.

'I managed to get everything done so I thought I'd head over,' he says. He follows me into the flat, where my bedroom door stands open.

'I won't be long,' I say.

Carl eyes my gaping rucksack, the open drawers and the clothes strewn on the bed. He laughs. 'It's fine. Take your time. I'll wait in the other room.'

He moves away from the bedroom door and I apply myself seriously to the task of packing. I've gathered up my stuff from the bathroom and am about to stuff another warm jumper into the rucksack when I remember my phone. Grabbing it from the bedside table, I run to the living room and throw it to Carl. 'Here!'

He gives me a questioning look as he catches it.

'Do something with it. Take it apart, do whatever it takes to stop it working. Then chuck it away, in the Thames or something.'

'Er, why?' Then his face clears. 'Right, I see.'

'They can find me, can't they? Through my phone, its location and stuff.'

'In theory, yes. But, Ellen...' He looks at me, and sees I am completely serious. 'Okay, okay, whatever you want. Not the Thames, though. We won't be in London for much longer.'

'No, well, somewhere. Please, Carl. I can trust you to do that for me, can't I?'

Carl nods, and slips my phone into the pocket of his jeans. 'I'll sort it later. Now stop worrying.' He smiles.

Later. I'll have to be satisfied with that.

Rosanna comes to my mind – like she's ever far away from it. By ditching my phone, I'll effectively be breaking off contact with her. But it's for the best, for now.

A dull ache fills my chest. *I'm so sorry, Rosie. For everything*.

Eventually, I'm ready, and Carl picks up my bulging rucksack.

'Christ, what've you've got in here? A dead body?' he says, then reddens, and gives me a regretful look as he realises his mistake. I let the moment slip by, pretending I didn't notice.

We take the lift down to the parking area outside the flats and Carl leads me to a blue Fiat Panda. I realise I hadn't given a thought as to how we were going to get to Sussex.

'I hired it this morning,' he says. 'The bloke who works at the hire place is a friend of mine. I get mates' rates.' He stows my rucksack in the boot, which is already fairly full. I add a couple of smaller bags containing the overflow.

Carl opens the passenger door. 'Hop in then.'

'I've got to pop back. Sorry.'

'Really?'

'Something I've got to do. Honestly, I'll only be a couple of minutes.'

Back upstairs in the flat, I open the kitchen drawer and take out three ten-pound notes and a twenty. I find a piece of paper and write a note: 'This is the money we collected for the animal charity. I took it from your desk. I don't know why I did because I didn't need it. It was a crazy, stupid thing to do. I'm really sorry.' I hesitate before adding my name. And then, because it would be wrong to compound my dishonesty any further, I do.

Then I put it in an envelope with the money, adding an extra fiver from my purse, and address the envelope to Paula at the office.

'Would you mind ever so much if we stop by my office on the way?' I ask, as I get into the car. 'I want to drop a letter off.'

Carl smiles patiently. 'Of course. No problem.'

TEN

CARL

Hartsbrook at first glance seems exactly as he remembers it all those years ago. The geography – the humpback bridge, the confident sweep of the road as it enters the village before it narrows and twists, the hotchpotch of buildings lining the road like a set of uneven teeth – all the same. But as he slows the Panda and looks further, the changes begin to show themselves. What was once a bank is now a bistro, the architecturally deficient pub is a Co-op supermarket, the family butcher's is a tanning and beauty salon. No doubt there's more, if he cares to look. He doesn't.

He is about to drive the length of the high street and take the left-hand fork that leads away from the village when he changes his mind, stops, and backs up a short way to park next to the church. The unfamiliar car jerks as he makes this manoeuvre, but his passenger remains silent, as she has been for practically the whole fifty-mile journey. It isn't an uncomfortable kind of silence and he doesn't want to press her into talking.

She comes alive as he unclips his seat belt and steps out of the car.

'Here?' She looks around, suspicion in her eyes.

He smiles. 'Yep. There's a bit of a walk ahead. I hope you're up for that.'

'Suppose I'll have to be.' She raises her eyes to let him know she's not serious, releases her own seat belt and climbs out of the car.

Carl opens the boot and lumps one bulging rucksack out after the other, together with Ellen's extra bags. From the back seat he retrieves a zipped holdall containing food and drink and other essential supplies. There are two more bags, but they can stay where they are for now.

'Are you going to be okay with that?' He eyes Ellen doubtfully as she shoulders her pack.

She says she's fine, and heaves up the holdall as well. He takes it out of her hand, and she smiles, then follows him across the road and through the lychgate. She doesn't question the route as they walk through the churchyard of St Wilfrid's, skirting drunken headstones and cracked grey tombs, then past a row of picture-book cottages to follow the public footpath sign.

The path is overgrown in places, almost disappearing altogether at its narrowest. But the route is imprinted on Carl's memory and he needs no other guide.

They arrive at a bumpy meadow studded with molehills. Ellen starts to cross it when he pulls her back.

'The quickest way from A to B is in a straight line,' she says. 'We learned that at school. Or were you away that day?'

'You have to follow the footpath around the edge. The fields belong to people. You aren't allowed to traipse across them.'

'Is that so?'

'Yep.' But then he looks around. 'Okay, there's nobody about to see so let's do it.'

She gives a triumphant smile, takes the lead and they cross the meadow diagonally. Back on the footpath, there's a stile, and she lets him help her over, although clearly she doesn't need any help. The next field they reach is ploughed – no chance of venturing onto the muddy ridges. Carl takes the lead again, following the narrow track alongside a wood.

'How much further?' she asks, as the footpath opens onto yet another field.

'Last one, I promise. Keep to the middle. Mind the ditch.'

The ditch lies between the field and the trees, and is partly obscured by nettles. Carl remembers falling into it when he was small. He was wearing shorts, and his legs were stung by nettles as well as muddied.

'Is this really the only way?' Ellen turns to him, her voice disbelieving. 'Not very convenient, is it?'

She's only raising these mild objections to cover her real thoughts. He's known her for less than a day but it's enough to understand that she's breaking inside. He wishes he could reassure her, tell her not to be scared; not of him, anyway. But words won't earn her trust. Only actions can do that.

There is another way to the house, of course. One of the roads heading out of Hartsbrook loops around and leads to smaller road – no more than a lane – which passes within yards of the front of the house. But the footpath is what he remembers best, and he needs to let his strongest memory guide him on this expedition – this backwards march through time – in case the next, vital, stage evades him: entry to the house itself.

The red-tiled roof, sagging in the middle, with a tall chimney at each end, appears above the trees, and Carl feels a shiver of excitement mixed with relief. Relief that the house is still there, and it actually exists outside his imagination; excitement at returning after so long.

And then, suddenly, he remembers the last, somewhat tense, weekend, he'd spent at Owl Corner with both his parents. It had been very soon after that weekend that his mother had upped and left without warning.

Carl puts the holdall on the ground rubs his arm, hard, as if he's rubbing an insect sting; the pain abates. He must focus on Ellen now, not himself. He only hopes he can be enough for her. He was never enough for Linnie, his mother – couldn't have been, otherwise she wouldn't have left.

Is this why he's scooped up this lost girl, hoping he can make things right for her? By doing so – if he succeeds – will it go some way towards allaying the guilt he feels at letting his mother down, not doing the very thing that would have made things right for her, whatever that was? Maybe it is; maybe it isn't. It's unlikely he'll ever know for sure.

What he does know is that, somehow, he was drawn to Ellen from the first time they spoke in the tunnel. If he'd walked on by, he'd never have forgiven himself.

Never have forgotten her.

She's waiting now, looking at him, not with curiosity but with gentle patience.

He picks up the bag and they walk on a short way. The trees end, the land opens out, and there it is: Owl Corner, exactly as he knew it then, and knows it now.

Ellen looks at the house, then at Carl. Her face betrays a trace of nervousness and he gives her what he hopes is a reassuring smile. He checks the time on his phone: 5.30. Sunset won't be for another couple of hours, but the day is overcast and the house and its surrounds are washed in shadow – not ideal if the power has been turned off. He had planned for them to be there earlier, but Ellen had barely started packing before he arrived to collect her. She'd looked askance when he'd told her to take just what she needed for the short-term, and they'd worry about it later, if needed.

Owl Corner looks like two houses joined together, which it possibly was originally – Carl doesn't remember the history now, except he knows the house dates back to the seventeenth century. The lower half of one end is brick, and timbered black-and-white above; the other end is all brick. Small lean-to outhouses are tacked onto each end. Slightly off centre, as if it belongs to the timbered side, is a green front door with a tiled porch held up by wooden struts. He sees this in his mind's eye, although not in reality as they've arrived at the back of the house.

A small wooden gate is set in a hedge. Beyond it, yellowing, overgrown grass fringes the house on three sides; the fourth side, at the far end, abuts almost directly onto a fence. He's surprised the grass isn't even taller. But perhaps there's a point at which grass stops growing if it's not tended; he has no idea.

He lifts the gate off its latch, although he needn't bother; one shove and the whole thing would collapse into the hedge.

'Come on, then,' he says, although he is really talking to himself rather than Ellen. This is harder than he'd anticipated, but as long as he puts this girl and her needs first, he'll be okay.

He pushes through the grass, Ellen following, rounds the building and offloads his luggage to the ground. There is no back entrance to the house. On the ground beside one of the posts that supports the porch, half hidden in weeds, is a large flattish flint. The stone is stubborn, bedded down in compacted earth, and it takes some effort to free it. He manages to lift it sufficiently to stick his hand in the gap, and after some painful scrabbling, his fingers find metal. The stone thwacks down again.

Carl holds the key, caked in mud, in his palm. He rubs it against the porch support, releasing some of the mud, but it's rusted, and the bit has a small kink in it.

He steps up to the front door and tries to push the key in the lock. The lock itself is discoloured. He waggles the key impatiently, fearful of pushing too hard in case it breaks off. It doesn't break, but it doesn't go all the way in. With nothing to lose, he shoves hard. The key is now in the lock but won't turn sufficiently to open the door. Carl rubs his sore fingers. He'll give it one more try, then it's on to his next option, which has as much chance of failure as the first.

Ellen makes a small sound. He straightens up and turns around to see her standing a few feet from him, her face passive, and he realises with a jolt that she has placed herself entirely in his hands. The pressure is like a physical weight dragging at his legs as he moves along to the far end of the house.

'Can't we get in? Did you know this could happen?' Carl gives her a look. 'Sorry,' she says, 'only if this isn't going to work, what are we meant to do next? Go back to London?'

'It won't come to that. Give me some credit,' he says, exuding an optimism he doesn't feel.

The small, square window in front of him is just low enough to reach without too much stretching. Pulling a tangle of ivy away from the glass, he grabs the two metal handles on the lower part of the frame and pushes upwards, hard. The handles dig into his hands, but the window gives an inch and he starts to heave it upwards. The frame creaks as the gap slowly increases. He needs it to be big enough to climb through, but he'll smash the glass if necessary. More heaving and the window's up, almost to its fullest extent.

'Wait there, by the door.'

He jumps up, grips the top of the window frame for support, and manoeuvres himself, feet first, through the gap. Once he's fully inside the room, he stands for a moment and looks around. This is the larder which leads off the kitchen. The shelves are empty, apart from some dubious-looking Kilner jars, an old meat safe, and a large oval blue-and-white china platter. Pictures flash before him: a large pink gammon joint on the platter, cooked at home in Surbiton and carefully transported; jars of blackberry jam his mother made, glistening like dark jewels beneath frilled paper caps; doughnuts from the village bakery in sticky paper bags, ready to be plundered by hungry children. Pictures stored in his memory bank forever.

Only nothing is forever. Certainly not memories.

'Carl? Carl! Hurry up, will you? I'm freezing out here.'

'I'm here. I'm trying to get the door open.'

The front door seems stuck fast, as if the house is protesting against the intrusion. In desperation, he yanks on the doorknob and kicks the bottom of the door at the same time. It opens with a whine of hinges.

'Hello.' He smiles.

Ellen's relief is as palpable as his own. She lumps her ruck-sack inside. Carl nips out and picks up his own bags, and by the time he's inside again, Ellen is halfway along the hall, peering into the rooms. Then she turns, and walks back a few steps.

'It's...' She bites her lip, regarding him with childlike appeal.

'Hey, come on. It's not that terrible, is it?' He knows this isn't what she means.

'Of course not. It's... Oh God, sorry, sorry...' She lets out a dry-eyed sob.

He closes the space between them and rests a tentative hand on her shoulder. So far, they haven't been tactile with one another, not even when he coaxed her out of the tunnel, and even this small gesture feels alien. Surprisingly, she hooks her arm up and covers his hand with hers. The contact lasts only seconds, but he senses her breathing slowing, and she seems calmer. That's a relief: he's not sure how he would cope if she were to break down in front of him.

He's beginning to feel out of his depth. This whole opera-tion has been accomplished in such a rush. So far, he's acted on impulse, which isn't something he usually does. But he couldn't leave her alone in the dark for another night. Neither could he leave her alone in the flat once she was out of the tunnel. In her troubled state, who knew what she might have done?

He could have walked away, focused on the practicalities, made sure she had the basics to survive, and left her to it. Instead, he parcelled up his life in London with surprising ease, claiming a family emergency to be granted compassionate leave from his job, and set off on this mission of mercy. He's aware how crazy it is, or would sound to somebody else.

In hindsight, perhaps he should have thought a little longer, a little deeper, before offering sanctuary to a complete stranger. Instead, he'd acted almost on impulse, letting one action lead to the next.

But it's too late now. He gives her a smile and rubs his hands together. 'Right, first things first. Light.' He flicks the only light switch in the gloomy hall. Nothing. This is not good news. 'Ah, well, we have candles and torches. We'll manage with those until I can sort out the power.'

'How are you going to do that?' Ellen looks doubtful, as well she might.

'I'll get in touch with my father. The services are in his name. I'll get him to reinstate them.'

This may not be as straightforward as he makes it sound, and hopefully it won't be necessary – the idea of having a conversation with his father about this house makes him a little uneasy – but he has responsibilities now, priorities he must honour.

'Your father who lives on Guernsey?'

'He's the only one I've got.'

'Does he ever come here?'

'He's not been back since my mother bolted, so I haven't either.'

'I'm sorry.' Ellen looks stricken. 'I shouldn't have asked.'

'It's fine. It was a long time ago.'

The doors leading off the hall are all ajar. Ellen chooses one – the one to the sitting room – and goes inside. She turns to Carl, genuine delight on her face. 'There's a fireplace! That's called an inglenook, right?'

'Yep. There's another one like that in the dining room, and

smaller fireplaces in a couple of the bedrooms. We can light this one when we need it and make it cosy in here.'

But Ellen's attention has already left the fireplace and she's circling the room, brushing careful fingers across the furniture, as if she's assessing precious antiques. Most of the stuff in this room is circa 1975, as it is in other parts of the house.

'I didn't expect it to look like this, inside. D'you know what I mean?'

'I do. You'd expect it to be full of old cottagey stuff, but this was how it was when Dad bought the house. The previous owners were moving overseas and left it almost fully furnished. I guess it saved my parents the bother of replacing it all.'

He rests his hands on the back of an olive-green chair with teak arms. Ellen pauses in her circling and begins playing with the switch of a table lamp with a mustard-coloured fringed shade. The lamp lights up.

'There you go. Leave these things to me.'

'Great! Dad must have kept up the electricity account. Or more likely he just forgot to cancel it and the bank keeps paying. The bulb must have blown in the hall.' He goes to the wall, flicks another switch and the ceiling lights shine out, two brass pendants with etched glass shades, suspended incongruously from centuries-old black beams.

'Can we have a fire tonight?' Ellen says, hopefully. 'It's a bit chilly.'

A basket containing what might be okay as fuel sits on the brick floor of the inglenook. Carl pulls it forward to see what's inside. There's scrunched-up newspaper in the bottom, a few logs, a handful of fir cones. He picks up a cone; it crumbles to dust. The logs might light, along with the newspaper, but not if they're damp. Logs used to be stored in one of the outhouses but he doesn't want to go outside again yet.

'We'll see later, when we've sorted ourselves out and had something to eat.'

Ellen is already on her way to the kitchen, taking with her the holdall they left in the hall.

'Looks okay in there,' she says, coming out again. 'It's a lovely big kitchen, isn't it? Your cooker's antiquated but at least it's electric, so it'll probably work. Can we see upstairs? The bedrooms?'

Carl's happy for her to lead the way up the narrow staircase, which twists round sharply at the top. The bathroom is at the back of the house. He opens the door for Ellen to see inside and waits for her to laugh at the avocado-coloured suite. But she just nods.

'It's fine. No shower, I take it?'

'We had a rubber hose thing attached to the bath taps, that's all. It's probably perished by now.'

Ellen wrinkles her nose. 'Oh, well, I like a bath. I brought some scented oil with me, expensive stuff. My sister left it behind.'

'Good to know you considered the essentials.' Carl winks, and turns across the hall to open another door.

This was his bedroom when they stayed here. It's small and boxlike, but has a view of the woods, which he always liked. He used to lie in bed and listen to the owls calling. The eerie sound didn't frighten him the first time he heard it, even though it was new to him. The owls were their friends, his father told him, as he tucked him in at night.

'You can be in here, or I can,' he says. 'Whichever. I'm not fussed.'

Ellen shrugs. 'Don't mind. It's up to you. It's your house.'

He shows her another bedroom. This one is larger, and has a small double bed. It also has violently coloured floral wallpaper that seems to advance across the room. It's funny how he's remembered some things about the house with complete accuracy, while others he's forgotten completely – like the décor in here.

'It's nice.' Ellen nods. It seems all she can manage for now. Her former determined cheerfulness has dissipated through tiredness and emotion, and probably her decision-making skills along with it.

'You have this one, then,' he says kindly, 'and I'll have the small one. Unless you want to see more?'

There are three stairs leading down from the landing to the main bedroom where his parents slept. He opens the door, peers inside, and is overwhelmed by an another rush of emotion. He pushes it away, fast.

Ellen is beside him. 'I'm good with the other one,' she says, turning away.

He can tell she's had enough now, as has he. It's been a long day.

'Right, then.' Carl leaps back up the stairs and onto the landing. 'If you want to bring your things up, I'll find the sheets and stuff.'

The beds have bare mattresses with dust sheets thrown over them. The pillows, sheets and blankets are in the tall wooden cupboard on the landing. He creaks the cupboard door open and begins tugging things from the shelves until he has a respectable armful of bedding. Dividing it into two, he leaves a pile on each bed then goes downstairs to help Ellen with her luggage.

The bags are unpacked for the things they need for now, and they've eaten a supper of soup and cheese and toast from the supplies Carl brought with him. Tomorrow, he'll walk to the village for more food and anything else they need, then come back in the car.

The immersion heater in the airing cupboard is on and the water has already reached a decent temperature. The only source of heat for the rooms, apart from the open fires, comes from cumbersome old storage heaters which don't seem to be working. Perhaps they never did; he can't remember now.

After several attempts, a fire is alight in the living room inglenook, using the scraps in the fuel basket. It won't last long, but it gives the room a cosy feel and welcome warmth. Ellen has inspected the beds and declared them too damp to sleep in after all. They agree it's too late to search the cupboards for hot water bottles, so they've brought blankets down and will sleep in there: Ellen on the sofa, Carl on one of the chairs. She seems pleased about this arrangement, as if she would rather not be alone. She doesn't say so, though. Carl is becoming used to guessing her thoughts, although he's probably getting it wrong most of the time.

It's a moonless night, and a fug of darkness envelopes the house, merging fields and woods with sky. The thick, olive-green living room curtains are closed halfway. Ellen asked him to leave them partly open, letting in the night. The darkness, she says, when he questions her, reminds her of the tunnel, the last place she felt safe.

Now she's curled up on the sofa, wearing red pyjamas and a blue fleece dressing gown. Several blankets are draped around and across her. Carl watches her surreptitiously. She's gazing into the fire, a faraway expression on her face. Behind her, the flames dance shadow-shapes on the wall. Again, Carl marvels at the trust she's placed in him.

He averts his eyes as she speaks, not wanting to be caught staring.

'Carl, why are you doing this for me?' Her voice is husky with emotion, and he realises how perilously close she is to breaking down.

It's not the first time she's asked the question. She needs solid reassurance, and he's prepared to give her that, as many times as it takes.

'You needed help. I was in a position to offer it. It's that simple.'

'Like the Good Samaritan.'

'Ha, that old cliché. I didn't see anyone passing by on the other side.'

'Fair point.'

'Anyway, I'm not that wonderful. You caught me on a good day.'

She chuckles. He's made her laugh, and he's glad about that.

But a moment later, her face is serious again. 'Carl, I'm still scared. I'm trying not to be, but I don't really know how safe this place is, and whether the police can track me down if whoever sent those horrible emails reports what they saw. You got rid of my phone – you did do that, didn't you?' He doesn't answer. Ellen hardly pauses. 'Is that enough, though? How do I know they won't come for me?'

'Nobody's coming for you, Ellen. You're safe here, and that's a promise.'

This is the truth. He knows the police won't find her here, or anywhere else, because they aren't looking, never have been – he only has to look at her to know that.

The more time Carl spends with Ellen, the more he's convinced of her innocence. She would never have got away with it; running from the scene, all the way up to the street. Somebody would have given chase, or at least spotted her and picked her up later. There would have been CCTV footage, if it had been working at the time.

Carl thinks about the emails she received, the creepy threats that finally broke her nerve and sent her into hiding. If they really indicated that somebody had witnessed the 'incident' and recognised her, that person would have contacted the police. It could have been done within hours and she would have been pulled in for questioning.

Those emails meant nothing. They were surely the work of

a nut job. It was only the timing of them that made Ellen take them seriously and link them to the crime she thought she'd committed.

Carl silently curses the guy at the centre of all this, who is surely out there somewhere, living his life, oblivious to the mayhem he's caused.

Ellen is not a killer, and the sooner Carl can convince her of that, the sooner they'll be out of there, and she'll be safely home.

'Settle down, get some sleep,' he tells her. 'Everything will seem better in the morning.'

ELEVEN
ELLEN

I must have woken up during the night, maybe several times, because I remember seeing Carl sleeping in the armchair, head lolling to one side, feet resting on a footstool. The blanket covering him had come adrift, exposing one bare leg and a foot with a sock still on. In my fuzzy-minded state I couldn't understand who this man was, what he was doing there, sleeping in the same room as me – a room I didn't recognise. I remember thinking he might be cold, and I should get up and replace the blanket, but I was afraid to wake him. Afraid of who he might be, and what he might do if he woke and caught me.

Once, I woke to find the cream and black tiled walls of the Tube around me, the arched roof with its defunct strip lights, the tunnel vanishing into blackness. I wasn't afraid. I didn't feel anything. I wasn't really awake then, of course. Dreams became intertwined with reality throughout the long night, and I couldn't tell which was which.

And then, as the room began to fill with powdery, early-morning light, I remembered where I was. I was in Sussex – exactly where, I couldn't have said. The journey from London came back to me, vivid and true. I saw the city slide away, the tarmac rolling ahead, folding beneath the wheels, and marching lines of traffic cones; I saw Carl's capable hands on the wheel, his trainered feet calmly operating the pedals as he drove us through the wintry landscape. It was as if remembering the detail of the journey was somehow important.

The chair where he slept is empty now, the blanket coiled on the floor. My heart races. Where is Carl? Has he gone, left me alone in a strange house? In a moment of raw panic, I leap off the sofa, scattering covers and cushions. And then I release the breath I was holding as he comes into the room, fully dressed in jeans and a chocolate-brown chunky-knit jumper. He stands in front of me, his back to the cold inglenook. I smile.

'Hey, you're awake. Snuggle back down and I'll bring you some tea—?'

He makes it a question, shifting from one foot to another, as if now he's brought me here, he doesn't know what to do with me. I feel a stab of sympathy for him, as well as deep gratitude.

I gather myself. 'I'm up now. I'll make the tea.'

'We'll do it together, then see about some breakfast. I brought long-life milk but I'll pick up some fresh when I go shopping this morning. You can come with me, if you like – take a look at the village.'

I follow Carl to the kitchen. He's brought along some little individual boxes of cereal, as well as bread and tins and stuff. He sets them out on the kitchen table for me to choose.

'Yes, please, to breakfast,' I say, picking up a box of Frosties. 'But no to the shopping trip. I can't go out, can I? I can't risk being seen.'

Carl's face tells me I've said something stupid. But what's the point of coming all this way only to parade around in public? Whoever *catcreep* is, whatever their motives in hounding me, they aren't messing about. In the cyber world, nobody is that hard to contact, which explains the emails. They must have seen me push Matt in front of that train, and recognised me. They may even have followed me home. How would I know? Okay, I got a taxi home; at least, I think I did – that part isn't very clear now – but it's not impossible.

I've thought and thought about it – I had plenty of thinking time while I was hiding in the tunnel – and it's the only possible explanation: *catcreep* saw me bolt from the scene and is determined to make me pay for my crime. And now they've played their little game and had their fun tormenting me, they'll have gone to the police with the information.

And what about CCTV? The Tube must be bristling with it. For all I know, the police may already have studied the footage and published grainy photos of me, in the papers, or on TV. The very least way, they'd have put out a description.

Somebody is out there looking for me, I just know it. Nobody gets away with murder. Not in today's world.

I suddenly feel shaky and sick. I put the Frosties back on the table. 'I'll use the bathroom first, before breakfast.'

'Okay. But, Ellen, think about it,' Carl says. 'Nobody around here knows you. They won't even notice you. Anyway, you were fine before you started getting those emails.'

Fine? I didn't tell him that, did I? He seems to be making it up as he goes along, as if he knows more about my situation than I do. How could I have been *fine*, after what I'd done?

'Of course I wasn't! I was a mess, Carl. I didn't know what to do. I was living with the biggest secret of my life and pretending everything was normal. It got a whole lot worse after Rosanna left and I was on my own.'

'I know. I get that,' Carl says. 'I'm so sorry, I wasn't thinking.' He rubs a hand across his head, making his hair stand on end. It's a gesture of exasperation and I find that slightly unnerving, as well as depressing.

. . .

Later, Carl goes out, telling me I'm not to worry if he's gone for a while. I wash up our breakfast things, and wipe down the kitchen surfaces and the shelves of the empty cupboards and fridge-freezer using the dampened tea towel. In the cupboard under the sink I find a cardboard box containing ragged dusters, dried-up tins of polish, a dustpan and brush, and a balding feather duster on a stick. I dust the surfaces downstairs with the best of the dusters, then tour the house with the feather duster and sweep the cobwebs from the corners.

The day is clear, bright and cold, and I open the bedroom windows as far as they'll go to rid the rooms of the musty smell and air the mattresses. The air that rushes in is fresh and sharp, and smells of damp grass. I carry out a search for hot-water bottles and eventually find two in the chest of drawers on the landing. They have pink fluffy covers, matted with age. I test them in case the rubber has perished but no leaks spring, so I leave one on each of our beds, ready to use later. Then I go downstairs, put on my coat and hat and sidle out of the creaking front door like the fugitive I am.

Carl has already assured me there are no near neighbours, the closest dwellings being a pair of former farmworkers' cottages some way along the lane which passes the front of the house. Owl Corner sits in a shallow dip, surrounded by fields and trees. Its situation makes it almost invisible from the main road and I couldn't have wished for a better hiding place. Even so, my throat squeezes dry and my heart thumps as I skirt the walls of the house and walk around to the back, my beanie hat pulled well down.

Yesterday, I saw only grass, as if most of the garden had been laid to lawn. But closer inspection reveals the sunken crescent shapes of what presumably were flowerbeds, with stumps and stalks of bygone plants spiking through the yellowing grass. Here and there, bright green spears of daffodils push up through the neglect, and patches of purple and white crocuses flourish. In a month or so, it will be spring.

But spring is the season of hope and promise, and I can't believe it will ever come again. However hard I try, I can't summon up any kind of hope for me, any sort of future. This is not self-pity, it's simple reality.

Words form in the recesses of my mind, words that constantly rearrange themselves. Words that will sound convincing when I present myself at a police station and confess to the murder of Matthew Leyton. If I'm not arrested first, this is what I must do, I know that now. But not yet. I'm not ready. Waiting a little longer won't change anything.

But neither will handing myself in. Confessing won't bring him back. It won't help Laura – Matt's wife – or his children. And it would hurt Rosanna in more ways than she could ever imagine. It would achieve nothing. I'm already punishing myself, and I always will. It's not as if I'm going to kill anyone else; I know I won't. Whatever madness took hold of me in that moment has gone. It's out of my system.

A crackling, rushing sound slices through the muddle in my head, startling me. My muscles tighten, ready to race indoors. But it's only birds, a flock of black rooks rising from the nearby wood. All is silent again, apart from the faint drone of traffic from the main road.

I cross to a corner of the garden and a cluster of stunted fruit trees, their bare grey branches flaking and discoloured with mould. Apples? I'll ask Carl later. I'm about to move away and head back indoors – I've been outside too long already – when something in the long grass beneath one of the fruit trees catches my eye. I brush the grass aside, revealing a little cross made out of twigs fastened together with string, stuck in a small pile of stones.

Time shrinks, the years concertina. Rosanna and I are

sprawled in the back garden of the Bexleyheath house, a scratchy tartan rug beneath us. The sun's too hot on the back of my head and I'm thinking I should go indoors, but I don't. Instead, I watch Rosanna. She's leaning back on her hands, face raised to the sky, eyes closed, like a sun-worshipper. A half-smile plays on her lips. She looks so assured, complacent, and I feel suddenly mutinous.

I shuffle across the rug, deliberately bumping my arm against my sister's. She opens her eyes and gives me an annoyed look. Now I have her attention, I use the only weapon I've got.

'Do you remember them dying?' I say, as if she could ever forget what happened to our parents. As if either of us could.

'Fudge and Flake? You made me look at them, after they were dead. I wished you hadn't.'

She thinks I mean the hamsters. She's looking towards the tree on the far side of the garden. In the long grass beneath it are the rotting remains of two miniature crosses made out of lolly sticks. We'd brought our pets with us to Bexleyheath but they were already getting on in hamster years and hadn't lived long after that.

Rosanna, wearing brief pink shorts and a white gypsy top, stretches out her bare, brown legs, and gives a little sigh.

The rebellious urge to stick pins in my sister is over as fast as it began, and I wish I hadn't said anything.

'Yes, them. Fudge and Flake.'

'You're mad, you are,' Rosanna says, and turns her face back to the sun.

The sound of a car engine close by sets the adrenaline pumping again, and I jog across the garden towards the house. Then I see Carl coming towards the front door. He's laden with carrier bags.

'Hi,' he says. 'Have you been okay?'

'Yes, fine. Did you have a pet here, a pet that died? Only I found a cross in some stones, over by the trees.'

'No, no pets. We only came here for weekends and holidays so we couldn't have kept pets.' Carl looks at me. 'That grave belongs to a bird, a robin we found dead in the lane, me and some of the village kids I was friendly with. The others said we should have a funeral for it. "Who Killed Cock Robin"? You know the rhyme? So we put it in a box and buried it. Somebody wrote a poem and we said it together.'

'Sounds like a lot of fun.'

Carl laughs. 'Oh, tremendous.'

We unload the shopping in the kitchen, then Carl returns to the car and comes back with his arms around a large box.

'I bought a cheap microwave oven,' he says, setting it down on the table. 'It'll save time.'

I'm about to say we don't need to save time – we have plenty of hours to fill – but that would sound ungrateful, so I just say, 'Great.'

'One more trip.' He sets off again and comes back lugging two sacks, which turn out to contain logs for the fire.

'I got these at the petrol station. They'll keep us going for a while.'

I offer him some money for my share of the supplies, but Carl gently refuses. 'I can do it. It's not like we're here for the long haul.' He catches sight of my face. 'Oh, Ellen, don't worry. I'm not going to kick you out. This house is yours for as long as you need it.'

I nod, unconvinced.

'Let's take it one day at a time, shall we?' Carl fishes in the pocket of his padded jacket. 'Here, I got you this.' He throws me a small package. I catch it. It's a mobile phone.

'It's a basic pay-as-you-go. I'll put my number in it, then we'll be in touch if we need to.'

'I can throw it away afterwards? When this is over, I mean?'

'If you like,' Carl says.

And again, his expression isn't how I expect it to be.

TWELVE

ROSANNA

Rosanna has never been to Cornwall in winter, and has decided she likes it. She can walk the lanes and coastal paths with Dolly, the dachshund, whose little legs seem to contain an endless amount of energy, and meet only other dog walkers and a trickle of open-air types in serious walking boots who rent the holiday cottages off-season.

Sarah and Jay moved there from London in search of a slower, more fulfilling way of life. Rosanna thought they were crazy at first, but now she kind of sees the point. Behind the old farmhouse is a large field, the only remaining part of the original farm not sold off separately. The plan was to set up a glamping business but there've been no signs of it happening, and Rosanna suspects it never will. Jay has a printing business in St Austell, and Sarah stays at home with their daughter, the cutest two-year-old called Chloe, who rackets around the farmhouse like a battery-operated toy that's gone out of control.

Sarah and Jay made it clear from the start that Rosanna is welcome to stay as long as she likes. They don't ask questions, but she has told them a little – it's only fair, since she's enjoying their hospitality. She's kept it vague, implying she's having a break from her boyfriend after a falling out but that it isn't over, by any means. She hasn't lied directly, only by omission. It won't do any good to tell them she's having an affair with a married man. They wouldn't judge – they'd never do that – but they might take the same stance as her sister, and however well-intentioned, she doesn't want to hear it.

Not that Ellen has ever said outright that she's fooling herself, and that Matt will never leave his wife for her. She never says it, only dances around it with her not-so-subtle questions and scraps of uninformed opinion, but it's written all over her face. This is one reason why Rosanna left London – to remove herself from her sister's watchfulness, as if she's waiting for her to fall, at which point she'll be there to catch her. It's been that way since the accident that took their parents away. As if Ellen has purposefully slid into the role of mother, which is totally ridiculous anyway, since she's the younger sister. And they had Aunt Margaret for that.

Rosanna sometimes wishes Ellen would get a life of her own instead of rummaging around in hers. Okay, that's not fair, nor strictly accurate. She casts her mind back to the day she found out Matt was married. They had only been seeing each other for a month, but she was already smitten, as he seemed to be with her. There was a West End show she wanted to see, and as she and Matt were passing the theatre on their way to a restaurant, she suggested going in to ask if they had any tickets left for the coming weeks. The show was popular, and she didn't think there'd be a chance. She couldn't believe her luck when they were offered two seats for the coming Saturday night.

Matt stood sullenly beside her at the box office.

'Saturday? I don't know, Rosie. I might not be free,' he said, while the box office assistant waited patiently for them to make up their minds.

'Well, why not? What might you be doing instead?'

He seemed to struggle to answer her. Eventually, he agreed to take the tickets, and paid for them. But he hadn't seemed keen and, for the first time, Rosanna held felt a streak of annoyance towards him.

She challenged him over dinner. 'If you didn't want to see the show, you should have said. I wouldn't have minded.'

'No, no, it's not that,' he said. Then he gave a big, regretful sigh. 'I'm so sorry. I should have told you right at the beginning. I'm not always free because I'm married, Rosie. If you want to walk away right now, I won't blame you. But I do have feelings for you, strong feelings. It's not the same with Laura, my wife. We aren't, well... But when there are children involved, you have to make compromises. You do see that, don't you, my love?'

Rosie wasn't shocked. Sad and disappointed, but not shocked. She hadn't failed to notice that their dates always seemed difficult to arrange – on his part, not hers. He'd always seemed restricted, too restricted for somebody supposedly free of commitments. Which, of course, as it turned out, he wasn't. He'd also said it was easiest if he phoned her when he was free to see her, and he would rather she didn't phone him. A dead giveaway if ever there was one. Only Rosanna had chosen not to acknowledge it, until that moment.

They talked about the situation a little more that night, but not as much as Rosanna would have liked, and not in any depth. There were so many questions swarming in her brain but Matt's demeanour effectively put up a barrier, one she couldn't find her way around, and they were never voiced.

She considered putting a stop to it, right there and then; of course she did – she had her pride, and some sense of self-preservation. But when Matt said he was falling in love with her, she couldn't do it, because she was falling in love with him, too.

'Oh, Rosie,' was Ellen's response at hearing the news. 'Don't do that, please. You'll only get hurt. What kind of man must he be to do that to his wife and children? Put a stop to it before it's too late.'

They argued a bit – well, quite a lot. Rosanna remembers accusing her sister of being prudish and always looking on the black side, while Ellen persisted with her warnings and gloomy predictions of heartbreak. They argued, on and off, for days, until finally Ellen announced that she wouldn't say another word on the subject, and it was entirely Rosanna's lookout if things went wrong.

She didn't mean it, of course, and Rosanna knew that, ultimately, her sister spoke out of love and concern for her. In the end they silently agreed to disagree, the best either could hope for.

Dolly tugs at the lead now, and squats on the grass verge. While she waits, Rosanna gazes across the hedgerow at the green and brown fields as they undulate towards the coast, her mind still on Ellen. Her sister will be better off on her own, for now. She might not see it that way yet, but she needs space to grow and move forwards, and she can't do that while the pair of them are stuck to each other like gum to the bottom of a shoe.

Besides, she doesn't want to be around to witness Ellen's disappointment when she finds out what else Rosanna has done. Or, rather, what she has, unbelievably, allowed to happen.

She thinks about Matt again, the shock and disbelief she felt when her messages shunted into a dead end and she realised he'd blocked her. She wasn't as cool with that as she made out to Ellen. How could he do that to her, after all they'd shared, all they meant to each other? Her brain, of course, came up with a rational explanation. Laura, his wife: the risk factor. But all he has to do is unblock her, or contact her from a different phone. He has her number, that's all he needs. He knows where she works, too, or used to. He may try and find her that way. If he does, and finds out she's left, he'll know she's not sitting around waiting for him to crook his little finger. She doesn't play those games, believes it's best to be upfront – but a little wondering and worrying on Matt's part can't hurt.

Her excruciating neediness on that last date in the restaurant still keeps her awake at night. She hopes Matt realises that wasn't her, not the real Rosanna, the fun, sexy girlfriend, the one who makes no demands. And what he said, about it – *them* – being over was entirely her fault. She didn't accept it then, and she doesn't now. She saw how he looked at her when they were outside the restaurant, the way his eyes followed the taxi as she swept off into the night, full of indignation but knowing he still wanted her, so much. It was only after that night that something had gone wrong and caused this hurtful separation. Matt would find the way back to her. They would find the way back to each other.

She's reached the outskirts of Mevagissey where the road bumps and twists and plunges downwards, to the harbour. Across the jumble of rooftops, the granite sea chops and churns. She stops walking, tugs lightly on the lead and looks down at Dolly. Two jet beads gaze mournfully back. She has such sorrowful eyes for such a happy little dog.

'Does Matt still love me, Dolly?' Rosanna says. 'Does my Matt still want me?'

But Dolly turns her liquid gaze on Rosanna's coat pocket, where she knows there are treats.

Dolly doesn't get it. Nobody gets it, only Rosanna herself. And Matt. Of course he loves her. These pinpricks of doubt are only because of the altered nature of time in this slow, quiet place. Time stretches out here, gathering in tangles among the stiff grasses, curling inside shells on the beach, hibernating beneath spiky hedgerows. It sees no need to hurry along.

It's beginning to rain. Rosanna turns around and they walk back the way they came.

. . .

As they cross the yard, the chickens in the coop flap and cackle. Dolly noses the wire fence but otherwise ignores them. They enter the farmhouse by the back door. The kitchen, a cosy mish-mash of old and new, is warm and welcoming. A shiny new butler sink has replaced the original and is backed by cheerful yellow tiles in place of peeling plaster. The ceiling beams have been lightened with trendy pale grey paint. Vintage blue-and-white china jostles happily with chunky lettered pottery and bold florals.

Sarah comes into the room. 'Cup of tea?' She switches the kettle on without waiting.

'Please.'

The dog laps eagerly from her water bowl, then flops into her bed in front of the wood burner. Chloe wheels into the kitchen, arms outstretched, and Sarah scoops her up and positions her on her hip in one smooth movement. The toddler has Jay's sunlit smile, his Afro hair, although hers is the colour of burnt toffee, not black. Her ocean-blue eyes are pure Sarah.

She flings out an arm towards Rosanna and waggles a golden-skinned hand. 'Hat!'

Rosanna takes off her bright blue beret and puts it on Chloe's head. The child giggles in delight, and Rosanna knows that this is the time, and if she doesn't say it now, she might never say it at all.

'There's something I need to tell you,' she says to Sarah. 'I'm pregnant.'

THIRTEEN
CARL

It's nine o'clock in the evening, and they're sitting by the inglenook in the living room, Ellen on the sofa, Carl in an armchair. Ellen's face glows pink in the firelight. The logs he bought won't last long at this rate, but the electric heaters still refuse to function, and the fire is essential. Ellen asked him to light it at four o'clock today, and he didn't have the heart to suggest leaving it until later to save fuel. She seems to feel the cold more than he does. They're getting through an extraordinary amount of food, too, because the two of them are here all day, although Ellen doesn't eat a lot.

It's not that he minds going out for supplies – it gives him a break from what is fast becoming a claustrophobic situation – but each time they run out of this or that, it reminds him of what's at stake here, and he ought to be doing something about it rather than whiling away the days making pointless assaults on the garden, reading, and generally drifting about.

But how? And where to begin?

Ellen is reading now. The shelves in the dining room are stuffed with books, most of which were inherited with the rest of the furnishings. The books smell like beached seaweed. The pages are foxed, the paper covers of the hardbacks ripped. Ellen says she doesn't mind, and it's a shame they've been neglected for so long. She's doing her best to rectify that, and as soon as she's finished one, she dives in and comes up with a nineteenth-century classic, a Mills and Boon romance, or a crime novel.

It's crime she's reading now – a Ruth Rendell. Her expression is intense as she scans the page. Reading probably takes her mind off her problems. Carl watches her, and feels the familiar weight of responsibility. He's thinking what to say to open the debate – there must be one, and soon – when Ellen raises her head, sighs, and closes the book.

Carl removes the earbuds attached to his phone, and waits.

'I keep thinking about Rosanna,' Ellen begins. 'How could I have taken away the man she loved?' She throws up her hands, a helpless gesture. 'How could I have hurt her that much? I'm no expert on love. I'm not sure I've ever been in love. Or if I have, it didn't last. Anyway, supposing Matt was *the one*, after all, and they would have ended up together?'

'Matt? That was his name?' Carl makes the question sound casual, when it's anything but. Ellen's never mentioned the name before, and he hasn't liked to ask in case he upsets her.

'Yes. Matt. Short for Matthew. Matthew Leyton.' Ellen waves away the interruption. 'I've ruined Rosie's life, haven't I? What kind of a sister does that? All I ever wanted to do after we lost Mum and Dad was protect her, be on her side, whatever. Well, I certainly failed there, didn't I?'

Ellen's face is clouded, her eyes darkening. Carl searches his brain for the right words, words that will convey sympathy and understanding without giving himself away – words that probably don't exist. Ellen is relying on his unconditional support. He can't snatch it away now. And yet something has to change.

'Ellen, the odds were stacked against him leaving his wife for her, because they always are, you know that. It's only guilt that's making you doubt the outcome of her relationship with Matt.'

She sighs again. 'I know, and you're right. But I took him away so fast. One minute he was hers, for whatever time they had left together, and then he was gone. Just like that. No warning.'

'She might have had a warning,' Carl says carefully. 'For all you know, she might have been expecting him to leave her, to disappear overnight without trace, in spite of what she said. I don't know what kind of relationship you have with your sister, but maybe she didn't want to lose face, and she hid what was really going on. What happened to him – what really happened – well, it fits with that, doesn't it?'

They've had this conversation before, something close to it, anyway. Carl feels the sensation of panic rising in his chest. He has to move this on, stop Ellen from treading round in circles. He has to slant her thinking, set her on a different pathway. It's a mammoth task, and he can't imagine now how he thought he was worthy or clever enough to take it on. She needs proper therapy, not his cack-handed pop psychology.

But he has to try. Nothing will change, otherwise.

'No.' Her voice is firm. 'You weren't there. You didn't see my sister waiting it out, checking her phone every five minutes. She never gave up on Matt, never lost faith that it would all come right. Okay, she's gone to Cornwall, but that doesn't mean she thinks it's over. It's me she's given up on, not him.'

Carl gets up and goes to the kitchen for a beer for himself and apple juice for Ellen – for some reason she hasn't touched alcohol since they came to Owl Corner.

'I don't know if I got it right about the robin,' he says, sitting down again. 'When you asked me about the grave, the robin came into my head. There was a dead robin at some time, but it might have been something else we buried and held the funeral for.

Could've been a field mouse.' He smiles to cover the outright lie. He forgives himself for telling it; it serves his purpose. 'Memory's a funny thing. It doesn't always work as you'd expect.' Ellen is silent. Carl ploughs on. 'You can be so clear about something that happened, you'd swear on it in court. And then... *pow!* You see a completely different scenario, and that rings true as well. Tru*er*.'

'What are you saying?' Ellen regards him with suspicion.

He ignores the question, talks a little more about what he's read, and what he knows.

'Memory's a fascinating subject. For instance, did you know that any memories you have of being a baby, under the age of two, or thereabouts, are almost certain to be false?' Ellen begins to speak but Carl rushes on. 'I've always had this picture in my mind of sitting in a highchair and being fed soft boiled egg, and I don't like it, and keep pushing the spoon away. But I know that what I'm remembering isn't real, it's made up from what I was told, or from a photo of me sitting in a highchair. Do you see what I'm saying?'

'Of course. You're saying that memory isn't perfect. But that far back, when we were babies... it's understandable if we get it wrong.'

'It is. But here's something weird I read. Princess Diana died in a car crash, in a tunnel in Paris, in 1997. That was before you were born, of course.'

'Yes, but Rosie remembers something, or thinks she does. She was only just coming up for three, but she says she remembers Mum crying because her favourite princess had died. My sister started crying as well. Of course, she had no idea what she was crying about.' Ellen smiles. 'Didn't want to be left out, I expect. It sounds about right.'

Carl smiles back. 'Could well be. Now, this is the interesting bit. A survey was carried out, a scientific survey, and forty-four per cent of the people who took part claimed to have seen a video of the actual crash on TV. But no such video existed. How could it have?'

'Yep, I get that.' Ellen looks at him, her head tilted to one side. 'Carl, why were you thinking about memory and stuff?'

As if she hasn't already guessed.

Again, he doesn't answer her directly. 'I read a book about it once. About how common it is to imagine you saw something, or were in a certain place at a certain time, when you couldn't have been. And how some people are more disposed towards having false memories than others.'

It's true, he has read a book on the subject and found it interesting; he doesn't mind Ellen knowing that. But he would rather she didn't know about the two hours he spent on the internet, reading articles and honing his very basic knowledge, the night before he brought her to Owl Corner. This was after he'd searched the internet for reports of any incidents at Victoria Tube station, and found nothing.

'You can convince yourself that memory is fact, if you're in a particular frame of mind,' he says, then immediately regrets taking things that far as Ellen springs up from the sofa.

'This is about me, isn't it? About Matt, what I did to him?' Her voice has fire, her eyes are like ice. 'You said you believed me! Not at first, but then you said you believed me. If you didn't believe I killed Matt, why did you bring me here?'

Actually, he never said that. He didn't tell her he believed her story, not straight out. It was what she wanted to hear, and her brain had skewed his words to make them right, for her.

He stands up, too. 'Ellen, please... I didn't mean to upset you.'

'Well, you're making a bloody good job of it, all the same!'

He wants to take her in his arms and soothe away her fear and pain. But they don't do touching, and he doesn't want to give her the wrong idea. Besides, he needs to keep this real if he's to make any progress, which is seeming more unlikely by the minute.

She stands before him, her arms limp by her sides. Her shoulders subside, the anger gone. She just looks exhausted, and sad, and that's partly his fault. He wishes he knew how to handle this properly. It was so arrogant of him to believe he ever could.

'I'm sorry,' he says. 'You're tired. Why don't you go up and have your bath, then go to bed?'

'I'm not eight years old,' she says, but her face says he's forgiven.

He's relieved, but annoyed with himself for pushing her too hard, and being clumsy about it. This will take time, and patience.

'I will go up,' she says. 'Is the immersion on?'

'Always. It's our one extravagance.'

''Night, then,' she says, from the doorway.

''Night, Ellen. Sleep tight. I'm sorry about before.'

Ellen nods, then she's gone.

FOURTEEN

CARL

They've been at Owl Corner for almost a week, and during that time the weather has turned from slightly chilly to ferociously wintry. The wind screamed in the chimneys, rattled the windows and squeezed under the front door in icy bursts. The trees in the woods whipped back and forth, snapping branches and casting them into the lane, and curtains of horizontal rain blotted out the landscape. Then, when they thought it couldn't get any worse, the blizzard arrived, and the world outside turned white.

Carl has made one expedition, cajoling the car along the snowy roads to stock up with food and more firewood from the petrol station. Other than that, neither of them has ventured outside.

The storms eventually abated, and the snow has gone. There's a noticeable rise in temperature. But Ellen still refuses to leave the house in daylight, other than to spend the odd half-hour in the garden, clipping at the bushes with a rusty pair of secateurs they found, and helping him uncover the flowerbeds and release the plants into the light. She wears dark clothes which don't show any flesh, the beanie hat pulled down over her forehead. She is ever-watchful, eyes darting everywhere. She jumps at the slightest unusual sound or sign of movement. She's like a frightened animal peering out of its burrow.

She isn't happy when he tells her a locksmith is coming to renew the front door lock, but it's essential if they're to go in and out with ease. She hides upstairs while the locksmith works. Carl gives her a key of her own, which she insists she won't need, but he makes her keep it, just in case.

Ellen will go out after dusk, and they walk along the footpath as far as the churchyard, skirting the woods where unseen wildlife rustles the undergrowth and owls call. She doesn't mind the sounds of the night, nor finds them threatening. She does say, however, that she finds the open countryside disconcerting; the expanse of fields around Owl Corner eerie and unsettling, even in daylight.

'I'm a city girl. I don't like all this green space. It unnerves me,' she says, bluntly.

There's nothing he can do about that. In a way, he empathises with her. He likes the countryside, even in winter; the quiet, and being close to nature. But he misses London: the continuous kaleidoscope of light and sound and movement, modern buildings juxtaposed with old, telling the city's story, hiding its secrets. He misses work, too, or if not yet, he soon will. He may only be a sales assistant but the shop and its environs thrum with life, making him feel at the centre of things. The loose tale he'd spun about a family emergency, without the thread of detail to hold it together, works for now, but he won't take advantage, especially as he's still being paid.

He wants to tell Ellen she'll get used to being in the country, but that would imply a longish stay, and he doesn't want her getting too settled, for her sake as well as his.

Carl watches Ellen reading quietly, or listening to music on his phone with a faraway look on her face, and wonders guiltily if this whole thing is a mistake. That if he'd left her alone and not interfered, she'd be back home in Brixton by now, living her life as normal. Whatever, it's too late now. She's here, and relying on him.

He has asked her to think about what happened at Victoria Tube station, to relive it through the images in her mind. He says he knows it will be hard, but it's important. Sometimes she nods, as if she agrees this is what she ought to be doing. Other times she brushes him off, making it clear she doesn't want to think about it. Whether she does or not, he has no idea; she doesn't say. It's a straw-clutching exercise, anyway. The idea that she shoved Matt Leyton under the train is so embedded in her brain, in every cell of her, the chances of a different story suddenly arising are practically zero.

It's becoming clearer by the hour that just talking and persuading isn't going to change a thing. He'd wanted it to come from her, the realisation that her 'memory' of killing her sister's lover is false, and for an entirely different scenario to present itself to her. Solving the problem for herself would have far greater impact and be much more satisfactory for her mental well-being.

But so far there's been no sign of that happening.

Rescuing Ellen from the tunnel and giving her sanctuary was only the start. He has to do better, be the person she can rely on. The only positive action he's taken so far is to look online for reports of a death on the Tube – he'd tried that in the little time he'd had before they left London, and found nothing. He has to up his game, nothing surer. He has to present Ellen with the indisputable evidence of her innocence, and there's only one way to do that.

He has to find Matt Leyton.

FIFTEEN
GEORGIE

Ellen Randall hasn't been at work for over two weeks. *Off sick,* Georgie's ears picked up as the lunch queue shuffled past.

Sick? Guilty conscience, more like. If the girl's gone down with something serious – nobody's said, not in Georgie's hearing anyway – that's a pity. But she did wrong, and if there's one thing Georgie can't abide, it's injustice. If Ellen has taken sick, it could be a case of divine intervention, and Georgie could have saved herself the bother.

There again, it galls her that Ellen didn't take her last message to heart, the one that gave her an ultimatum. If she's been off work, she couldn't have confessed, could she? Or perhaps she has, and now she's afraid to face anyone. It serves her right, in that case.

It wasn't until Sonny, the teenage boy from next door, and Georgie, were hunched over the laptop in the living room, along with the faint whiff of chlorine and chewing gum, and he was teaching her how to set up a new email account, that she mentioned the thing she really wanted.

She's not a complete dinosaur with technology, and she isn't stupid. Who was the first one to get the measure of the new till at work? Georgie Smith, that's who, and then she had to show the others. She could have worked out how to set up a new email identity for herself, with a little patience. But without *her* email address – her personal one, not her work one – the whole operation was doomed to failure.

She fetched Sonny a can of Coke from the kitchen, put some chocolate biscuits on a plate and then explained what else she needed besides a new email address.

He wasn't too keen at first. 'Can't be done,' he said, with a firm shake of his head.

'Can't it? That's a shame. I'd have thought a bright boy like you would have been up to speed on that sort of thing.' Georgie gave Sonny a little smile. 'Oh, well, if you say it can't be done, I shall have to take your word for it.'

Georgie picked up a biscuit and nibbled the chocolate round the edge.

'When I said it can't be done, I meant not by just anyone,' Sonny said, straightening his back. 'You need something called a Lookup tool and that means setting up an account and jumping through a load of hoops. And you need to know what you're doing.' Sonny tapped the side of his nose.

Georgie gave him a sideways look and a little wink, and waited.

Sonny smiled. 'Okay, okay. I guess I could give it a go. Not here, though.'

Then he said that if he did what she asked, she wasn't to tell anyone. And she looked at him and said that if he did it, he wasn't to tell anyone she was asking. They high-fived on the agreement.

Which is when he went back next door to use his father's computer.

Sonny's dad's in the legal profession; Georgie isn't sure in what capacity exactly, but it must be something close to the top.

There aren't many houses in this street with just the one family in them.

He was back within the hour with what she wanted written down on a scrap of paper. She pushed a ten-pound note into his hand.

'Ta,' he said, before he skedaddled back up the steps.

'Hush money,' Georgie said. They laughed at that.

As it's Saturday, she's giving herself a little treat and nipping over to Oxford Street, to Marks and Spencer at Marble Arch, for a bit of a browse and a spot of lunch. The queue in the café will be a mile long but she's got all day, and there's always someone pleased to chat. 'Are you saving this seat for somebody? No? Mind if I sit here then?'

Opposite Georgie on the Tube are two girls, about the age of Ellen Randall and her sister. Dressed similar, too. Double-breasted woollen coats, like Georgie's school coat, dresses peeping out from underneath, thick woolly tights, clumpy boots. These two don't look alike, Georgie thinks. They'll be friends, then, not sisters. Their chatter drifts across the aisle, like leaves blown in the wind. From what she can gather, they're off to look for something to wear to a party.

The last party Georgie went to was a girl at school's four-teenth birthday party. Unless you counted Georgie's own wedding reception, which she didn't. Anyway, she was only allowed to go to the party because her sister, Charlotte, who was in one of her 'up' moods at the time, persuaded Dad to let Georgie go. Their mother never had much say in these matters.

The girl whose party it was – her name escapes Georgie now – wasn't a particular friend of hers, and she had no idea why she'd been invited. Unless it was to make up the numbers – there was a flu epidemic at the time, half the class was down with it. It was probably that.

The party girl was one of those shiny types, all eyes and hair, and coltish legs; the 'in crowd' flocking around her much the same. But Georgie made herself have a nice time, ignored the behind-hand stage whispers about her knee-length skirt and blouse coming out of the Ark, took full advantage of the buffet and bopped around to Donny Osmond with the best of them. She only tripped over the coffee table once. It shouldn't have been left there in the first place, in Georgie's opinion.

If she thought she'd escaped total humiliation, she was wrong. At nine o'clock on the dot there was a hammering on the front door. It was a wonder anyone heard it above George Harrison belting out 'My Sweet Lord' on the record player at full volume. But Georgie did, and so did somebody else. A call went out. 'Georgie, your dad's come to collect you!'

Her mind skates over what happened next, except for the stupid tittering that followed her and her father all the way through the streets to their front door. And up the stairs to her bedroom, come to that.

According to Dad, she'd taken advantage of her freedom, stopping out till all hours. The names he called her didn't bear repeating, inside her head or out of it. It wasn't even as if there were any boys at the party, so none of them made sense anyway.

But it doesn't do to dwell, does it? The girls get off the train at the same station as Georgie. Silently, she wishes them success with their shopping, and hopes they enjoy the party.

SIXTEEN

ELLEN

Time spools on, although my mind makes little sense of it. Past and present seem like one mass of moments, with no distinction between them. As the days lengthen, the weather lifts, interspersing short, sharp showers with longer spells of mild sunshine that turn the brick walls of the house strawberry pink. Baby ferns sprout beneath the window ledges from the cracks in the mortar, spindly daffodils bloom acid yellow and fat buds appear on the fruit trees, which Carl says are apple, pear and plum.

I pass the time by reading my way through the books on the dining room shelves or listening to music on Carl's phone. I also do most of the cooking, the little cleaning that's needed – we don't disturb the dust much, the two of us – and peer through the porthole of the elderly washing machine, praying it will reach the end of its cycle before whatever is making that ominous grinding noise wins the battle.

Carl spends most of his day working on the garden. He's invested in some new tools because the handles on the old ones were loose, and the tines of the fork kept breaking. I watch him digging, quite manically at times, resurrecting the submerged borders, tending the scraps of plants that still grow in them. This rebirth seems to please him, but I wonder what the point is, considering the house will be left to its own devices once we've gone. Sometimes I work alongside him, forking out the weeds and ridding the soil of the larger stones. I've made a pile of these in a corner of the garden; the miniature stack looks like a leftover from some sort of ritual.

In the evenings, Carl lays the fire in the living room, using the logs he bought from the petrol station, eked out by whatever dry sticks he finds in the woods, and we eat our supper from trays on our laps, then read, or play sevens and rummy with a pack of dog-eared playing cards we found in a drawer. It feels as if we're playing house, like children expecting to be called back to real life at any moment.

'I bought us this,' Carl says one morning after one of his trips out. He places a worn-looking box on the kitchen table. It contains a small, silver-grey radio. 'It's second-hand but in good working order, so the woman in the shop said. Sorry I couldn't run to a telly. Anyway, we never had one here, so there won't be an aerial or anything.'

'It's lovely. Thank you,' I say. 'I didn't bring much cash with me but I'll pay you back for all the stuff you've bought, when-ever... I can.'

Carl smiles. 'Don't worry about it.'

I twiddle one of the knobs and a rustling sound fills the space until it finds a channel. I switch it off again. 'But...'

'But what?'

'The news. I might be on it. Okay, okay, I know how crazy that must sound to you, but it doesn't to me. I can't help the way I think, or feel.'

Carl, who has been the last word in patience all along, drags out a chair, drops into it and puts his head in his hands, elbows on the table. I feel afraid to speak. Eventually, he looks up. 'Ellen, this can't go on.' He sees my face. 'Sorry, sorry. I'm just not sure where we go from here. You won't be on the news. You said it yourself, there were no reports of anyone being... of any such incident in the Tube on that day, at that time. No news of any deaths. Not even accidental ones.'

'There was no *accident*! Don't you think I'd have known if he'd fallen in front of the train?'

He doesn't reply. He just looks at me. Heat travels down the backs of my legs. If Carl is starting to doubt me, I don't think I can cope.

My voice is thin, stretched almost to breaking point, like an over-tuned guitar string. 'There were no reports at the time, not that I found, and God knows I searched hard enough. But that was then – before the person who witnessed what I did decided to send me threatening messages. I've not been online since then – I didn't dare. And no, I don't know why they took so long about it, they just did, okay? Carl, you know all this. You know why I had to get away.'

He looks at me, and there's a difference in his expression, a kind of distance that wasn't there before. As if he's moving slowly, inch by inch, away from me.

'I know what you told me, Ellen.'

'And what's that supposed to mean?'

'Nothing, nothing. I'm tired, that's all. Pretty exhausted, as it goes.'

'Oh.' I drop into the seat opposite him. 'I'm sorry, Carl. Of course we can have the radio on. That was just me being para-noid. You should try and get some rest today. You've not stopped with the garden, and rushing around in the car.' He gives me a look. 'Sorry, I know you only go out to get us food and stuff. Anyway, why shouldn't you go out? I'm the one in hiding.'

In hiding. Carl's right. This can't go on indefinitely. He was so kind, bringing me here, offering me exactly what I needed. But perhaps it's time I moved on. Found somewhere else to go, anywhere that isn't London. But where? I rub the side of my face despairingly. I'm tired, too. I've seen the purple smudges under my eyes in the mirror, badges of stress and strain. But Carl shouldn't be suffering. It's not his problem, and it's unfair.

'You've done so much for me, more than anyone else in the world would have done.'

'I'm not so sure about that.'

'Well, I am. You've done enough. I was a total stranger and yet you rescued me. Now I've got to work the rest out for myself. I'll think of something.'

Carl's head snaps up. 'Ellen, don't even think about it. Don't think about leaving. You're to stay here, where you feel safe, and where I can keep an eye on you. Right?' He smiles.

'Right. But...'

His palm faces me. 'No *buts*. I will have to nip up to London at some point. I have to return the car, for one thing, and check in with my boss at the shop. You'll be all right here, won't you?'

'Of course.' I smile, but my stomach's quaking. *I'll be fine on my own*, I tell myself. *Nobody's coming for me here. I can do this.* 'You go and do what you need to do.'

'Thanks. I can leave it a few more days. If there's anything you need from your flat, I can collect it while I'm there.'

The mention of the flat jolts electricity through me, as if I've touched a live wire. Naïvely, I'd believed my secrets were safe within its walls. Instead, they were on the outside, hammering at the windows to be let in, like displaced ghosts.

I don't want Carl anywhere near the place, as if opening that door might in some way taint him.

'I'll have a think,' I say.

He mentions it again later, as if he wants to do me a favour by dropping by the flat – as if he isn't doing enough for me already. So I tell him I don't need anything bringing from home but if he has a minute to call in and check that everything's fine, and I haven't left the gas on or anything, I'd appreciate it. It's the sensible thing to do, and of course there's no harm in Carl going to the flat. My vivid imagination can be a curse at times.

I fetch my bag and give him the keys while I remember.

He holds them up, dangling them between thumb and forefinger. 'Ta. I won't lose them, I promise.'

'Okay. But I've got another set. I always carry two, because you never know.'

'Why doesn't that surprise me?' Carl says, and we laugh.

SEVENTEEN
ELLEN

Carl hasn't said any more about his proposed trip to London and it's a shock when, two days later, he mentions it again.

'How will you get back?' I say, fearful of being left alone for too long, no matter how confident I sounded before. 'You're dropping the car off at the hire place, aren't you?'

'There are these things called trains and buses. We're only in Sussex. Same planet, and everything.'

He laughs, making gentle fun of me. I can't for the life of me see anything to laugh at, but I must try and hold it together, for his sake as well as my own.

I find a grin. 'Yes, okay. Point taken. When will you go?'

It's early afternoon, and we're in the back garden, perched gingerly on sagging, ripped canvas chairs we found in one of the outhouses. They look as if they might give way at any moment. It's a sunny day, but not that warm, and we're cosseted in coats against the spring chill. I was reading but Carl clearly has something he wants to say, so I put the book down, and wait.

'In a day or two. Tomorrow, perhaps. I haven't decided yet. Ellen, there's something I need to talk to you about before I go.'

My stomach wavers. This is it. Despite his promises, this is where Carl tells me I have to leave, that I can no longer count on his protection. My mind scrabbles frantically for a solution. Other than returning to the flat where I'd be hunted down in no time, I can't think of one.

'Not that,' he says, shaking his head. 'I said you can stay here as long as you want... need to, and I meant it.'

'You're a mind reader.'

'I don't have to be. It's written all over your face.'

'Is it?' I rub my cheek and pretend to scowl. 'I shall have to watch that.' I'm playing for time, and Carl knows it.

'As well as taking the car back, I'll go into the shop and see my boss. I have to explain why I've not been back to work, and that I need a little more time.'

A little more. My heart crashes.

'Will he be okay about it, your boss?'

'She. And yes, she will. She's good on the people stuff. She's the understanding type, lucky for me. She can't hold my job open indefinitely but I'm fine for now, so don't start worrying about it.'

'Okay,' I say, feigning a lightness I can't feel.

Carl looks at me pointedly. My heart flickers.

'I don't know how to say this, Ellen, but I also need to do something about your situation.'

'My situation? In what respect?'

He sighs, as if I've irritated him in some way, though I don't know how. 'You know what I mean. You believe you committed the ultimate crime and you ran away. And now here you are and, as I said, you're welcome to stay as long as you like, but is it *right*, Ellen? Is any of this right?' I go to speak but Carl continues. 'Did you do what I asked? Have you gone over the incident in your mind, seen it any differently from before? I'm sorry, but I have to ask if anything's changed.'

'Of course nothing's changed! Why would it?' *This, again.*

This awful doubt in Carl's mind. 'You don't think I did it. You don't believe I killed Matt.'

The silence that follows seems interminable. Eventually, Carl speaks. 'I don't believe you're capable of killing anyone, Ellen.'

I lever myself out of the chair. I can't look at Carl, I just can't. 'I'll go. I can't stay here if you're not on my side.'

'Sit down,' Carl says, quietly and emphatically. And I do. 'Please try to understand it from my point of view. As far as I can see, there's no record of anyone called Matthew Leyton dying, being killed, committing suicide, having an accident, whatever. You were right about that.'

'You checked? You've been looking?'

'Yes. *Yes.* I am entitled to do a little digging under the circumstances, don't you agree?'

Of course he is. He's giving me shelter, protecting me from the outside world; he has a vested interest. And then something comes to my mind that I'd not considered significant before.

'I saw you taking your laptop, when you went out to the village. Is that why? Were you researching Matt's death, in secret, without telling me?'

Carl drops his gaze. 'I know it was underhand, I admit that. I've been going to a café, using the wi-fi there.' His eyes reach mine. 'So far I've found nothing about a Matthew Leyton, alive or otherwise. Nobody of around his age, nothing that remotely fits with what you've told me about him. Ellen, do you see what I'm saying?'

I sit bolt upright. 'That the whole thing's a figment of my imagination. That's what you're saying, isn't it? Well, thank you very much for your faith in me. And in my sanity, come to that.' I push up from the chair and stomp across the grass. Standing by the fruit trees, arms folded, my back to Carl, my mind grapples with this turn of events. A quiver of fear passes through me: fear of Carl himself. If he isn't hiding me from the police, and whoever else is out to get me, what am I doing here, in the back end of beyond? Nobody knows where I am, not a single soul.

Which is the whole point, but is that now working against me?

I sense Carl's approach, and turn to see him standing a few feet away, his eyes soft and kind, his mouth working anxiously, silently, and I know that was a ridiculous thought and I have nothing to fear from him. He's not the enemy here. There's only one of those, and that's me.

'I'm sorry,' I say. 'Sorry I got in a strop. Of course you have every right to want to know more. I just wish you'd told me you were looking, that's all.'

'I know. I should have trusted you to take it as it was meant, and that I did it for your own good.' He claps a hand to his forehead. 'That sounds patronising, sorry.'

'It's fine.' I sigh heavily.

'So, I'll go to London tomorrow and while I'm there, I'll make some discreet enquiries. You needn't worry, I won't do anything to leave you exposed, or in danger of any sort.'

We walk across the grass, back to the house. Carl's genuine kindness towards me is reassuring, but at the same time I feel defeated, as if this whole exercise is totally pointless and I might as well take myself off to the nearest police station, confess all and let them do what they like with me.

'You're cold,' Carl says. 'We shouldn't have stayed out so long. I'll get the fire going and we'll have tea.'

And this is what we do. Carl fetches wood from the outhouse, adds it to the twigs, dry leaves and odds and ends foraged from the woods, and soon the fire catches and orange tongues flicker brightly against the sooty black of the fireplace. I make the tea, toast a couple of crumpets under the grill, and we sit companionably side by side on the sofa.

'I'll need to stay in London for a couple of days, if you're okay with that?' Carl says, after a while. 'We're well stocked up with food and stuff, and I'll bring some more firewood inside. There shouldn't be any problems. But if there are, you can ring me and I'll come straight back.'

I nod. I can't be anything else but okay, can I? Carl's entitled to do what he likes. He doesn't need me clinging to him like a barnacle to a rock.

'Ellen,' he begins carefully, 'is there anything else you can tell me about Matt? You said he was an architect, and where he worked, but what about his home, the places he went? Anything that would give me something to go on.'

'You want to look for evidence... that Matt is dead?' My voice is a whisper. This is what Carl meant by 'discreet enquiries'. Of course it is. What else could it be?

'Tell me what else you know about him, even if it's some small detail,' Carl says, not answering my question directly.

I want this to stop now, but I can see it's not going to. So I think about what I know about Matt, other than the fact he was the most abhorrent man who used my sister mercilessly.

'Rosanna didn't tell me much. I wasn't interested enough to ask those kinds of questions.'

Carl gives a small sigh, and asks me to describe Matt. This is hard. I don't want to see his face, the twist of his mouth as he snarled at me. I don't want to see any part of him in my head, ever again. Carl waits. I make vague references to Matt's height, his colouring. From Carl's point of view, it's not much to go on.

I remember something else. I don't need to mention it because it's not relevant now, but I do anyway.

'Rosanna sent me a couple of photos of him. Not that I wanted to see them, but she was so smitten she wouldn't have understood that.'

'You have photos?' Carl grabs at this, his face alert.

'Not now. On my phone, which has gone, of course. You took care of that.' I glance at my new phone on the side table, the one Carl got me. A burner phone. Who would ever have thought I'd need one of those?

Carl fidgets awkwardly. He doesn't look at me. My stomach knots but I don't know why. He's on my side, and I don't doubt that for a second, not now. Yet, there's something going on here, and all I know is that I don't like it.

'I didn't get rid of your phone. I intended to but I didn't, in the end.'

I stare at Carl. My face burns, my mouth goldfishes uselessly.

'You're angry with me. I understand that. I was going to do what you asked but I thought you might regret getting rid of it. I'm sorry.'

Neither did he think it was necessary – that's as plain as day.

I want to shout and scream at him, hit him, even; but I do none of those things. I'm so mired in disbelief that my reflexes have atrophied.

Eventually, I find my voice. It emerges loud, and challenging. 'Where is it then? My phone. If you kept it, where is it?'

Carl gets up, goes upstairs, and returns with my phone. He hands it to me and I immediately drop it onto the sofa, as if it's white hot. Which it might well be. I can't chastise him any more; not after all he's done for me, and coming back here with the painful memories of his mother's abandonment still intact. Yet I am *so* angry, so fucking angry. I ball my hands, digging the nails deep into my palms, to suppress it.

'It's flat, of course. I might have a charger that fits,' Carl says.

'I've got one. I packed it with my stuff. But why? Why would you bring my phone here when anyone could trace me through it? You *know* that's why I needed it gone.'

Carl walks to the window, turns, walks back again. 'Ellen, nobody has traced you through your phone, have they? You really don't need to...'

I stand up. 'Don't tell me I don't need to worry! If you do, I'll...'

What? What will I do?

Again, that sensation that all is lost. I feel as if I'm trying to swim through black, glutinous mud.

We eat dinner in awkward silence. My phone is charged and I check for messages. There are none of any significance: no threats from nutcases, nothing weird at all amongst the stream of spam and jokes and sales pitches. I don't know whether to laugh or cry. I don't know how I feel any more, about anything, or anyone. I ping the three photos of Matt across to Carl's phone. He looks, and nods, and says thank you. Then he goes upstairs to pack a bag for tomorrow.

I sit at the table for a while, my hands steepled to my mouth, and try not to think about anything. Carl doesn't come down, and I hear sounds from the bathroom above.

Eventually, I find the energy to move. I decide to leave the washing-up till morning; it will give me something to do when Carl's gone. I go to bed and lie on my back, gazing through the window at the cloud-shadows shredding the opal disc of the moon.

EIGHTEEN
ROSANNA

She knows exactly when it happened.

It was a mild, misty night at the end of October. They'd been to an early cinema showing, then pressed into a pub where the din of the crowd competed with the pulsating beat of the music so that they had to shout at each other. Not that they wanted to talk.

Okay, she'd probably had two vodkas too many, and bar snacks rather than a proper meal. Matt hadn't held back on the alcohol either. But they were having the best time, and a lot of fun, so why not? It was a Friday night date, for a change, and she didn't need to get up for work in the morning.

They were all over each other, snogging in the corner of the bar like a couple of teenagers. Rosanna felt as carefree as she could ever be. And loved. She felt loved and wanted, because Matt made her feel that way. She didn't want to lose that feeling. Ever.

'Let's get out of here,' Matt mouthed eventually. They pushed their way out into the street and, minutes later, found themselves in an alleyway where, pressed into a convenient, dark doorway, they had urgent, frantic sex. Thrilling. Breathless. Fast. He didn't use anything. She was vaguely aware of that at the time, but her desire overcame any worries.

'I love you,' she said afterwards. Because she always did. And Matt said it back, because he always did. So, yes, that was when baby Leyton had begun.

She's as certain of that as she can be. She tries not to think about how drunk she got at Christmas – there's nothing she can do about it now. The baby should feel like a mistake; in fact, it's the opposite. The bond is already there, unshakeable. She'd never have imagined it would be like that, but at least that's one choice she doesn't have to make.

Sarah says Rosanna should decide where the baby is to be born, because she needs to be properly checked out and get herself 'in the system'. Not the best way to put it, Sarah agrees when Rosanna demurs, but she needs to have at least some idea, if not a hard and fast plan.

If only she could think that far ahead. Okay, July isn't light years away, but she's only just starting to get used to the idea of having an actual baby, becoming a mother. How is she supposed to make those sorts of decisions, the list of which is growing by the day? Sarah and Jay are being so kind, spoon-feeding her the information she needs, but, ultimately, this is her responsibility. She has, at least, faced up to that.

Tied up with the decision about the birth, of course, is an even more urgent one. Cornwall was meant to be a break, an extended holiday, while she waited for Matt to deal with whatever the problem was and get in touch. Then she'd have taken herself back to London, and... what? Her mind seems incapable of filling in the blanks now. But London, definitely London, and the flat. Home, that's where she would be.

So, should she go home now? Which would mean telling Ellen, and then she'd feel guilty and ashamed and stupid for having got herself pregnant, because her sister would make her feel that way, even though she may not intend to. If she stayed in Cornwall, at least for the time being, she could keep it secret a while longer.

If Rosanna had noticed any signs that she might be pregnant when she'd jumped on that train at Paddington, she'd chosen to ignore them. The possibility was too weighty a subject to be dealt with then. It wasn't until she'd found herself passing by the same chemist in the same little Mevagissey street on her daily walks, Dolly trotting along beside her, that she knew what was needed to set her mind at rest.

Except it didn't. None of the three positive test results did that.

Rosanna refolds a gorgeous blue jumper, whisper-soft, that a recent customer has handled, and replaces it in its correct display cubbyhole. She'd never considered working while she was in Cornwall, but Sarah's friend, Lowena, who owns the shop, needed a part-time assistant and Sarah mentioned it to Rosanna. She didn't have to think about it for long. She doesn't like being beholden to her friends, and this way, now she's earning, they are happy to accept some payment towards her keep. A win-win, as they say.

Lowena's Cornish name means 'joy', which fits with her happy disposition. She's cool about the pregnancy, and having a job is something to pass the days rather than just walking Dolly and swanning about like the tourist she really isn't. Not any longer. Not since things became, well, serious.

The little shop, a cornucopia of treasures for the memento-seeking tourist as well as being popular with locals for its small but beautiful collection of clothes and accessories, isn't very busy at this time of year. But Lowena has elderly parents living nearby, and with Rosanna there to mind the shop, she is free to call in on them and do their bits of shopping.

It's one of those times now, and Rosanna plays a game with herself, standing behind the till and pretending she owns the shop. A child's game, which makes it even more amusing. She scans the shelves with a critical eye, noting anything out of place. At quiet times, she likes to rearrange the shelves to show the pretty china and other bits and bobs to their best advantage, and she's organised the knitwear cubbyholes by colour and tone – it was all rather haphazard before. Lowena gives her a free hand, and doesn't mind what she does. She tells Rosanna she has a good eye for colour, and good taste.

But not in men, apparently. Oh, she still loves Matt, of course she does. If he walked through that door now, she'd throw herself into his arms and... Wait! She sits down on the stool behind the till. If by some miracle he did pitch up – it would be a miracle, since he has no idea she works here – there'd be no 'throwing' about it. Matt has let her down, big time. Ellen knows it – knew it all along, apparently. But Ellen doesn't know everything; she doesn't know how loving Matt is, how he whispers love words into her ear, tells her how wonderful she is, and how he thinks about her all the time when they can't be together.

This is the thing. Rosanna is still thinking about Matt in the present tense. But if he loves her, truly loves her, as he said, then why hasn't he been in touch? Okay, she accepts he had to cut her off when he had that wobble with his wife; he wanted to protect Rosanna, as well as himself. But now? It's been an age. He has her number, and even, if he cares to resurrect her old messages, the address of the farmhouse. And nothing.

I've lost him, haven't I? The words say themselves inside her head, but it's as if they're a rehearsal, in case she has to say them for real. It's not been that long, not in the great scheme of things. Time here has a way of distorting itself. One moment it feels like the hands of the clock are whizzing round, cartoon-style; the next, a week seems like a lifetime.

Memories are all she has. Memories of the time spent with the great love of her life. And even those are becoming less reliable. Scenes change colour, words take on different meaning. Love is less like love and more like lust.

Rosanna swallows back the lump in her throat. If only she could talk to Matt, she could make him see how much she loves him, how much he needs her. But the truth is, the more days that drift by, the less likely it seems that she will ever talk to him again, let alone set eyes on him.

She has to be brave about it. If she can survive losing both parents at the age of ten, being uprooted to live in a new place with relatives she hardly knew, and virtually starting her life all over again, she can survive this. The only fly in the ointment – one of Uncle Derek's pet sayings – is the baby she's carrying. Sarah and Jay think the father should be told, and in any other situation, Rosanna would agree. But this is complicated. She hasn't so far told them Matt is married, although by the tone of the conversations, by what has not been said rather than what has, they have probably worked it out.

Assuming she could find a way of contacting Matt, it would seem as if she's trying to trap him, wouldn't it? As if she's using the baby as a means of emotional blackmail. She can't have that, not at any price. If Matt wants to be with her, it has to be because he loves her, not because she's having his child. Oh, it's all so confusing!

Lowena is back. It's mid-morning, and Rosanna greets her, and goes out the back to make the drinks – coffee for Lowena, ginger and lemon tea for Rosanna, as she can't stomach coffee at the moment.

As she waits for the kettle to boil, she thinks about her sister. Perhaps if she told Ellen about the baby, it would somehow pave the way to telling Matt. What could Ellen do, hundreds of miles away? Not fuss, for a start: making sure Rosanna keeps her check-up appointments, watching what she eats, gets enough sleep. Etcetera, etcetera. That's how it would be, if she went back to London now. Ellen would be so disappointed in her, and she really doesn't want to face her, not yet.

The decision as to whether to stay in Cornwall suddenly seems a lot easier.

Rosanna waits until half past six, when she knows Ellen will have been home from work for a while, sits on the bed in her room beneath the eaves of the farmhouse and calls Ellen's number, her original one. It goes straight to voicemail. Ellen still hasn't found her phone, then. Trust her to lose something as important as her phone. Although, actually, it's well out of character, but Rosanna has stopped wondering about that.

She calls the other number, the one Ellen gave her of her new, cheap phone, the one she bought to tide her over. At this point she hasn't decided whether to tell her about the baby or not. If she does, so be it. If not, then there's always another time.

Her sister answers immediately, as if she'd been waiting for a call. 'Oh, hi, Rosie.'

'Yep, it's me. No need to sound so disappointed.' The old friction snaps readily into place.

'I wasn't. How's Cornwall?'

Rosanna resists the temptation to say it's the same as the last time she asked. 'It's good. I like it here. I've got a job, believe it or not.'

Ellen laughs. 'I'm not sure I do! What kind of job?'

Rosanna tells her about the shop, and then she finds herself describing the quaint, cobbled street it sits in, and how, after work, she goes down and watches the fishermen on the pier, and the boats bobbing in the chilly harbour. As she talks, she realises how fond she's become of this little seaside village, and the peaceful life it offers.

'I miss Brixton, though. Too bloody quiet here by half,' she adds, to compensate. She's a London girl, always will be.

Ellen asks when she plans to return, but there's something else behind the question, a caginess that sets Rosanna on edge. She tells her she isn't sure when she'll be back, expecting disappointment from her sister.

But, no.

'Well, it doesn't matter because I'm not there anyway,' Ellen says, breezily.

'How d'you mean, you're *not there*?'

'What I said. London's not the centre of the universe,' Ellen replies, crossly.

'Well, I know that, don't I? So, where are you then?'

A small silence, then: 'Sussex. In the country. A friend has a house we could use and we fancied a winter break. So...' An awkward little laugh. 'Here we are!'

'*Sussex*? What friend?'

'Oh, just someone from work. You don't know them.'

Since when did Ellen have friends Rosanna either didn't share or know about? She can't help feeling slightly put out. 'Oh, well, have a good time, then, little sis.' Another thought. 'How did you get time off work? I thought you didn't have much holiday left.'

'I quit. Sent in my notice. You're not the only one who needed a change.'

The call ended, Rosanna sits staring down at her phone. She revises her image of Ellen going to work, coming home again, sitting in the flat, marking time until Rosanna returns, but it's not easy. She can't remember a time when her sister did something so out of character, or in any way surprising.

Automatically, she presses a hand to her abdomen. She's glad she didn't say anything about the baby now. If Ellen could have secrets, so could she.

NINETEEN

ROSANNA

'Rosie, I don't want to interfere,' Sarah says gently, 'but don't you think the father should be told? I gather all's not well in Camp Romance, but a baby... Do you really want to keep it a secret from him?'

It's Monday morning, just after nine, and the three of them – four, counting Dolly – are in the yard. Chloe is learning to ride her new scooter and insists on an audience, although the scooter has now been discarded on the ground in favour of puddle-jumping.

Sarah scoops up the dog and fondles her velvety ears. Chloe immediately runs to Rosanna and asks to be picked up. She swings Chloe up onto her hip and takes her over to look at the hens.

'Be careful. She's heavy,' Sarah warns. 'Her wellingtons are muddy.'

'She's fine,' Rosanna says, but Chloe is already wriggling towards freedom, and she sets her down. The child races away and retrieves the scooter, her face screwed up in concentration as she tries to co-ordinate her feet in order to push forward.

'It's too big for her really. A friend whose daughter had outgrown it passed it on. It keeps her quiet, though it won't last.'

'She'll soon grow into it.'

'She will, all too soon.' Sarah looks pointedly at Rosanna.

Rosanna crosses her arms around herself, as if she's cold. She isn't. 'I haven't heard from Matt and it doesn't look as if I'm going to now. I've been so stupid, Sarah. He told me it was over but I didn't believe him. I thought he was just having a wobble about... well, being married and everything, and he'd come back to me, in time.'

'Ah.' Sarah nods. 'I guessed it was something like that. Do you want to tell me about it? Not if you don't want to. Only it might help to talk.'

'I'm not sure. I don't know what there is to say. I don't know how I feel about him any more.'

'Oh dear. You sound so sad,' Sarah says, her eyes softening. She calls Chloe. 'Let's go inside, anyway.'

Sarah makes tea, and they sit at the table in the cosy farmhouse kitchen. Rosanna tells the story, including what took place on that last night, when she'd worn the special dress because she'd believed – truly believed – that with Christmas coming up, Matt would make some kind of commitment to her, and they would make plans for the future. Far-off plans, okay, but Rosanna had convinced herself that her future would include Matt, because anything else felt totally impossible. She'd brushed off his unkind words and refused to accept he was leaving her, convinced she had enough power to jolly him out of it. Who the hell had she been kidding? Only herself.

She feels better straight away for telling Sarah the story. Better, but not much clearer in her mind. Her friend is sympathetic, and totally non-judgemental, as Rosanna knew she would be. She doesn't offer advice, just a listening ear.

'I'm glad I've told you. I didn't tell you before because I didn't want you to think badly of me. You and Jay.'

'Well, I don't, and I never would. Neither would Jay.'

'I know. Thanks, Sarah.' For some reason, she's close to tears now. Tears she's been holding back for too long.

'Don't be daft. Just let me know if there's anything I can do, that's all. I'm over the moon you're having the baby in Cornwall.' She grins. 'I can't say I'm not.'

'It's the only sensible decision I've made in a long time,' Rosanna says, pulling a face.

'What about your sister, though? Have you told her yet?'

Yet. Of course, it would be natural to bring Ellen in on the secret, as far as Sarah is concerned. But she doesn't know how Ellen can be, and it's not as if Ellen has been in touch with her.

'She lost her phone. She gave me another number when I tried, it went straight to voicemail.'

This is true; she has tried to ring Ellen, but after several attempts, an hour between each, and still no reply, she'd given up. She hadn't left a message. If Ellen couldn't be bothered, neither could she. In any case, she isn't really looking forward to telling her sister about the pregnancy.

'Is there a landline at the flat?' Sarah asks.

'That's just it,' Rosanna says. 'She's not there. My sister has packed in her job and taken herself off to some place in Sussex to stay with a friend, so she says.'

She realises she sounds resentful. It's not fair of her, but it's how she feels.

'Like you, then.' Sarah eyes Rosanna.

'Yes, I know. Ellen can go where she likes, do what she likes. We aren't joined at the hip.' She laughs. 'Actually, that's exactly how we were. When we lost our parents, we made a kind of silent pact that we'd face whatever came together. Life's not like that, though, is it? Stuff happens. People grow apart, and we're different people, Ellen and I. I miss her, though, Sarah, even though she's a pain in the proverbial, forever watching me like a bloody hawk, telling me where I'm going wrong.'

Sarah laughs too. 'You don't mean that. Not the way you said it, anyway.'

'Maybe not. But Ellen needs her own space. She needs to find her own way. She's better off without me, for now.'

Sarah is silent. Rosanna can guess what she's thinking. Ellen is her sister; she deserves to be told about the baby. And she will be. But the longer she leaves it, the harder it becomes. She doesn't need Ellen's disapproval, no matter how she wraps it up.

Telling her sister wouldn't, of course, be as hard as telling Matt. If it ever happens – the likelihood is diminishing by the hour.

Rosanna is working today; she needs to be at the shop by eleven. Sarah offers her a lift but the sun is finding its way through the early morning murk, promising a mild spring day, and she enjoys the walk. It's so different from being in London, where she hardly walked at all, unless it was around the shops. Or beside the Thames, where she and Matt used to stroll, stopping to kiss every few yards like a couple of love-struck teenagers.

He never seemed to worry about being seen with her in public; there was nothing furtive about their relationship when they were out together. There'd been none of that surreptitious casting about to see if there was anyone he recognised before they waltzed into a pub or restaurant. Matt's daring was part of his allure, she couldn't deny that. But there was daring, and there was recklessness. She doesn't know why she didn't question it at the time.

As she strolls along the lane leading from the farm, she tries to push Matt from her mind. But, after her talk with Sarah, she can't seem to shake him off. Her friend is right, in theory. A man should be told if he's going to become a father. But even if she finds a way of letting him know, can she stand the humiliation and fresh heartache when he tells her he's not interested? Does she want to hear it spelled out for her that Matt is under no circumstances prepared to wreck his marriage, even if that marriage is only continuing for the sake of the children who already exist?

Lowena smiles her usual welcome when Rosanna arrives at the shop. There are customers: two women, chatting delightedly over the range of silky scarves in jewel colours; and an elderly couple scanning the miniature framed prints of Cornwall. Visitors, probably. It's nearing Easter, and Mevagissey's tourist season is beginning in earnest.

The rest of the morning brings a steady trickle of customers, while the street outside is lively with passers-by and window-shoppers.

At one o'clock, Lowena heads off to call on her parents. The shop is closed for half an hour and Rosanna is left in peace to eat the sandwich she brought with her. Again, Matt hijacks her thoughts. She has to do *something*, even if it ends in more tears. Five minutes on her phone, and she has the number of Trubridge and Jensen, Design Architects.

Her voice is steady and confident as she asks to speak to Matthew Leyton. Well, why shouldn't she phone him? He doesn't call all the shots, not any more.

The female voice on the other end is hesitant. 'Leyton, did you say?'

'Yes, Matthew Leyton. He's one of your architects.'

Silence. Rosanna checks the time while she waits. Lowena will be back any minute. Rosanna's free to make personal calls but she'd rather this one wasn't overheard.

Eventually, the woman speaks. 'There isn't a Mr Leyton here, I'm afraid.'

Rosanna senses the call is about to be disconnected. 'Hold on. Do you mean he's out?'

'No, I mean we don't have anyone of that name.'

'But you have, I'm sure of it. Could you check again, please? It's very important.'

'Can I put you through to someone else on the team?'

'No, I only want to speak to Matt... Mr Leyton. It's a personal call.'

Surely there's some mistake? Rosanna hears faint voices in the background, the tinkle of a phone, a door closing. She imagines Matt at his drawing board, oblivious to the call. Or he's out on site, or visiting a client. The woman clearly has no clue who Matt is. Perhaps she's new in the job.

The answer comes back: 'Sorry, I really can't help.' And she's gone, leaving Rosanna staring at her phone.

She takes several long breaths. There must be a simple explanation. Matt could have left Trubridge and Jensen. He'd talked about setting up his own practice. Okay, it couldn't have happened in the time since they'd last been together, but he could be making preparations. Or he might have taken a job in another company. Either is possible.

But not likely. Not in such a short space of time. Rosanna's had enough practice at rationalising Matt's actions, making excuses for him. She's not going down that path any more: it only leads to disillusion.

There's another possibility, one she hardly dares think about, but it makes sense: Matt has instructed the receptionist, or whoever she is, not to pass on any calls, personal ones anyway. He'll have charmed her into that, no problem.

Damn it! She stuffs the phone in her bag. Why is she even bothering? If Matt thinks so little of her, she refuses to waste another second of her time fretting over him. Her hand automatically finds the small swelling below her ribcage, smoothing its way over the needlecord of her dress.

'It's just you and me now, kid. Just the two of us. And we're gonna be fine.'

TWENTY
ELLEN

My first thought was that it was Carl on the phone – my new phone. I've kept the other one switched off; it feels safer that way, although it probably doesn't make a jot of difference.

He's been gone all day, since eight this morning. I could ring him but he doesn't need me on his tail. He knows I'm safe here – hopefully that's true – so he has no reason to ring. All the same, I had hoped to hear from him. Instead, it was Rosanna.

The day has dragged without Carl here, and I was pleased to hear from her, although I don't think I came across like that. She sounded odd, if I'm honest – different. A strange mixture of the old devil-may-care Rosie and something new, less assured; especially when I told her I was in Sussex. I hadn't thought about telling her before, but of course she needs to know. If she turned up at the flat and found me missing, she wouldn't be happy. And she is my sister, after all.

Darkness closes in around the house, soft, impenetrable, like a thick woollen cloak. The morning mist didn't clear completely today, and the treetops merged with a grey, dismal sky. No stars tonight, and only a pale patch where the moon sulks behind the clouds. It's mild for March but I laid the fire before sunset and got it to catch on the fourth attempt.

I sit in the chair Carl normally uses, my dinner on a tray – beef casserole. I cooked a large batch and this is the remains from our last two meals. I find cooking comforting, and it makes me feel as if I'm doing something useful. The radio is on, but the music playing sounds too loud, too intrusive, in the silent house, so I switch it to Radio 4 and half listen to an actor with a familiar voice reading from *Silas Marner*.

The evening darkness is fine; the night will be, too. It reminds me of the tunnel, and I have flashbacks of camping on the bench in my sleeping bag, the breath of a thousand long-gone passengers wafting past, the ghostly thrum of train doors, opening and closing, opening and closing. I was never frightened in the tunnel, although Carl said it wasn't safe. I *felt* safe, and that was all that mattered.

I'm safe now, too, tucked up in Owl Corner. There's a small part of me that still says otherwise, but even that is starting to fade now. But I don't want to get complacent. I need to stay on my guard, just in case. Matthew Leyton is dead, and I killed him. Whoever sent those messages knows that. It was still me, and I am still that person, although saying the words inside my head makes me shudder.

Carl said he would be away for a couple of days. At the time, I interpreted it literally, but he sounded vague when he said it. How long he intends to stay in London must depend on how his investigations pan out. I can't even think about what he's doing, where he's going, or who he's talking to without fear grabbing at my insides. I don't understand what he hopes to achieve by digging around in Matthew Leyton's affairs. The man's dead. What more is there to know?

But I have to trust Carl. He hasn't let me down so far – apart from the phone thing but I've forgiven him for that – and I know that whatever he's doing, he has my best interests at heart.

He's right about one thing: this can't go on forever. I have to find a way forward. If only I could see that happening.

A sudden sound startles me, but it's only rain peppering the windows. I take my dinner things to the kitchen and decide to wash up in the morning. Back in front of the fire with a glass of Sauvignon, I huddle down in the chair, pulling an old crocheted blanket around me. The radio programme has switched to the news. It seems as if they're talking about a different world, one I used to belong to and perhaps never will again.

Turning off the radio, I gaze into the fire and think about Rosie. I wonder if it's raining in Cornwall. My sister's never been much of an outdoors person, and Cornwall is largely about the outdoors – rocky coves, pretty villages, clifftop paths, crashing waves. It seems strange to think of her there. She has a job! That was a surprise. Clearly she has no plans to leave Cornwall any time soon. There again, this is my sister: impetuous, often selfish, doing what she wants to do, when she wants to do it, and hang the consequences. She's perfectly capable of walking out on the job and her friends and winging it back to London tomorrow if the mood takes her.

My mind automatically flies from Rosanna to Matt. Is she still pining for him, convinced that she only has to wait it out? Surely the penny's dropped by now. My heart leaps, and I want to wrap Rosie in my arms and tell her everything's going to be all right, and she deserves so much better than a lowlife like Matt Leyton.

A thought swings through my brain: *I did the world a favour.* I rein it in, fast, before my musings run wildly out of control. Nothing excuses what I did. Nothing.

Carl asked me to relive it all in my mind, run over what happened, examine every detail. To what end I couldn't imagine at first, but he's right. If he's going to help me, release me from the trap I set for myself, he needs every bit of information I can muster. Why he's helping me is still not clear, but I suspect it's because he sees something of himself in me, because of the way our lives have paralleled. His parents are alive, unlike mine, that's true, but his mother's abandonment of him clearly left its mark, almost like bereavement. It's the only explanation I have, apart from his innate kindness.

The fire is beginning to die but I'm not ready for bed yet. I close my eyes, take myself back to London, and that night, and force myself to concentrate, hard.

The blast of cold air as I push through the revolving doors of the Printabilly building. Traipsing along Victoria Street, past brightly lit shop fronts, nothing in mind but getting home. The neon blue sign above the underground station entrance. The slow descent of the packed escalator. The fight for space in the swarming tunnels. And then...

Wait. Something else before that. Before I reached the station. My mind gropes for the missing fragment of memory as if for a jigsaw-puzzle piece lost down the back of the sofa; a small, unimportant piece, not part of the main picture. My brain urges me to leap over this and return to the platform, and Matthew Leyton, smug in his overcoat and Rupert scarf. My burst of anger, red-hot, uncontrollable. The confrontation and what happened afterwards. The inescapable, unalterable truth which, no matter how many times I relive it, remains as terrible, and as terrifying, as before.

Again my train of thought slams against the buffers. I need to find that missing piece, insignificant or not. And then it comes to me, as my brain flashes back to a black and white baker-boy cap bobbing in front of me as I walk. It's Georgie, a catering assistant from our staff restaurant. She's a little way ahead, keeping pace with the crowd. I'm not one of her favourites – she has favourites among the staff, she makes that clear – and I don't try to catch up with her. Too many people, anyway.

Georgie Smith. She would have been on her way to the

Tube as well. It wasn't her usual time of day. The restaurant closes at four; the catering staff have almost all gone home by then, unless there's a meeting or something in the building. It was her, though. She always wears the same hat in winter. I knew it was her at the time. I know it now.

Did she see anything? Was she there when the emergency services came, and the whole station was thrown into chaos?

I don't remember seeing her on the platform. If she'd been close by when I remonstrated with Matt, I'd have noticed, wouldn't I? Or was I so far gone, so focused on my outrage against that man, that I wouldn't have noticed if I'd been surrounded by a gang of laser-toting police officers?

I get up from the chair and cross to the window. Tugging the sleeves of my jumper down, I clutch them tightly in my palms. My reflection in the blackened glass, marbled by rain-drops, stares back at me. *I don't believe you're capable of killing anyone.* Carl's words repeat themselves as loudly as if he were standing right here. His misplaced faith in me rips my heart in two. My thoughts spin inside my head like a fairground ride, then shatter and cascade to the ground in a zillion coloured frag-ments. I piece them together to make a picture.

But it's a different picture from the one I saw before.

Nothing's working as it should, and what I thought was real no longer seems as clear as it did. Suddenly, my safety doesn't seem paramount any more.

If Georgie Smith has something to say, I want to hear it.

TWENTY-ONE

CARL

Carl spent last night at his flat, a ground-floor conversion in a scruffy but quiet Camberwell street. He went home straight after dropping off the Fiat, feeling the need for some breathing space, time to gather his thoughts.

Tim, his flatmate, didn't come home last night. Judging by the unaired state of the place and the rock-hard half-loaf in the bread bin, he hasn't been around for a few days. A text exchange reveals his whereabouts – his girlfriend's place, unsurprisingly. Carl feels vaguely disappointed, but he probably wouldn't be great company at present. His head is too full of other things.

He hasn't told Tim exactly why he suddenly needed to go to Sussex, but couched it in the same vague terms as he did to Blythe, his boss at work. A friend in crisis, he'd said, without mentioning any names. With Blythe, he'd swapped *friend* for *family*. Both accepted his non-story easily, which made him feel guilty. He hated lying, especially to his boss because she was lovely, the best, but he didn't have much choice.

Setting out after a scratch breakfast, his first port of call is the shop, a twenty-minute walk away. Blythe is welcoming, slightly disappointed that he hasn't come to work, but they have a talk in the back room, and she agrees to his suggestion of taking the next two weeks as unpaid leave. Pinning down a time limit will help him focus on Ellen's problem, although he hopes, quite desperately, to have her out of hiding and home before that.

Leaving the shop, he remembers he hasn't called her. She'll be waiting and, knowing Ellen, worrying, and he doesn't want that. He calls her as he walks the short distance to his usual barber's. She's fine, she tells him, sounding bright, which makes his heart squeeze. He tells her he's staying in London again tonight at least, and hopes she doesn't mind. He'd already warned her he might be away a few days but it's best to remind her. She assures him he must do what he needs to do, and not to worry about her.

After the haircut, he makes for the nearest Costa where he sits with a coffee while contemplating his next move. Actually, there's not much contemplating to be done. It's more a way of putting off the inevitable. He has to find Matthew Leyton in person, or at least, some trace of him. Having exhausted all virtual avenues, this is all that's left.

He remembers he promised to go to Ellen's flat. Brixton isn't a great distance from Camberwell, but because of the time factor he hops on a bus rather than walking.

Ellen's flat smells of her, or rather, that expensive bath oil stuff she uses. Clothes are strewn across her bed: rejects from her packing. He makes a quick tour of the rooms, finds nothing amiss apart from a dripping tap, and minutes later he's back in the street, and heading for the Tube.

The nearest station to where he needs to be is Victoria. He tries not to think about the connotations as he bounds off the train, through the tunnel and up the escalator. Using the map on his phone, he finds the turning he needs which leads off Victoria Street. A few streets on, he passes Printabilly, where

Ellen used to work. The name springs out at him, and he stands for a moment, looking up at the windows and imagining her inside, safe at her desk. Where she ought to be. The thought spurs him on. He mustn't fail at this. He can't go back to Sussex empty-handed.

The building housing Trubridge and Jensen, Design Architects, is as Ellen described it: tall, peppermint-green, angular. He finds it easily. A list of the companies in the building is engraved on a slate-grey plaque beside the entrance. A twentyish guy with floppy blond hair, wearing black chinos, white shirt and red tie, stands behind an enormous, curved desk in the shiny-floored lobby. A security pass on a lanyard announces him as Alastair Hill. He smiles enquiringly at Carl.

'I've come to see one of the architects. Mr... Matthew Leyton.'

'Company?' Alastair sits down and faces a computer screen.

Carl frowns.

'Which company? There are two architects' practices in the building.'

'Oh, right. Trubridge and Jensen.'

Alastair taps the keyboard. 'Leyton, you say? Have you got an appointment?'

'Not as such. Well, no, not at all. I was in the area and I hoped I might catch him.'

Feet tap across the shiny floor; a short, middle-aged woman in a navy trouser suit enters a code into a security panel, vanishes through a door next to the reception desk, and reappears in the office behind reception.

Alastair looks up from the screen. 'I can't see the name listed. In any case, you can't just swan up there on spec. That's not how it works.'

'I wasn't planning on swanning anywhere,' Carl says, trying to hide his impatience. 'Maybe he could come down and see me?'

The look on Alastair's face tells him this is not how it works either. He swivels round on his chair and faces the office. 'Monica, heard of a Matthew Leyton? T and J? Nothing on the list but he could be new, I suppose.'

His colleague taps at her own keyboard, then looks across at Carl. 'How are you spelling the surname?'

Carl knows this, but how? Oh yes, Ellen wrote it when she sent him the pictures. He spells it out for Monica.

'Leyton? As in the area of East London?' she says.

'That's it, yes.'

'No Leytons. No Matthews, either. I looked at the technicians as well. And the arch assistants. Are you sure you've got the right name? Or the right architects?'

'Pretty certain on both counts,' Carl says. He considers showing them the photos of Matt on his phone but that would seem kind of weird.

'Will you excuse me a sec?' Alastair nods at a phone with a flashing light.

'Sure.'

While Alastair deals with the phone call, Monica comes out to the desk. 'Would you like me to look up the name on the register? The list of registered architects? That should put you right. I've got five minutes.'

'That would be great, if you could. Thanks,' Carl says, wondering he'll ever be put right again.

Time slows. His neck and shoulders prickle. This whole thing is starting to feel eerily unreal. Across the lobby, the lift purrs, the doors open with a ping and people emerge: two men and a woman. They talk to each other in low tones. Carl watches their back view as they head for the door. Alastair ends the phone call and returns to his screen-gazing.

After what seems like hours, Monica approaches the desk. 'There are a couple of Leytons, spelled your way, but wrong initial. In any case, one's in Bristol and the other's in Milton

Keynes. I tried other spellings but again, nobody local. Certainly not around here, anyway.'

'Cheers, Monica,' Alastair says. Then, to Carl, 'Sorry we couldn't help.'

'It's fine. Thanks, anyway. I'll... make other enquiries.'

And how, precisely, is he going to do that? He pushes through the door and stands outside the building, casting his eyes up and down the street, as if the answer might appear out of the fog that is making its insidious way along the tarmac.

It's cold, and he's hungry. He heads for the Tube and home.

While the chilli con carne he picked up from the corner shop is revolving in the microwave, Carl considers phoning Ellen to ask her if Rosanna's lover might have been using a false name, then thinks better of it. She's already told him everything she knows, and she doesn't truly support this mission. She only went along with it to please him, he realises that, and he doesn't want to upset her by quizzing her further. Besides, if Rosanna knew her lover by that name, Ellen won't know any differently, will she? If the bloke has been going around incognito, Carl's scuppered before he's barely begun. It's a depressing thought.

Over his meal, Carl thinks around the problem, trying to approach it from a different angle. The only idea he comes up with is even more depressing: that Ellen's story is true, and she really did push Matt in the path of the train. Okay, murderers don't exactly go round with it written across their foreheads. They look like anybody else.

But Ellen? No. Never in a million years.

Supposition, educated guesswork, and pure gut instinct – when it comes down to it, these are the only weapons he has in the fight to bring Ellen back to the real world. But even if he's stopped believing in himself, he won't stop believing in Ellen –

the real Ellen, not the one who for some reason thinks she's a killer.

He pushes his plate away, leans his elbows on the table and puts his head in his hands. Back at the house in Sussex, he tried as many times as he dared to convince Ellen that her memory of that night is distorted, or at least make her question it, but she wasn't having any of it. She was – *is* – so sure of what happened, she won't consider any other version, and he finds that so frustrating at times he could shake her.

But he is not Ellen. He can't see inside her head. Loneliness – yes, Ellen is lonely; he realised that early on – can affect the mind in all kinds of strange ways. The tragic loss of her parents would have had a long-lasting effect and probably explains her attachment to her sister and her determination to protect her. Other than that, he can't second-guess her thoughts. But he has to help her. He cares about her too much to walk away now.

Getting up from the table, Carl wanders through to the sitting room and stands at the bay window. Across the narrow street, he can see straight into another room. A family, gathered around the flickering light of a large TV screen, a dog romping around. The ordinary domestic scene calms his mind, pushes his thought processes onto more fertile ground. He thinks about today, his visit to the green building. It must mean something that Rosanna, and therefore Ellen, knew the name Trubridge and Jensen. Perhaps Matt's left the company, and the records the office held didn't go that far. Or he's an associate rather than a direct employee of the company. And, of course, there is such a thing as Data Protection. But there's more to be learned from there, he feels certain.

It's Saturday tomorrow. The offices will be closed. He may as well go back to Sussex and spend the rest of the weekend with Ellen. Then on Monday, he'll come back to London, perhaps with some fresh ideas to work on, although the chances of that are getting more distant by the minute.

. . .

In the morning, Carl gets up early and, leaving a note for Tim, sets out for the station. On the train, he texts Ellen to let her know he's on his way. She doesn't answer but it doesn't matter. He'll be seeing her in a couple of hours.

At Horsham station, he can't face the long bus ride to Harts-brook and instead splashes out on a taxi to take him directly to Owl Corner. He finds himself smiling as he pushes open the creaky gate. But as soon as he unlocks the front door and goes inside, he knows.

Ellen has gone.

TWENTY-TWO

ELLEN

If only I knew Georgie Smith's actual address, it would be so much easier. But you can't have everything, as Aunt Margaret is fond of saying, and my journey's gone smoothly until now.

Smoothly, but it ate up far more time than I'd have liked.

Having hiked to the village along the footpaths, I caught a grindingly slow bus to a town called Horsham, then a train to London Victoria.

Almost two o'clock now, and all the Pimlico streets are starting to look the same so that I can't be sure which ones I've been to and which not. It's Saturday, so I'm hoping to catch Georgie at home. If there's the slightest chance I can talk to her and gather even the tiniest scrap of information, it's not an entirely pointless exercise. It's time I took control of my own fate, even if it means... well, I can't think about that now.

I hate lying to Carl, but I haven't really lied, only by omission. I didn't want to hear him tell me this was a bad idea, even if it's true. My phone's switched off. If he's back at Owl Corner before me, I'll deal with it then, but I've finally realised I can't just sit on my backside and wait for him to solve all my problems for me.

My mind wheels back to the Christmas before last. There'd been a raffle at work – when was there not? – and Georgie's ticket had been picked out for second prize, but she wasn't there to claim it. She was off sick, recovering from a chest infection. The prize was a hamper of Christmas goodies, some of them perishable, and not the sort of thing you'd want to keep hanging around. Three of us from our office decided we'd deliver it to her personally – any excuse for a bit of extra time off work – even though Georgie made it clear she didn't approve of me. But I had nothing against her, and it was Christmas.

So off we set at lunchtime, armed with Georgie's address. We went by bus – the hamper, all done up in cellophane with a massive red bow on top, perched on my lap – then walked a short distance to her street.

I sort of remember the direction we walked in, but not the street name, and none of the names have jumped out at me so far.

But I do remember the house. It's tall – okay, they're all tall around here, and of similar style – but hers is painted a rather horrible green colour in sharp contrast to next door, which is pin-smart with pristine white walls, subtle grey window-frames, and shutters at all the windows; a complete house, not sliced up into flats like most around here. I admired that house, thinking how totally Instagrammable it was and that I'd love to live in one just like it.

I also recall that below street level, on the strip of concrete outside Georgie's basement flat, stands a collection of garden ornaments – cats of various colours, the paint chipped and worn; a windmill; and a girl in Dutch costume. All old stuff, and not in a good way. Stuff that looks as if it's been there for years, but perhaps loved in some way by Georgie. The three of us laughed unkindly at the ornaments as we walked down the steps.

This is what I see in my mind now as I try another street:

the cats, the windmill, the Dutch girl. Of course, the ornaments might have gone and the green walls been repainted but, feeling newly hopeful, I walk along to the middle of the terrace.

The white house comes into view first, its walls glowing in the sun. And, yes, the ornaments are still there next door, in front of what I'm absolutely certain is Georgie's flat. Even the green walls are the same.

I hang back for a moment, nervous at the thought of confronting Georgie and asking my questions, which will seem odd to her. Who knows what sort of reception I'll get? I'm half hoping she's out, but I don't really. I've come this far, been brave enough to leave Owl Corner. I can do this.

She opens the door slowly and carefully, as if she's expecting it to be somebody bringing bad news. Behind her, in the hallway, I see the baker-boy hat on a hook with a row of coats.

'Oh, it's you.' She looks taken aback, perhaps a little shaken. 'What is it? What do you want?'

I ask if I can come in and talk to her for a minute. She seems to be thinking about this, but eventually lets me in with a nod of her head and I follow her into a sitting room, which is more stylish and inviting than I'd have imagined. A fake coal fire flickers in the grate, despite the mild day. A large-screen TV shows its black face in the corner. On a side table stands a framed photo of a group of determinedly smiling people posing against a background that looks like the set of a TV soap.

Georgie waves me to a turquoise velvet sofa but doesn't sit down herself.

'And to what do I owe this pleasure?' she says, making it clear it's anything but.

My heart plummets, along with my spirit, but I rattle off an explanation that I hope sounds vaguely plausible. I give her the date and approximate time I saw her ahead of me in Victoria Street, when we were both heading for the Tube, and ask if she saw anything unusual once she'd got there, or witnessed an incident of any kind.

Georgie says nothing. She sits down on an orange button-back chair and looks me over with undisguised curiosity, as if I'm an exhibit in a museum.

I sigh. 'I'm sorry, Georgie, bursting in on you like this. Only it's become sort of important. It's to do with... somebody I know, somebody I'm trying to help. As a friend.'

'Oh?' She's not buying this.

I wouldn't either.

I press on. 'I want to find out what happened that night, and I think we... I saw you on the way to the Tube station.'

She gives a small laugh which is more like a snort. 'Taken up amateur sleuthing, have you, now you've left Printabilly?'

I realise this is her attempt at humour, and I smile. 'Something like that, you could say.'

'How's your sister?'

The out-of-the-blue question floors me for a second. I wasn't even aware Georgie knew I had a sister.

'Rosanna? She's fine. She's on holiday at the moment, in Cornwall.'

'Cornwall? Is she now?' Georgie dwells on this for a moment. 'Very nice for some, I'm sure.' Then, when I don't reply, 'That date you said – the second of January? A Tuesday?'

'Yes, that's it.'

'Wait there.' Georgie leaves the room and comes back holding a wall calendar. She flicks the pages back. 'Worked late. Had to put on coffees and stuff for one of their meetings. Yes, you're not wrong there. I might have been around Victoria, same time as you. Can't swear to it, mind.'

'Do you always come home by Tube, Georgie?'

'Of course. It's quickest. Anyway, I like it.'

'Do you?' I must have looked puzzled.

'I do. So there. Look, what's this all about?'

I suppress a sigh. I've already explained, at least I thought I had. 'Do you remember seeing an accident? Somebody falling off the platform, going under the train?'

'Can't say I remember anything of that nature.'

'But you would, wouldn't you, if it happened when you were there, on the platform?'

'There'd be a kerfuffle, sure as eggs. I might've remembered. On the other hand, I might not. Why? Did you see anything then?'

'Sirens. I heard sirens. Somebody shouting. That's all.'

Georgie makes a dismissive puffing sound. 'Sirens? That's nothing unusual, is it?'

'No, of course not. The trains, though. Was your train delayed? Was there a hold-up on the line?'

'I don't remember any hold-up. Nothing to write home about, anyway. Who had this so-called accident, then? Somebody you know, you said?'

I realise I have to stop now before I tie myself up in knots. Georgie clearly knows nothing about it, nothing she remembers, anyway. She confirmed she always goes home by Tube, but I didn't actually see her enter the station. She could have caught an earlier train and was gone before I arrived. Or she went to the shops before getting the train home.

And then it hits me, the fatal flaw in this incredibly thin line of investigation: Matt was on the northbound platform. Georgie, on her way home to Pimlico, would have been on the southbound. I curse myself inwardly for my stupidity. But the main station entrance leads to both lines, and if there'd been a problem on one, the ensuing mayhem would surely have spilled over. The emergency services would enter via the main tunnel before it split off, which means Georgie could still have seen something.

I shake my head to clear it. She's just said she didn't see

anything. North or south, it's all academic. And completely pointless.

'Not exactly,' I say. 'Look, I'm really sorry, Georgie. I'm wasting your time...'

'So why did you do it?'

The question flies across the small space and pierces me like a knife. *She knows!* Georgie does know something. Has she been playing me along, waiting for me to say the wrong thing and give myself away?

I take a moment, swallowing hard, struggling to level my breathing. This is what I've come here for, isn't it? To hear somebody else's version of what happened that night, gather some detail to corroborate my own story. But I can't deal with it. How did I ever think I could? I wish Carl was here – I wish it with every cell of my being. But he'd never have agreed to let me come in the first place.

'What? What did you say?' My voice is husky, hardly there.

Georgie leans forward and jabs a finger in my direction. 'You don't need money. You girls, you and your sister, living the life of Riley. You've got good jobs, and the wherewithal to walk out on them any time you like, as I'm seeing it. Born with silver spoons in your mouths, I shouldn't wonder. So why did you do it? Go on, tell me that.'

'Money?' Now I'm really confused. Except it seems we've careered away from the subject of what happened in the underground and onto something else entirely. 'Why did I do what, Georgie?'

'You know what. Pretending to be all innocent.'

I almost laugh. Innocent is something I never pretend to be. Far from it.

Georgie continues: 'The charity money that was meant for the dogs' home. Oh yes, I was there, in the corridor outside. I saw you, through the glass, have no doubts on that score. You stole the money from Paula's desk.'

The charity money. I'd almost forgotten about that – the further evidence of my shortcomings, if ever any was needed. Georgie saw me steal the cash. But what she didn't see was me pushing Matt Leyton to his death. Which doesn't prove a thing. It simply means she wasn't in the right place at the right time to have witnessed my greater crime.

My mouth opens and shuts. I can't believe the way this conversation has twisted and tightened and spiralled right out of control.

Georgie rears up. 'You're a wicked, evil girl! That's what you are.'

Evil. My mind picks out the word, outlines it in black, frames it with fire.

You've got an evil streak in you, Ellen Randall! An evil streak that runs all the way through, like the writing in a stick of rock.

Rosie said it. Georgie knows it. And I know it, too.

'I know. I'm so sorry. It was a spur of the moment thing. I don't know why I stole the money. I saw it there and I took it before I knew what I was doing. I wasn't myself at the time. That's my only defence.'

'You should have owned up. I gave you time but you didn't do that. Not to my knowledge, anyway.'

'*You* gave me time? Oh...' My hand flies to my mouth. 'It was you. *You* sent me those emails. You're *catcreep*.'

Georgie looks momentarily shamefaced before she lifts her chin and her expression hardens. 'I did, as it goes. I wanted to frighten you, make you dwell on your sins. Want to make something of it, do you? You were the one who committed the crime, remember that.'

'I did give the money back. I sent it to Paula, all of it.'

'Anonymously, I'll bet,' Georgie says, scornfully.

'No. I put a note in, with my name.'

Georgie looks taken aback. 'Oh. Well, that's something, I suppose.'

I close my eyes for a moment. When I open them, Georgie's staring at me, waiting to see what else I've got to say for myself. Nothing, as it happens. I'm beyond speech, beyond logical thought.

'I had a sister once. Charlotte, she was called.' Georgie's tone is light and conversational, as if the last five minutes never happened and we're acquaintances, chatting over afternoon tea. 'She got the Brontë name, you see. I got the Heyer, for my sins.'

I follow her gaze to a small bookcase in the corner, its shelves stuffed tightly with shabby hardbacks from a range of eras: Georgette Heyer, Mary Stewart, Agatha Christie, Arnold Bennett, the Brontës.

'Right.' I nod. 'Did something happen to your sister?'

Georgie speaks quickly, rattling the words out. 'Killed herself with sleeping pills and a bottle of gin. Left me to my own devices.' She rests her hands on the arms of her chair, as if she's about to get up, but she doesn't. 'All in the past now. Leaves its mark, though. Can't say otherwise.'

A wave of shock and sadness passes over me. 'I'm sorry, Georgie.'

'Yes, well, like I say... Anyhow, you ought to be going now.' She stands up.

I stand up, too. 'Of course. I'll leave you in peace.' I hitch up my rucksack, which is on the floor beside the sofa. I still have my coat on.

We're in the hall, near the front door, and I turn to Georgie. 'For the record, there were no silver spoons. Our parents were moderately well off because they worked hard, and Rosie and I inherited when they died. It doesn't make up for losing them.'

'No, well, it wouldn't.' Georgie's face softens with the kind of emotion I've not seen since I got here. She opens the door. 'Off you go now.'

TWENTY-THREE
GEORGIE

Well, that was a surprise. Shock, more like. What was it all about? The Tube? An accident or something, which was meant to have happened back in January?

One journey home is much like all the others. She could hardly be expected to remember the detail, not even if it was last week, never mind months ago.

Georgie returns to her sitting room and sits down on the sofa. That girl, Ellen, the one whose life should have been hers, coming here and asking all sorts of questions, but not saying why she wanted to know. Not the done thing, is it? Turning up out of the blue. Almost forcing her way in here.

No, no. Georgie corrects herself. There wasn't any of that. The girl was politeness itself; Georgie couldn't say otherwise. Of course, she'd let her in, out of curiosity; let her waffle on about an accident Georgie knew nothing about. And then she'd seen the opportunity to mention the other thing, and before she knew it, she'd gone right in there and asked the girl why she'd done such a bad thing. Ellen hadn't seemed to understand what she meant. They'd both sat there, looking at each other, wondering what the heck the other was talking about. For a while, they'd been talking at cross-purposes.

Georgie bites her lower lip, twists her hands in her lap. She shouldn't have raised her voice, said those horrible things. True, though, weren't they? Well, at least the girl knew now that what she'd done was wrong, no matter if her head was all over the place at the time. She'd more or less said that, hadn't she? It hadn't washed with Georgie, though. Not then. But now she's had time to think about it, pinching that charity money wasn't the sort of thing she could ever imagine a girl like Ellen doing, so something must have gone wrong to make her act like that. All the more reason, then, to make her understand the severity of her crime before she went and did something else out of character and got herself into real trouble.

Georgie stops her biting and twisting and gives her head a little shake. In a way, she's done the girl a favour by sending her those emails, letting her know someone was onto her – they'd given her a bit of a scare, Georgie could tell – and now she's told her to her face exactly what she thinks of someone who could stoop so low as to steal from a charity collection. She'll think twice before she does something like that again, that's for sure.

There is something Georgie regrets about the visit, though. She accused Ellen of being a poor little rich girl. As if it would be her fault, even if she was. Give Ellen her due, she was good about it. Georgie wondered at the time if she'd taken in that crack about silver spoons, or even knew what it meant. But then she'd slid in the reference to losing her parents, and it had been all Georgie could do not to pull her in for a hug.

If Georgie did hugging, which she didn't. No reason to, not for years.

Sensing movement in the street, Georgie goes to the window and looks up, and there's Sonny from next door, coming home from somewhere or other. The sports centre, probably. He padlocks his bike to the railings. Georgie taps the window and Sonny glances down and gives her a little wave before he vanishes up the steps of his house, out of sight.

Georgie sighs and looks at the clock on the mantelpiece. It's too late to go to Oxford Street for lunch in Marks now. She'll see what's what in the fridge, then she might take herself for a little walk this afternoon. It's a fine day. Shame to waste it. The towels she washed yesterday are on the clotheshorse, still damp. She could pop round to the laundrette, finish them off in the dryer. There are always people there on a Saturday. Always someone who'll strike up a conversation, even if it is only that peculiar man with the twitch.

Georgie goes to the kitchen, opens the fridge and takes out the cheese and buttery spread, and the cream crackers from the cupboard. As she spreads the crackers and slices the cheese, she imagines somebody – a friend – asking her why she didn't go to Marks today. And Georgie would say, 'Oh, I didn't have time for that. I had a visitor!'

TWENTY-FOUR

CARL

He walks around the house, calling her name, then checks the back garden in case he's mistaken. He isn't. He peeks inside her bedroom. There are clothes discarded on the neatly made bed: jeans, a black hoodie, a pair of thick socks. This feels too much like an invasion of Ellen's privacy, and he closes the door and goes back downstairs.

He checks the hooks in the hallway. Her dark green parka is there but her navy-blue coat is missing. As far as he knows, she hasn't worn it since the journey down from London. Her boots, the ones she wears in the garden and when they go for their walks, are on the floor, traces of mud stuck to the heels. She might have gone shopping in the village. That would be a first, and a welcome development. But, somehow, he knows that's not where Ellen has gone.

Standing by the kitchen sink, looking out over the garden, which is bursting with new life, he takes out his phone to check if she's replied to his text, but there's nothing. He sends another. *'Hi Ellen. I'm at OC. Where are you?'* A beep sounds from the sitting room. He goes through, and there's her phone, the cheap one, on the sofa. He thought she was still using it – she was when he called her on it from London – but obviously she's changed back to her proper phone, a sign that Ellen is returning to normal. At least, he decides to think of it that way.

He scrolls to the number on his phone, begins texting but changes his mind and calls. Voicemail. He doesn't leave a message. She will see the missed call and perhaps call him back.

He doesn't own her. She's free to do as she likes, go where she likes. She doesn't need his permission. Yet he can't help worrying. He also feels disappointed. He'd been looking forward to spending the weekend with Ellen, cosied up in the house, going for a walk tomorrow, perhaps. He wanted to check she was okay, too. Arrogant, maybe, but he's felt responsible for her for so many weeks it's hard to shake off the feeling.

He fills the kettle for coffee and bangs it onto the base. He has no right to be cross with her, but it would have been nice if she'd have let him know she was going out. And why is she ignoring his call? She must have spotted it by now.

He watches the back gate constantly in case she has gone to the village after all, and she'll appear with shopping, her face lighting up as she sees him at the window. He has a sudden thought that something might have happened on the way. Perhaps she's fallen into the ditch and sprained her ankle. The footpath is muddy and slippery; it's a possibility.

He leaves the house, crosses the back garden and follows the footpath around the fields, as far as the churchyard, but the only person he meets is an elderly man who lives in one of the cottages down the lane.

It's early evening and Carl's in the kitchen fixing himself something to eat when, finally, a text comes through. *'Sorry I missed your call. I've gone to see a friend. Don't worry about me. I'm okay.'*

He can't believe he's trekked all the way back here to see

her and she's swanned off somewhere. Who is this 'friend', and why can't she say where she's gone instead of making a mystery of it? He flings open the oven and slides the pizza out, catching his fingers on the oven shelf. He drops the pizza onto the waiting plate and holds his burned fingers under the running cold tap.

When, minutes later, he calls Ellen's phone, it goes to voicemail again. He sends a text, keeping the tone light, which isn't easy. *'I'm at OC would you believe! Thought I'd surprise you. That worked well. Glad you're okay. When are you back?'*

At 11 p.m., having had no response to his text, Carl tries calling. Again, voicemail. Remembering Ellen's state of mind and the way she's suffered, he isn't angry any more; he couldn't stay angry with her for long, even if he wanted to. At least she has made contact. Clearly, she doesn't want to talk to him for some reason, and he must respect that.

Making sure the fire is out, he switches off the lights and goes upstairs. It's only when he's in bed, attempting to read but finding it impossible to concentrate, that it occurs to him where Ellen might have gone – the police. She could have gone to confess to the murder of Matthew Leyton. From the way she spoke, she'd considered this option a number of times, and dismissed it. But that doesn't mean she hasn't changed her mind again.

His heart races at the thought of her being so overwhelmed with guilt that she couldn't see any other way out. He shouldn't have left her on her own. It was too soon. He should have stayed around to protect her, as he had set out to do in the first place.

Can it be true? Has she really gone to the police? They won't believe her. Where's the evidence? She'll be out of there in no time. But it won't be as simple as that – he's watched enough TV crime dramas to know how it works. There'll be checks, investigations, procedures to be followed, psychology reports to be filed. It won't be as easy as turning her round and sending her on her way. Is she, even now, lying on a hard, narrow bed in a police cell because nobody has worked out what to do with her?

Another version of Ellen's story climbs into his brain. He's thought of it before, even half-suggested it to her in a bid to end her nightmare. Could the scuffle between Ellen and Matt have caused him to fall onto the electrified rail? In which case, if he really was killed that night, was it an accident? She's always been so adamant of her intentions she would never hear of it, but supposing that is what really happened? Would she still be to blame?

If she has gone to the police, that is an angle they would surely raise with her, once they'd located the record of the death. The only crime she would then have committed would be one of omission, of failing to report the accident and admitting her part in it. Of course, there'd be no way of knowing that's what happened after all these months, nor even at the time, given the crush of people on the platform.

The problem with the accident scenario is that he doesn't believe it, any more than he believes Ellen pushed Matt on purpose. It doesn't align with there not being any reports of an incident on the Tube at that time, no apparent ensuing chaos; and that, surely, makes it implausible. But if there's the remotest chance it happened that way, it still isn't good news for Ellen. It wouldn't make her feel any less guilty.

He doesn't sleep: his racing mind refuses to let him. He lies there listening to the owls calling in woods, and by morning he's convinced himself that Ellen has walked right back into trouble when he's trying so hard to get her out of it. Well, he'll just have to try harder.

Sunday creeps along with excruciating slowness. Carl feels edgy and impatient. He could do some work in the garden, but everything is damp and rain has turned the soil to mush. He chooses one of the old books from the shelves in the dining room but after a few pages he loses interest and his attention wanders. He can't seem to settle to anything.

St Wilfrid's church clock strikes twelve as Carl sets off to walk to the village along the footpath. The air is fresh and sweet, and he feels a lot better for being outside. He buys the last newspaper from the rack at the shop and some bread and bacon for tomorrow's breakfast. Back at Owl Corner, he makes coffee, opens the paper on the kitchen table and begins to read. For a while, he's absorbed in catching up with what's happening in the world. And then his thoughts divert again, and he remembers Ellen being scared of listening to the news on the radio. She couldn't really have thought she'd get a mention, could she? Deep down, she must have known how unlikely it was, even if she had actually murdered Matt Leyton. It was just her frazzled mind, enlarging her supposed situation and blowing the whole thing out of proportion that was making her afraid of her own shadow.

Carl waits out the rest of the day and still there's no word from Ellen. He feels for her, he really does. He wishes she was here so he could talk to her, try to calm her fears. He doesn't send any more messages or try to ring her. Whatever is going on, either she wants to be left alone, or, God forbid, she has no choice in the matter. There's nothing for it but to carry on with his pathetically amateur investigations, and pray he unearths something of use before it's too late.

He eats late, using up what's left in the fridge to put together a scratch meal, then clears away and tidies the kitchen in readiness for the morning. At 10 p.m. he thinks he may as well go to bed when he has an idea. Well, half an idea, but it's enough to make him pick up his phone. Glass of wine in hand, he sits in the armchair by the ash-filled inglenook and clicks and scrolls, clicks and scrolls. After fifteen minutes of this it looks like he's wasting his time. And then, just as he's about to give up, he hits on a result.

He blinks at the screen, bright in the half-light of the living room. Okay, it's a long shot, but he has nothing else. It has to be worth a try.

With a couple of glasses of Merlot inside him, he sleeps soundly, and in the morning he locks up Owl Corner and begins the journey back to London.

TWENTY-FIVE

ELLEN

It feels strange, other-worldly, being back in the flat. I didn't make a conscious decision to come home but something led me here, just the same. I realised from the moment I left Georgie's flat and walked along her street that I couldn't go back to Sussex – I've taken advantage of Carl's hospitality for far too long – so it wasn't a surprise to find myself jumping on a bus to Brixton.

Staying in London is a risk, knowing Carl's here. But it's a big city and the chances of running into him are virtually nil. Besides, where else would I go? I wasn't shocked by Georgie's forthright opinion of my character. The words stung, but she was right. Hadn't I heard the same from my sister? It's only a matter of time before Carl – dear, lovely Carl – sees the light and reaches the same conclusion. I hope he can forgive me for running away from Owl Corner when he's been so kind. But it's best I stay away from him, from everyone.

This includes Rosanna. Is this why she really went to Cornwall, to put some distance between the two of us, and why she shows no signs of coming back? I miss her so much, especially now I'm back in the flat. I should ring her, let her know I 'found' my real phone. I love my sister dearly, in spite of our scratchy relationship, and in time I will let her know I'm back in London. But my instincts tell me to leave her alone for now and let her enjoy Cornwall in peace – hopefully she has found peace, and she's over Matt Leyton.

I think about my visit to Georgie and our crazy conversation, spinning off in unexpected directions at every turn. I should be angry with her for scaring me half to death with those emails, but none of that matters now. Carl was partly right; those threats were the work of a nutcase. But I can't think of Georgie Smith in those terms. She must have had her reasons for wanting to lash out at me and, apart from her discovery of the theft, I don't know why she hated me enough to bother and I doubt I ever will.

I wander around the flat and find myself in Rosanna's bedroom. I open the wardrobe, and there's the pink dress – her special dress – on its hanger, squashed in amongst other dresses she used to wear for dates with Matt. No call for those in Cornwall, obviously. I reach inside and touch the delicate layers in the skirt of the pink dress, then jump back as if I've been stung. It's only a dress, but it encapsulates my thoughts and feelings about Matt, and about my sister. And about myself. Mostly about me, and that is the most frightening of all.

I close the wardrobe door and go to my own room, where I unpack my rucksack with the things I brought with me from Sussex: leggings, my favourite jumpers, some socks and underwear, my watch, face creams, toothbrush. When I left Owl Corner I had every intention of returning today, and yet I packed these things 'just in case'. But then, I am a 'just in case' sort of person. 'You think too much, Ell,' Rosanna once said. 'Stop worrying and let it happen.' Whatever the 'it' was at the time. I can't help smiling at the memory.

The smile switches off as the other memory races back, the one that never leaves me. Except it's changing. It changes every time now. It's like replaying a film that's being constantly edited. Every time I run it through my brain, the starting point is different. Sometimes it begins when I'm hurrying along Victoria Street, Georgie up ahead – she isn't always there, but mostly she is. Other times, it begins as I'm swallowed up by the rush-hour crowd at the mouth of the Tube; or it takes me straight to the platform, as if I've been whisked there by magic and not by my own two feet.

Sometimes I see the train appearing from the tunnel and hurtling straight past, not stopping at the station at all. Or it slides alongside the platform with a grind and a squeal, and the hum of its doors opening. The details of what happened next have become confused, and my memory offers up two versions: either I pushed Matt in front of the train, or under it. I want to see it clearly, relive it as if it were yesterday, but I can't, and it frustrates me.

I deserve the punishment of perfect recall.

I don't leave the flat for the rest of the day. There is food in the freezer and cupboards, although there's no milk or bread. No wine, either. A glass or two would help take the edge off, but for some reason I dare not go out. Force of habit, I suppose. I look down from the window at the bustling street and see danger on every corner. Stupid, I know, after I've travelled all the way from Sussex and miles across London, but that's how it seems. I can't get past that feeling, and there's no point in trying to fight it.

I keep thinking about Carl, and his quest to find Matt Leyton. Okay, I admit that when he first mentioned making enquiries, I automatically assumed he was going to search for evidence that Matt Leyton had died. Then, soon after, it hit me that the opposite was true – Carl intended to find the man himself, alive and kicking.

I was so sure he believed my story – why else would he have

brought me out of the tunnel and found me another hiding place? He'd begun to have doubts later, I could tell by the questions he asked me, and the talk about false memory, a subject he raised so carefully, but so transparently. Now I wonder if he ever believed me at all.

I dismiss my own doubts at this point. I was there. Carl wasn't.

It's early evening. The TV is on with the sound turned low. I put my mug of black coffee down on the floor, pick up my phone and switch it on. There's a missed call from Carl. I think about him haring around London on his futile search and feel deeply sad, as well as extremely guilty. I can't let him think I'm still at Owl Corner; it would be too dishonest. But neither do I want him to know I'm in London. He may work that out for himself, of course; I don't know. I only know I don't want to see him or talk to him, not now.

After a minute's thought, I text him to say I've gone to see a friend, and not to worry about me. What he will make of that I have no idea, but it might please him to hear I've been brave enough to go out. I switch the phone off again straight after I've sent the text.

My eyes fill with tears. *Sorry, Carl. I'm so sorry, for everything.*

When I wake in the morning, it takes me a moment to remember where I am, and what day it is. The familiar shapes of the room and the way the light slants across the walls nudge my brain into gear. I'm at home, and it's Sunday.

After my shower, I'm dressing in the bedroom when I hear sirens – *police?* – in the street outside. The sound is muffled because of the double-glazing, but I can tell they're close, and my heart rate shoots up. I try telling myself nobody is coming to arrest me. It's been too long. My phone was there, at Owl

Corner, all the time, although I didn't know it, and I wasn't tracked down. Besides, they wouldn't use sirens, would they?

I'm trying to think logically, but there is no logic to all this, none that I can get a grip on, anyway. The sirens fade, but the panic in my gut continues to rise. If I hadn't given in to my wild notion about Georgie Smith knowing something of what happened in the Tube, I'd be in Sussex now, surrounded by empty green fields with only the owls for company. Safe. Or at least, safer than I feel here.

I remember something else, something I should have thought of yesterday: Carl has the keys to the flat. Supposing he comes today to check on things, as he'd offered? He didn't mention it when he rang on Friday. It could be today. I can't be here when he comes. I can't face him. I can't face anyone.

TWENTY-SIX

CARL

The construction site is harder to find than he thought it would be. He doesn't know the area well, and Shoreditch is in the midst of a major regeneration. Every street has its share of demolition sites, skeleton buildings, scaffolding, hoardings, cranes, builders' lorries and dumpers. One depressing stretch of graffitied hoarding looks much like another, and as he turns the corner into another street he wonders if he made a mistake and the website he found is way out of date; the complex up, the workers gone, ages ago.

But no, here it is. 'Sharpwell Court' the large green and white sign beside the gates proclaims. 'A development of 120 well-appointed 2- and 3-bed apartments, gym and wellness centre, retail arcade, communal gardens.' Another sign alongside gives the name of the construction company – W. H. Graves Construction Ltd. – and a list in smaller text of the subcontractors and other associates, including Trubridge and Jensen, Design Architects.

Carl puts his face close to the metal mesh of the tall gates. Inside is a welter of activity: white hard hats move along walkways; cranes swing slowly against a backdrop of grey sky; clouds of chalky dust billow from huge skips into which corrugated metal tubes are directed, like flumes at a water park. A notice swings from one of the gates: *No entry to unauthorised visitors*. Already the futility of this mission is imprinting itself on Carl's brain. Even if he could get inside and find somebody to speak to, what is he going to say that would sound even halfway plausible? He'd thought no further than getting to this place with its remote connection to Matthew Leyton. No plan other than thinking on his feet.

Standing a little way along the pavement, he checks his phone again in case there's any word from Ellen. Nothing. He hopes that wherever she is, she's safe and well. He leans against the hoarding, watching the flow of people going about their Monday morning business. Everyone looks purposeful, even the old woman wearing slippers and carrying a bundle of old newspapers under her arm, rheumy eyes fastening on Carl as she shuffles past.

He walks back to the gates. They are pulled almost shut, but there's a gap. If he pushes, no doubt they will open further. Okay, there may be security alarms or something, but probably not in the daytime, when vehicles need to get and out. It's a building site. He's not breaking and entering, for God's sake. After a minute, he stops prevaricating, shoves the gates open wide enough to pass through and then he's standing on stone-strewn concrete alongside a flat-topped mountain of copper piping. Nobody takes the blindest bit of notice of him, even though a couple of hard-hats are crossing the square around which the new development is arranged.

Carl looks around to get his bearings and sees what he's looking for: the site office – a yellow oblong box sitting on top of a platform. Other similar boxes lead from it. Carl makes for the perforated metal steps, and, moments later, he's tapping on the filthy glass door.

The stocky, fiftyish man who opens the door is wearing

khaki trousers, a checked flannel shirt, and heavy-duty boots. He frowns at Carl. 'Yes? Can I help?'

A second man, slightly younger, and dressed similarly, comes out from behind a desk. He addresses the first man rather than Carl. 'After a job, is he?'

'Give us a minute. He's not said yet.' Then, to Carl. 'Looking for work, are you?' He looks Carl up and down. 'Not much of you, is there? Labouring's heavy work, you know.'

The men exchange glances, shaking their heads, as if they're communicating in code.

'No, nothing like that.' Carl smiles politely. 'I'm sorry to barge in like this, but I was on my way to see my... an architect. He works for Trubridge and Jensen. He's doing a job for me. He said something about working on this project, so I thought as I was passing I'd call in and see if by any chance he's with you this morning. Before I trek all the way to his office, that is.' He hesitates as the men's faces look blankly at him. 'I live round here. Not far.' He nods his head vaguely, as if to indicate the direction.

This is madness, his excuse for being there sounds so far off the mark as to make him look as if he's lost the plot completely. Which, possibly, he has. But Ellen's face, her wide-eyed frightened face, swims into his mind. She is worth any number of wild goose chases.

He thinks for a moment about the photos of Matt in his phone, and makes an instant decision not to show them. He absolutely can't, even less so here than he could at Matt's office. He'd seem even more like a nut job, and probably be marched off site by Security. Who on the right side of sanity carries around photos of their architect?

'Okay, I can see that's not the case. No worries. Worth a try, I thought.'

The first man has already gone back to his desk. The second man, who Carl can now see from the badge he wears, is the project manager, or one of them, comes forward, narrowing his eyes. 'What's the name? This architect you're wanting?'

'Matthew Leyton.'

'Who's he after?' A voice calls from across the other side of the site office. Carl looks over as a young woman's face appears from behind a large computer screen. Her desk is littered with plans weighed down with a yellow hard hat.

'Leyton. From Trubridge and Jensen.' The project manager turns towards the woman, then back to Carl.

The woman shakes her head. 'Don't know him.' She begins leafing through the plans. 'No. No. Nope, no Leyton given on these.'

'Ah, well, never mind,' Carl begins, and turns to leave. 'Thank you anyway.'

The project manager rubs his chin thoughtfully. 'The only architect we deal with from Trubridge's is called Malone, and he was only here last week. No doubt he'll grace us with his holy presence again in a day or two.' He raises his eyes and grins at Carl. 'No use to you, though, is it? Guess you'll have to make your trip after all. Or get him to come to you. That is usually how they work. You shouldn't have to go chasing about.'

Carl thanks him again and retreats down the metal staircase before this gets even more complicated. Perhaps he should have accepted what he was told at Trubridge and Jensen's offices – that they didn't have a Matthew Leyton working for them. But the link to the company was all he had to go on. Ellen – or rather Rosanna – hadn't conjured up the name from nowhere.

Back in the street, he berates himself for being so ignorant when it comes to tracking down a complete stranger – a stranger to him, anyway. Good job he isn't leaning towards private investigation as a career, then. Or the police.

Ellen falls right back in his mind at the association. She'll be fine, Carl assures himself, though it's more like a fervent wish than anything based on fact. Perhaps it's Ellen he should be

looking for, not Matt Leyton. But she won't thank him for
following her around, will she? If she wanted to talk to him she
would phone, or acknowledge his calls. He has to remember
that Ellen is an adult, with a will of her own. For all he knows
about her, there'll be a zillion things he doesn't know.

It's a little after two. Plenty of the day left, although he feels
heavy with exhaustion, physically and mentally. This comes, of
course, from being on high alert all the time. Firstly, because he
is worried about Ellen, and secondly, because in some small,
twisted corner of his mind, he's constantly expecting to walk
into Matt Leyton at any moment, and to recognise him straight
off.

If only.

He buys a take-out coffee and drinks it sitting on a convenient wall. A young man swathed in a grubby sleeping bag sits
in the nearby doorway of a boarded-up shop. Carl returns to the
café, buys tea, a packet of sandwiches and a cake, and quietly
sets them down in front of the homeless guy, who mutters a
'Thank you' and half smiles up at Carl.

Having located the right stop, Carl boards a bus to Camberwell. Tim will be at work. He'll have the flat to himself, his
laptop to hand, and the space and peace to think clearly about
what he's doing, and how else to go about finding the bloke who
Ellen would swear in a court of law is dead.

TWENTY-SEVEN
CARL

The bus journey from Shoreditch had taken ages, and when he finally arrived home, Carl sat about lethargically, wasting time. Tim came back early, bringing his girlfriend, Debbie, with him. They'd been shopping and bought enough food for Carl to share, which was just as well as the fridge was looking bare, as usual. Relaxing with friends over dinner and a couple of beers, then watching a film, took Carl's mind away from Ellen and her problems, at least temporarily. He'd needed the break and felt less fraught about it all by the time he went to bed.

He had, however, spent an hour or so with the laptop before Tim and Debbie arrived, with the same dismal results as before. It seems unbelievable that there's no digital trail. No social media accounts, no business link-ups, no photos that might remotely match the ones he has. Nothing. Even if Ellen's wild assertion that she killed Matthew Leyton were true, there would be some remnant of his existence somewhere. There are other Matthew Leytons, of course – it's not that uncommon a name – but none with a profile that in any way matches the one he's after.

So... supposing the bloke's using a false name, or rather, he was during his relationship with Rosanna—? Maybe he should have thought of that before, but hearing Matt's name tripping off Ellen's tongue meant he hadn't considered the possibility. Now, though, the idea lodges in Carl's brain, gathering more credence by the minute. The Trubridge and Jensen part, he feels fairly certain, is true. The information is too precise to be made up. Of course, he could be totally wrong about that, but for now it's all he has – the name and whereabouts of a company which does exist, and for which said anonymous person may work.

Standing in his kitchen now, having slept in longer than he'd intended, Carl slaps a hand to his forehead in frustration.

An hour later, he's back in the street where he was on Friday, looking up at the green façade of the office building. It has to be worth another shot. He has the photos of Matt on his phone, and he's past caring what the guy on reception thinks.

Further along the street, he sees a pub sign, which gives him another idea. Passing by the green tower, he walks along to the pub. It's just opening and the landlord, if that's who he is, wishes him good morning and holds the door back for him. Carl orders a coffee at the bar and when it arrives, takes out his phone and scrolls to the clearest photo.

The landlord shakes his head. 'No, sorry. Don't recognise him. Mind you, that doesn't mean much. Who is he, then?'

'An old mate of mine. We lost touch and I'd like to track him down. I think he works around here somewhere, or he used to.'

'We get plenty in from the offices round here,' the landlord says. 'Lunchtimes, and after work. You could pop back later, when the bar staff are in. It might ring a bell.'

Carl thanks him, finishes his coffee and leaves. There are two more pubs further along the street, as well as a coffee shop, and another serving take-out sandwiches. He visits them all, not bothering to buy anything else. A female bartender in one of the pubs looks at him with suspicion. Perhaps she thinks he's a cop, or a private investigator. He finds that funny. The assistant in the sandwich shop stares at the photo for ages. She could have seen him, she says. He looks vaguely familiar, but she really can't be sure. She hands the phone back with an apology. Carl thanks her, and saunters back along the street, in no hurry to return to the office building.

Once he's been back there and probably drawn another blank, he'll have run out of ideas.

Reaching the building, he doesn't enter straight away but crosses the road, perches on a low wall outside a dry-cleaners and brings up the photo of Matt on his phone, the one he used for his enquiries. It's taken from quite close up, although the man's gaze is fixed way off to the side. He's not smiling. The rim of a wine glass is just visible in the bottom left-hand corner. A waiter obscures much of the background but it looks as if there's a bridge, and distant buildings. Carl guesses it was taken somewhere along the Embankment. None of that is relevant, but it keeps his mind occupied for a minute more.

He keeps the phone in his hand, the photo a click away. Traffic trickles by. There are few people about. The constrained quietness of a London side-street prevails. Carl is thinking he should cross to the green building and get this over with when he senses movement behind him. He glances round to see the door of the dry cleaners closing on a tall, dark-haired man with a plastic dry-cleaning bag slung over his arm containing what looks like a suit. He looks annoyed, and impatient, as if he's had to wait a while to collect it. He marches past Carl, glancing left and right as he nears the kerb.

Carl stares at the guy's face, looks at his phone and clicks, stares again. He's sideways on but he's almost sure.

He stands up. 'Excuse me...'

The man turns, and stares back at Carl. 'Yes?'

Carl raises his phone, flicks buttons, clicks, clicks again, and again.

'Hey, stop that! Who the hell are you?' Matt – it's definitely him – advances, his hand outstretched towards the phone. 'Give me that!'

Carl backs away, clicks again, framing Matt's face, then focuses lower down, where a security pass swings on a red lanyard. 'Never mind who I am. I know who you are. The elusive Matt Leyton!'

'What the *fuck* is this?' The suit in its shiny plastic bag slides to the ground. His face and manner are a complete give-away, and there's no doubt left in Carl's mind.

Matt moves. The distance between them closes. 'Wait a minute. You were here yesterday. You were in my building. I saw you hanging about in reception.'

'So what if I was? No law, is there?' Standing his ground, Carl slides the phone into his pocket. He has what he wants. It's time to leave. But curiosity, as well as anger on the girls' behalf, holds him back. This man is the cause of all their grief. The whole sorry mess is down to him. He broke Rosanna's heart – clearly, he just dumped her when he got tired of her – and incensed Ellen to the point where she wanted to kill him, a feeling so intense and compelling that the memory of that moment in the underground became hopelessly entangled with imagination and sent her to the edge of despair.

He steps forward. 'Enjoy it, do you? Getting your ego-trips by treating women like dirt?' He's so close now, he can feel the man's breath. Matt is a few inches taller than Carl, broader in the shoulder, and Carl's movements are slightly hampered by the backpack he's wearing. But he launches himself forward, grabbing Matt by the lapels of his jacket and shoving him.

Matt staggers and reels back, then rights himself, and before Carl knows what's happening, Matt lands him a punch full in the face. The force of the blow knocks Carl off his feet, and as he hits the pavement, Matt delivers a sharp kick to his ribs.

Carl is vaguely aware of Matt muttering under his breath as he retrieves the suit in its bag from the pavement and jogs across the road to his office. Picking himself up from the ground, he sits on the wall until his breathing slows and his heart rate normalises. He feels pain in his chest and wetness on his upper lip. He searches his pockets for a tissue. There isn't one, so he tugs his T-shirt free from the waistband of his jeans and uses the hem to dab at it. It comes away spotted with blood. He takes a few more minutes to gather himself, then sets off towards Victoria Street, checking his phone as he goes.

There's still no word from Ellen. He no longer believes her story about going to see a friend. It doesn't ring true now, if it ever did. Neither does he really think she's gone to the police. If she was going to do that, she'd have done it before now. She's certainly brave enough to walk into a police station and confess to her imagined crime, but she'd be thinking of the effect on her sister, and a rift that could never be healed. Perhaps she's back in Sussex. But if she's at Owl Corner, waiting for him, surely she'd have picked up the phone and let him know? There'd be no reason not to.

He needs to find Ellen, not only to present her with the proof of her innocence but because he's afraid for her.

But where is she?

At Victoria Tube station, he stops on the busy concourse, hitches the backpack down and scrabbles inside. If Ellen isn't in Sussex, or visiting some mythical friend, or, God forbid, sitting in a bleak police interview room, she'll be at home in Brixton, won't she? He can't be certain, but it's the best guess he has. His fingers close around the keys to her flat. Transferring them to his pocket, he moves forward with the crowd, onto the escalator.

TWENTY-EIGHT

CARL

Carl presses the buzzer on the panel at the main door to the block of flats. Nobody answers, so he lets himself in and takes the lift to the second floor. He knocks on the door of the flat, just in case, before he unlocks it and enters. Empty silence greets him. He makes a swift tour of the rooms but he can already sense that Ellen isn't here.

He goes to the kitchen. The tap he turned off when he came here on Friday is dripping slowly into the sink – the hot water tap. Yes, he's sure it was this one. He turns it again to the full 'off' position and the dripping stops. The mugs that were face down on the draining board have been put away, the dishcloth draped neatly over the sink edge. He touches it; it feels damp. He checks Ellen's bedroom again. It's neat and tidy, no clothes on the bed now. Obviously, she's been back. So why didn't she stay? Why leave again when home is the one place she should be? It's where she belongs.

Flummoxed and frustrated, Carl returns to the kitchen and drinks a glass of water. He's not feeling so good now. He goes through to the living room, flops down on the sofa with his feet up and takes out his phone. The photos he took of Matt are better than he'd hoped. There are several full-face shots, the closest-up one especially clear. He compares them with the slightly out-of-focus shots Ellen gave him, and the match is evident, as he knew it would be. He squints at the last picture, the one he took of Matt's security pass. He swipes the image into close-up and looks at the name on the pass: 'Isaac Malone'. And beneath it, the logo of Trubridge and Jensen.

Got you! Carl pulls himself upright. It's a glorious moment, but it doesn't last. The proof that Matt – Isaac – is indeed in the land of the living is reassuring in case there was the tiniest shred of doubt lingering in his mind, but no use unless he can show Ellen. He glances towards the door, listens carefully, longing to hear the key turning in the lock, and for Ellen to step into the hall with bags of shopping. He sighs. She hasn't simply popped out to the shops. The flat is too pristine, the atmosphere all wrong.

He looks at the time on his phone. It's only a quarter past three, but it seems a whole lot longer than five hours since he stepped off the train this morning. His head is throbbing, his ribs are sore, and he feels faintly nauseous, probably because he hasn't eaten since an early breakfast. He needs to go home to Camberwell before he does anything else – whatever else there is to be done. Right now, he can't even think straight.

He levers himself off the sofa, and as he swings his backpack onto his shoulder, he notices a piece of white paper on the table by the window, weighted down with a glass candle votive.

He goes over, picks it up, and reads.

Dear Carl, I want you to know I'm so very grateful for your kindness and for taking me to your beautiful house in the country and keeping me safe. I can't thank you enough. Please could you do one more thing for me – don't waste any more of your time on me, on all of this. I know what I did and that makes me a bad person. But you saw only good in me and I will always love you

for that. I am all right, or I will be, so please don't worry. I hope
your life is everything you want it to be. I won't ever forget you.
Thanks again. Love, Ellen.

The bus stops and starts, stops and starts. One more jolt and
he may very well throw up in the aisle. Eventually, he's
decanted onto the street and makes his way home. He's
rummaging in his backpack for his key on the doorstep when
the door opens.

'Christ, what happened to you?' Tim says.

Carl can't think what he means for a moment. Then he
looks in the hall mirror. A purple and yellow bruise is germi-
nating nicely on the cusp of his swollen left cheekbone and his
left nostril is plugged with congealed blood. There's a smear of
dried blood on his chin.

'I had a slight altercation with a mad man, that's all.'

'Looks like it. Want to tell me about it?'

And Carl does want to. He realises if he doesn't tell somebody about Ellen, and Matt – who turned out to be Isaac – and
the whole ludicrous-sounding saga, he might lose the plot
altogether.

Which, in fact, he's probably already done.

Tim goes out and comes back ten minutes later with burgers
and chips from the takeaway and sets two bottles of beer on the
table. Carl talks and Tim listens, and gradually he feels the
weight slide from his shoulders.

'So where is she now, d'you reckon?' Tim asks, after making
it plain he thinks Carl was crazy to have got involved in the first
place.

'No idea. I have to find her, though.'

Tim raises an eyebrow. 'Because of the murder thing? Only
that?'

'Of course. Why else?'

Tim gives him a sideways look. 'Never mind. Look, if I can help, let me know. Can't see how, though.'

'Nor me.'

Around half past six, Carl goes upstairs and lies on his bed, intending to have a rest then go back down.

He must have fallen into a deep sleep because when he wakes and checks the time, it's gone nine. Feeling strangely disorientated, he goes to the bathroom and downs some water. His face is sore and he looks a fright, but his head has stopped thumping and his brain is beginning to clear. He thinks about Ellen and the note she left. It sounded so final, as if she's given up. When Ellen gives up, she withdraws from the world; he's learned that about her.

Suddenly, he knows where she is.

TWENTY-NINE
ISAAC

He should be out on site this afternoon. The last time he was at the Sharpwell Court development, a couple of queries on materials were left hanging. But it's nothing that can't wait. He's not in the mood now, and definitely doesn't fancy hiking all the way to Shoreditch. He calls the construction manager and tells him he'll be over early next week. Then he picks up a pencil and continues work on the design of an art gallery extension that's sitting on his drawing board.

He feels surprisingly shaky after the encounter in the street. The bloke deserved what he got, though, following him around, *stalking* him. Taking photos of him, for God's sake! He'd known immediately what it was about when the guy called him Matt Leyton. The same way he'd known what that rumpus in the Tube had been about just after New Year, when that girl accosted him and called him all the names under the sun. At first, he'd thought she was a nutcase, picking on a random stranger to spew her bile, until she said the name. And then all roads led to Rosanna Randall. He'd not used that name with anyone else.

The Tube incident was so long ago he'd all but forgotten it, until that unsavoury business today brought a sharp reminder. He'd been waiting for the train, nothing on his mind except the home comforts of Islington, until she'd appeared at his side and started shrieking at him. She tried to grab hold of his arm but only succeeded in plucking at the material of his coat. He'd been in the front line of the crowd, behind the yellow line at a practised safe distance from the track. But she was jigging about, obviously not realising how close to the edge of the platform she was. He'd had to manhandle her to move her back to safety.

And then the train whooshed into the station, and luck was on his side because it stopped at exactly the right point and a set of doors opened in front of him. He'd leapt on board and, when he glanced back, disbelieving of what had just happened, she'd vanished into the crowd.

He shouldn't have been surprised there'd been repercussions; Rosie was a sparky little thing. Unless she'd had nothing to do with it, and her sister – Helen? Ellen? – had spotted him on the platform by chance and taken it upon herself to right what was seen as an unforgivable wrong. It seemed the more likely scenario.

The girl was almost certainly Rosanna's sister; the likeness was pretty strong. He had met her once before, briefly, when the three of them collided outside Selfridge's. He'd allowed the introduction then hurried on, pretending he was late for a meeting.

What she'd hoped to achieve by yelling at him and making a fool of herself in public he had no idea. It wasn't even as if the affair was ongoing. He'd made as clean a break of it as he could. It was hardly his fault if Rosanna hadn't believed him.

The skirmish on the underground had struck a discordant note, which was a shame, really. Rosanna, with her sunny disposition and her brilliant little body, forever ready for him, was one of his better conquests and he'd rather not have had his memories soured by unpleasantness. They'd had some good times together. She seemed to get off on the thrill of ostensibly illicit date nights, fitted in whenever he could escape the confines of domesticity. Or so his story went.

Isaac selects a different grade pencil and works on the detail of the front elevation. His mind rewinds further to a Monday night back in December, and what was to be his last date with Rosanna.

Monday nights had become theirs. Light years away from the commitments of Friday and the weekend, Monday was a social wasteland, purpose-built for working late at the office or holding a business meeting. And how easy it was to forget the time and let the meeting overrun until it was so late he may as well crash in a convenient hotel rather than go home and wake everyone up when he got in. This useful little narrative had become such an intrinsic part of their relationship – all his rela-tionships – he almost believed it himself.

That Monday it was just dinner, not the whole night. He'd had a hectic day at work and, unusually, wasn't in the mood for anything more energetic. He apologised gently, reminding her that he couldn't push it too often – another genuine-sounding little get-out whenever he needed one.

She shrugged, smiled into his eyes and said, 'Fine by me.' Or something like that. Then she'd gone on talking about some-thing else. But the pressure was there, all the same. The sweeter and least demanding Rosanna was, the faster the time approached when he'd have to act. It wasn't something he'd planned for that night, more a natural progression of events.

Perhaps it was the way she was dressed. She always made an effort to look beautiful for him – not that much effort was needed. But that night, he remembers now, she'd worn a pale pink dress he hadn't seen before; silky, sparkly – and expensive, if he was any judge in these matters.

As soon as he'd helped her out of her coat and seen what she was wearing, he'd had half a mind to whisk her off to a classier restaurant with real candles, not battery-operated ones. There was no shortage of such places in Mayfair. But then he'd have had to cancel the table and make his excuses, which might have been awkward. The restaurant he'd chosen might have been a rung or two below fine-dining standards, but it wasn't exactly McDonald's either.

She sat opposite him in the low-lit booth. His gaze followed its habitual trail, sweeping over the whole alluring picture before alighting on a full, delicious mouth, light brown eyes soft as velvet, cheekbones blushed and highlighted to feline perfection. He remembers how she twirled a strand of dark brown hair around one finger before uncurling it and flicking it back over her shoulder, leading his eye to the thin strap of her dress and the dip beneath it where so many times his tongue had found a home.

She chattered on, switching as usual from one unrelated topic to another – something that could cause him to lose the plot if he let his mind wander and missed a bit. He didn't miss the mention of Christmas, though. It stirred something in him, as if somebody had poked a stick into his mind, urging him to get on and do what was necessary.

They were having a party on Christmas Eve in the flat, she and her sister, she told him, as she pushed the ice-cream sundae dish towards him – she liked sharing desserts, enjoyed the intimacy of it, presumably. Personally, he thought it unhygienic. Then she asked him, casually, as if she wasn't that interested in the answer, what he would be doing on Christmas Eve. He gave her a jokey reply about wrapping up scooters in the shed in the dark, and making a last-minute dash to the supermarket for some little extras Laura was panicking about.

It was always 'Laura'. Keeping it simple meant less chance of a slip-up. His own current identity was enough to remember. Matthew, Mark, Luke and John, which became Jon, short for

Jonathan – John sounded middle-aged. Then back to the beginning. He'd stopped being Jon when he finished with Esme, a month before he met Rosanna. His real first name being Old Testament, it seemed logical to switch to the New. He had a system for picking the surnames, too. He stuck a pencil in the map of the Tube in his desk drawer – Finchley, Kilburn, Hyde, Leyton – ringing them round as he used them.

As ever, Rosanna wasn't fazed by the wifely reference. 'Got you,' she said.

He thought she was about to invite him to her Christmas Eve party. Not that it would ever happen. He'd never been to her flat, wasn't even sure where it was, although he had a rough idea. Neutral territory was the order of the day, otherwise things could get severely out of hand.

And then he discovered what was really on her mind when she talked about the two of them having their own festive celebration in a hotel. Between Christmas and New Year, if he could get away. She spoke dreamily about log fires and Christmas trees in the foyer while Isaac's mind whirred away on a mission of its own. He hailed the waiter and ordered coffee to buy himself breathing space.

And then, in one, heartfelt, sentence, he told her it was over.

She was upset, a little tearful; he was prepared for that. He wasn't prepared for her blatant denial. They were in love, weren't they? He was having a moment of doubt, and guilt, she insisted. That was all. To give Rosanna her due, the tears were soon gone. She didn't whine or plead – well, only a little. That was never her way. But neither would she accept his decision.

'Let me know when you're over it, Matty,' she said. *Matty*.

He didn't bother to argue. The icy glitter in her eyes and the stubborn set of her chin told him it was futile. Instead, he gestured to the waiter for the bill, signalling not only the end of the evening but the end of the affair. Telling him to get her an Uber, she scooped up her Marc Jacobs bag, the one he'd bought her for her birthday, and swept across the restaurant to fetch her coat.

That was how it ended. As far as he was concerned, anyway.

Isaac brings himself back to the present. He sits back, reviews the second draft of his drawing and is pleased with the results, despite his mental meandering. Few architects these days draw by hand, but he prefers it as a way of communicating his ideas to the client who, in this case, will be happy. He's good at his job, damn good. Work satisfies him like nothing else.

Who that guy was today was anybody's guess, except obviously he also had something to do with Rosanna. Was she really still so angry, after all this time, that she'd lined up some geek to hound him? Try and scare him? Like that was ever going to happen. He hadn't been scared since he was twelve and his father took his belt to him for telling tales about his mother. Never since. Nothing scares him now.

It was mystifying, though, what took place today. All he knows is that if the guy turns up and harasses him again, he'll get more than a bloodied nose.

THIRTY

ELLEN

It's already 10 a.m. by the time I leave the flat. I don't dare leave it any later in case Carl arrives. I have a plan in mind if I can just get through Sunday. I need this time to gather my thoughts, but I can't stay here, so I get a bus out of Brixton that takes me to Trafalgar Square.

It's a fine day, and I spend some time watching the people and the pigeons, then walk the short distance to the National Portrait Gallery. The hush inside aligns with my mood, which is a whole lot calmer than it was in the flat. I gaze at the faces in the frames. The faces gaze benignly back. Nothing threatening here, nothing to be afraid of. I've been afraid for so long I've forgotten how to be anything else.

I walk, and I sit in coffee shops, losing myself amongst the Sunday crowds, until eventually I decide it's safe to go home. If Carl was going to check on the flat, he would go there in daylight. At least, common sense tells me that, although it may not be the case. Whatever, I can't wander the streets until night-fall, and I take the bus back to Brixton and let myself into the flat around seven.

I make myself some dinner, then put the TV on, but I don't

switch on any lights. Later, I pack my rucksack, ready for the morning, and make general preparations for my exodus, then go to bed at ten, set the alarm on my phone and try to sleep.

It's almost 7 a.m. when I arrive in Maystone Road.

I'd intended to be here earlier, while it was still dark, but I underestimated the time it took to walk here, and my rucksack and sleeping bag – concealed in a Selfridges carrier bag I found in Rosanna's wardrobe – hampered my progress.

But it's fine; the Monday morning buzz hasn't begun and there are hardly any people about. The secret door doesn't budge when I use two hands to push it. It was stiff before, but now it's wedged tightly in its frame and I wonder, a little desperately, if someone from the authorities has come along and sealed it. I put my foot to the bottom of the door and kick hard, and eventually it gives way. I use the handle to pull it shut behind me and descend the two long flights of concrete steps.

My footsteps echo as I walk along the platform, using my torch to guide me away from the edge. I hunker down on the bench in the alcove, my sleeping bag draped over me.

It's weird, but being in the tunnel feels different from before. The vibe is different, as if there's something in the air that wasn't present last time, although the smell is the same: a mixture of dust and grime that isn't actually unpleasant. I keep telling myself there's nothing to be afraid of. I've never been scared of the dark, and yet somehow the darkness seems thicker, blacker, more complete than before. It presses in on me, as if it's a living thing, an enemy I need to keep at bay.

The grimy tiled walls and arched roof enclosing me are keeping me safe, and separated from other people, specifically Carl, who needs to get on with his life and forget all about me. I know this, but it doesn't stop the swirly sensation deep in my gut, and the slight tremor in my hands, which are cold despite woollen gloves. I lift the sleeping bag from on top of me and shimmy into it fully, pulling it up as far as my chest, snuggle down, and try not to think about anything.

My little illuminated Timex tells me I've been here for almost two hours now. Even in this subterranean secret world, time passes; I don't know why I find that surprising. I thought I might doze – I didn't get much sleep last night – but I'm obviously too wired for that. I may not have slept but I've certainly been dreaming, waking dreams in which I see myself as in a film, tailing Matt through the northbound tunnel at Victoria, yelling at him to stop. But I didn't do that, did I? I didn't speak to him until we were on the platform. Did somebody shout when I pushed him over the edge as the train came in? Or was that as I was running away? Whichever, I heard that shout so clearly in my mind before. So why can't I hear it now?

And, as before, the scene plays out in a slightly different way. I can't feel the wool of Matt's coat on my palm any more – the memory of that touch went long ago. It's as if a gremlin has wiped the recording, leaving my brain struggling to keep the story alive.

Yet here I am, back in hiding, because obviously it's where I need to be.

If nobody else sees fit to punish me, I must do it for myself.

I feel air on my face, a distinct current, out of nowhere; a spectral breath. I curl up tightly, hiding my face in the folds of the sleeping bag. When I raise my head again, the air is still, but the tunnel has lost its innocence, somehow. So much life has passed through these tunnels. I found it comforting before, visualising the trains shunting in and out of the station; the passengers making their everyday journeys to work, the city, the shops, or onwards to link up with other trains, above and below ground. Now the atmosphere feels threatening, malevolent.

All this, of course, is my imagination doing its dirty work. But telling myself this aloud, as I do now, doesn't quell my fear of this place, irrational though it is. Urban explorers, people like Carl and Leo, come in here for fun, for the thrill of it. There can't be anything bad about it, can there?

I'm not convincing myself.

I pick up the torch. I'm rationing its use because of the battery – I didn't think to bring a spare – but if I read for a while, it might help settle me.

Of course, I could just take myself out of here, give it up as a bad job and go home. But what then? Will Carl come, or try to contact me? Or Rosanna? I can't talk to either of them. I can't explain it, but with them it's as if I'm putting on an act all the time, and they don't deserve it. They deserve honesty.

I tried with Carl, I really did, but although I loved being with him when it was just the two of us at Owl Corner, I was pretending, going along with his determination to help me when all the time I knew he couldn't, and that nothing he could do or say could change what I was – what I am: a killer.

As for my sister, how can I ever face her again? The strain of keeping my deadly secret would break me, break the pair of us.

So, no, I can't leave, I can't go home. Not until I've worked out how to live, and how not to hurt the people I care for most.

I manage to read for a while, then unzip my rucksack, take out a box of apple juice and pierce it with the straw. I drink about a quarter way down, then stand the drink on the end of the bench, wary of taking in too much liquid so as to delay my foray to the surface, and the public toilets. The drink soothes my nerves a little.

As I'm feeling in the rucksack for a chocolate bar, the torch slips sideways in my hand, throwing the beam across the track. I scream as the light picks up something moving, fast, along the rusting rails. A rat. Then another, and another. Three lithe bodies, scampering silently, intent on some deadly night mission – down here, it's always night.

There weren't rats the last time. Not that I saw, anyway. Another flies past. I scream again and press myself against the cold tiles as I give way to fear. I can't stop the feeling. It engulfs me, turns me into a quivering mess.

My thoughts loop around, back to the scene of my crime. I need the details. I need to hang on to them and see what I did, experience the shock and horror of it again, because my unaccountable fear of this place is nothing in comparison.

If I can gain some sense of perspective, I'll be okay, as far as I can be, anyway.

But I can't do it. My mind seems to be losing its reason. *I killed Matt Leyton.* The words no longer ring true. Matt was tall, broad-shouldered. Did I really have the strength to push him off that platform?

I remember shouting at him; yes, I do remember that. And his face when he turned and saw me. I remember the crush of people. And the train coming. So why can't I remember pushing Matt, seeing him fall to certain death?

Why can't I?

I take several deep breaths, then make myself sit up straight and shine the torch around. No more rats. Even if there are, they're doing no harm. They're just living their lives, doing what rats do. I wave the torch, drawing light patterns across the arc of the roof, the walls, the concrete floor of the platform with its worn-away yellow markings. Nothing has changed. It's just a tunnel, going nowhere. There's nothing to be frightened of.

I switch off the torch, drink a little more juice, eat the chocolate bar, and start to feel better. I'm not cold any more.

I decide against reading because of the potential battery problem. Snuggling down in the sleeping bag, I try to nod off but it's not happening, so I pull my mind back to sunnier days, simpler times.

We're on a beach, Rosie and I. We arrived there from a path alongside a wood, which intrigued us, as the only beaches we knew then were backed by a stretch of promenade guarded by hotels and festooned with traffic islands. This one is bordered by a wide stretch of grass and the fringes of the wood.

It's a golden day, a day of soft yellow sand and blue skies and a gentle, twinkling sea that feathers our feet with foam as we dash in and out of the shallows. We're somewhere on the Isle of Wight, I think – our first holiday with Aunt Margaret and Uncle Derek. The hotel is full of old people sitting about in a fusty lounge with overstuffed chairs. Rosie and I are made to sit up straight at the table, not chatter noisily, and say please and thank you to the waitress. My sister isn't happy to be so restrained and wants to get down and wander off between courses. There's some sort of altercation about this, conducted in fierce whispers from our aunt and whiny tones from Rosanna while I sit still and silent, trying to make up for my difficult sister.

Looking back, it must have been an expensive hotel, but probably not exactly suited to the holiday needs of two small girls. I remember enjoying the beach, though, and being allowed to play in the big garden of the hotel. I don't remember much else about that holiday, except for overhearing what I thought was a curious conversation between our aunt and uncle when I sneaked up behind their deckchairs on the beach, intent on jumping out of the shadow and surprising them.

'Poor little devils,' Uncle Derek was saying. 'Think what would have happened to them if we hadn't stepped in. They'd have gone into care and been swallowed up by the system. Open to all sorts, not given proper guidance. Heaven knows where they'd have ended up.'

It hadn't dawned on me he was talking about me and my sister, until Aunt Margaret realised I was there, and shushed Uncle Derek with a finger to her lips.

The words hadn't meant much to me, apart from the bit about 'care'. Where was that? And what was this 'system' that swallowed children up? Whatever it was, it seemed to be something to avoid at all costs.

I think it was then that I started watching Rosanna, feeling anxious and miserable whenever she did something naughty, in case she was taken away to this 'care' place and I would never see her again.

It felt like a heavy burden, keeping my sister on the straight and narrow, sheltering her from harm – harm as I saw it, anyway – but it was one I shouldered willingly. Once I'd started, it was hard to shake the habit.

Hard, but not impossible. Clearly, it's time I stopped blaming my shortcomings on the circumstances of my life, and let my sister make her own mistakes. I can't rewrite the past, but perhaps time does that, all on its own.

I pull the sleeping bag up around my ears and picture Rosanna and me, as adults, on another beach; not the Isle of Wight, but an unknown tropical beach, with turquoise water and dove-white sand, our skin warmed and tanned by the sun.

We turn to each other and smile.

THIRTY-ONE
ELLEN

When I look at my watch again, it's 2 p.m. I must have slept, which is good in a way, but I will need to sleep later, when it's actually night. I blink myself fully awake, and it shocks me how dark it is, as if my brain has forgotten to warn me. I feel hot and panicky, and I reach for my juice, but the box is empty. I find another in my rucksack, stick the straw in and take a long drink. Which is when I realise I need the toilet. It's a risk, getting in and out of the tunnel without being seen, or rather, without anyone in the street taking an undue interest, but it has to be done.

I'm there and back in no time, particularly as it's begun to rain. I was astute enough to leave the door a tiny bit ajar, so that when I came back it didn't take so much effort to open again. I even went to the 24/7 minimart while I was out, as there was nobody else at the counter and it didn't take long. So now I have more sandwiches – I've already eaten the ones I brought with me – and a spare torch battery.

I settle down to read, and gradually I become absorbed in the book, which is one I've read before but there is comfort in the familiar.

I'm disturbed by a rustling sound. I gasp, look up from my book and switch the torch off. The sound comes closer, and I dare to switch the torch on again and shine it around. I feel almost faint with relief when I realise that what I'm hearing is the carrier bag I got from the minimart, empty now, moving around on the ground below the bench. I can't feel a draught, but I guess there must be one at ground level.

Just a bag, rustling in the air current. But it unsettles me again and I feel shaky inside.

The day wears on. The Timex becomes my friend, with its little green hands and numbers – a comforting reminder of my teenage years, and my ordinary but safe little life with my aunt and uncle in the ordinary but safe Bexleyheath house.

I read and doze the hours away, or just sit in my sleeping bag and wonder what Rosanna is doing now. And Carl, who has demons of his own and shouldn't be fighting mine as well. Is he still in London? Has he been to the flat since I left it? I hope he goes there, then he'll know how grateful I am for all he's done for me.

And he'll know I've set him free.

It's nearly six o'clock when I need the loo again. The toilets I use are tucked away in a small green space and nobody bothers to lock them at night. I can nip to the minimart for a bottle of water and more food while I'm out.

I take my hairbrush, toothbrush and paste, and a packet of wet wipes from my rucksack and put them in my coat pocket, then make my journey up the two long flights of stairs to the door. I listen for a moment in case there's anyone directly outside, although the wood is thick and muffles the sounds from the street. I tug on the corroded metal handle. The door doesn't open. It doesn't give at all. I think back to my earlier trip. I didn't shut the door fully when I went out, but I must have closed it right up when I came back. There was no reason not to, and I probably wasn't thinking about it too much.

I pull on the handle again. The wood creaks but the door doesn't open. I examine the edge, putting my palm against it. I can't feel air, and there's no telltale chink of light. Okay, so the door was very stiff when I arrived this morning. The wood is probably swollen and warped by the passing of time, as well as the recent rain. It's not locked – there's nothing to lock it with. I must be losing my strength. I grasp the handle firmly and pull. Another creak. No movement.

Stepping back from the door, I stare at it, breathing hard, trying to contain my rising panic. I got in this morning, and I've been out, and in, since. It must be possible to do it again. I step up to the door, take hold of the handle and jiggle it a bit, taking it nice and steady. Perhaps that will do the trick.

It doesn't. The door is stuck fast. Sickening heat sweeps over me as I place both hands on the handle and give one almighty tug. There's a rasping sound, and the handle comes away from the door, leaving two raw holes in the wood, like wounds.

I drop the handle with a clang, bang my fists on the door, and yell. My voice echoes in the stairwell. I doubt if it carries outside, and even if it does, who's going to take any notice?

'*Oh*. Oh God!'

I tell myself to keep calm, use logic. But my heart's pumping like crazy and my chest hurts with the effort of breathing. Retrieving the handle from the ground, I force one end into the crack of the door and try to lever it open. But it's hopeless. The door is too thick, the ends of the handle not thin enough.

I bang and shout again, and, after a while, I run back down the steps, two at a time. On the wall opposite the track is the old Way Out sign, with an arrow in a red circle. It points right, the opposite way from my bench, towards the main exit of Maystone Road station. I know what Carl, and Leo, said about the station being inaccessible, but that's from street level. Perhaps from down here there's a way.

I'm running now along the platform, not caring that it's dark, but keeping close to the wall. I haven't gone very far when I almost smash into a metal grill. I blink, forcing my eyes to see. The grill is part of a huge gate. As far as I can tell, it fills the tunnel, from top to bottom, and side to side, stretching right across the rail track. I grab the bars and shake them, but they don't even waver, and I can already tell there's no way through.

I'm crying, great, wrenching sobs, as I run back along the platform, past the steps, past the bench, and all the way to the brick wall that cuts off my section of platform. There's a gap in the wall, Carl said. I didn't stop to pick up the torch so I feel my way to the gap at the edge. It's barely wide enough, but I squeeze through.

My eyes have become more accustomed to the dark and I only have to jog a short way along to see ahead of me what I already knew was there.

Another wall, this time one that seals off the tunnel completely.

This is it. This is how it ends. Nobody will find me till it's too late. Maybe not even then.

I can hardly breathe. I squat down on the platform and relieve myself, then squeeze through the gap, walk back to the bench, scramble into my sleeping bag and shake with sheer terror.

THIRTY-TWO
CARL

Carl glances up and down the street, then nudges the door with his shoulder, the way he always does. Nothing happens. He tries again, placing his hands in different positions and pushing firmly, but it's no good. The door is truly stuck. It was already warped by years of neglect. Now it seems that time has defeated it.

He steps back on the pavement and checks his watch. It's nearly ten, an hour since he left home. He should have taken an Uber instead of the bus, but he hadn't thought; after his sleep he probably wasn't fully compos mentis. He'd called out to Tim to let him know he was going out, then walked round to the bus stop. As it goes, there wasn't any need to hurry.

He gazes up at the red brickwork with its decorative arches, the architecture of the underground forever imprinted on this insignificant street, as if the answer might be up there some-where. A police car sits at the traffic lights at the end of Maystone Road, and he waits until it drives past him out of sight before he tries again. But no amount of shoving and kicking makes any impression. If only he'd brought Tim with him – their combined strength might have had the door open, although he suspects it wouldn't have made any difference.

Turning round to face the road, he leans against the door. If Ellen isn't in the tunnel, where the hell is she? He was so sure that's where she would be. Obviously, he was absurdly wide off the mark. There's no way into this section of the station other than through this door. No way in at all now.

After a few minutes, during which he mentally berates himself for having misread the situation, he walks along Maystone Road and turns into a wider, busier street. The 24/7 minimart is doing a brisk trade. An oldish man wearing a filthy duffel coat comes out with a carrier bag, the neck of a bottle poking out. He mutters a swear word as he almost cannons into Carl. Further along, the smell of kebabs and chips wafts from the door of a steamy-windowed takeaway.

On the next corner, there's a pub with stained-glass windows and a surround of dark green ceramic tiles. He makes the bar just in time for last orders, finds a seat in the corner and nurses his bottle of lager as he thinks about Ellen, and what might have been in her head when she wrote that note. It was addressed to him; a goodbye note. As long as that's all it was. Whatever else she might be, Ellen is a fighter, a survivor. She wouldn't do anything stupid.

Would she?

He's been wrong about so much else. Is he wrong about that, too? Trusting his own instincts is all very well, but isn't it as unreliable as trusting memory?

So... Carl tries to think clearly and positively – not easy, as his head is starting to feel as if it's twice his bodyweight – *so, if Ellen didn't go back into hiding in the tunnel, did she go somewhere else for a while and is now back home in Brixton?* He won't say 'safe' because he has no more idea now of her state of mind than he did the day before yesterday, when he discovered she'd left Owl Corner.

The pub is closing, the punters trooping out, leaving a trail of 'goodnights' behind. Carl follows them, his bottle still half-full on the table. He walks a few yards along the pavement, away from the groups of evicted drinkers laughing and talking loudly to one another, takes out his phone and rings Ellen's number. Voicemail. He leaves a message, aware, too late, that he sounds hysterical. But there's always the hope that she'll see it and call him back. He feels inside his pocket in vain, already knowing the keys to Ellen's flat are in his backpack at home. Anyway, it's too late to go there now. If she is at home, she probably won't answer the door buzzer at this time of night. She mentioned before the annoying number of food-delivery guys getting the flat number wrong, and off-their-heads strangers stabbing the buttons at random. But if he doesn't go and check, assuming she is there, how will he know if she's okay?

Besides, if she's not responding to his calls, who knows how long it will be before he can show her the photos of Isaac? He thinks about emailing them to her in case she checks but suspects it would be too much for her to handle, all at once. He really needs to be with her when she sees them.

He gazes up and down the road, which is beginning to quieten down. Ellen's flat is within walking distance; perhaps he should head off in that direction anyway. His feet are dead weights. It's been a long, intense day and he's exhausted, despite the few hours' sleep he managed earlier. His head's banging like a bass drum. He's probably concussed from the punch. He could just hail a passing cab, get home and start again tomorrow.

While he's debating his options, he walks, and finds himself back at Maystone Road. Now he's here, it won't hurt to have one more try at getting into the tunnel.

Once he reaches the door, he doesn't waste time. The traffic's thin, no pedestrians close by. Carl stands on the kerb facing the door, takes a deep breath, launches himself across the pavement and channels all his remaining energy into one almighty kick with the sole of his boot. Wood cracks.

The door gives; his earlier attempts must have weakened it. It opens only a fraction, but it's enough. Hooking both hands around the door edge, he pushes, and the gap widens sufficiently to let him through.

A pain in his foot shoots up his leg as he descends the stairs, two at a time, but he hardly notices. Remembering the torch in his inside pocket, he pulls it out and sends the beam across the platform. He calls her name. It bounces back to him, ghostly, metallic. He calls twice more. If she's in here, she must hear him.

There's no answering call, no sound at all, except the laboured scrape of his breathing.

THIRTY-THREE

ELLEN

Are my eyes shut? Are they open? Can't see. Everything's black. Is it night?

Metal on my tongue. No, not metal – orange. Something dry at the back of my throat. Gritty.

My hands. So cold. Where are they? Here, somewhere. Inside... what is this? My bed?

Don't think it's a bed.

Have I been asleep? Am I asleep now?

I felt myself falling.

Like Alice, down the rabbit hole.

Must have been dreaming. If I'm awake now, why has nothing changed?

Can't get out. Need to get out. I can't see the way.

Light. I had a light, before. Can't find it now.

I'm lost. Lost in this dark place.

Mummy! Come and get me. I need you. Mummy, where are you?

Noise. Coming from... where?

Voices in my head. Not outside. Only silence in here. And the ghosts. But they don't make noise.

A voice again. An echo. I'm dreaming. Drifting...
Light beyond my eyelids. Piercing. Forcing them open.
Blinking. It's hard, blinking. Too hard to keep my eyes open.
But I do, and I'm dazzled by brightness.

THIRTY-FOUR
CARL

'Ellen. Ellen!' He grips her shoulder, gives her a shake.

The torch beam swings across her face and the hump of the sleeping bag, then reveals, to his horror, a squashed packet of paracetamol and next to it, a small carton of orange juice.

Her eyes flicker as she recoils against the light but he keeps the beam focused until her eyes begin to open.

He waves the packet in front of her face. 'Have you taken these? How many?'

'*Oh!* Oh, Carl! It's you.' She bursts into tears. 'I couldn't... the door got stuck and the handle came off. I thought I was going to die. I'm not dead, am I?'

He laughs at this, out of sheer relief. 'No, you're not dead, and I'm no angel. Ellen, listen to me.' He waves the packet again, which has clearly been opened. 'How many of these have you taken?'

She blinks. 'What are they?'

'Paracetamol.'

'Oh. Yes. I got them at the shop, I think. Or did I bring them with me?' Her voice is slurred with sleep.

'Never mind that. How many did you take?'

'Four? No, five.'

'No more?' It's only a small packet but he needs to be sure.

'That's all there were left. I thought... I wanted to go to sleep. I thought if I went to sleep I might not wake up and it would all be over.'

'What would all be over?' He needs to hear exactly what she'd intended.

'This...' She lifts an arm from the sleeping bag and waves it. 'Being trapped down here in the tunnel where no one would ever find me.' She gives a small sob, releasing fresh tears. 'I didn't want to die. I was so scared.'

Carl edges onto the bench and gathers her up in his arms. She sobs quietly against his shoulder as he smooths her hair and whispers 'shush' sounds. Then he remembers the door. Supposing some idiot comes past and pulls it shut?

Gently, he lifts Ellen away from him. Her eyelids are heavy with sleep but they have to get out of here, now. With some effort, and half-hearted compliance from Ellen, he pushes the sleeping bag down to waist level and pulls her free.

She's able to stand, just about. He slings her backpack over his shoulder, leaving the sleeping bag behind, and together they make their way up the two long flights of steps.

Once they're through the door and into the street, Ellen wakes up a little more, but he keeps hold of her arm to steady her.

'I'm sorry,' she says, her voice catching. 'So sorry for all the trouble I've caused. I don't know how you knew where I was but thank you. Thank you for rescuing me. I'll go home now. I'll be fine.'

'You're going nowhere except home with me, to Camberwell. No arguments.'

Her face in the sickly yellow glare of the streetlight is colourless, streaked with dirt and tears.

She says nothing, just nods.

. . .

'I was only going to stay down there for a while,' Ellen says, when they're in the back seat of the Uber. 'I needed to sort things out in my head, how to go on. It wasn't working, being in the flat. I was scared all the time, in case somebody came to get me. Or you came and thought you had to look after me. I didn't want... I couldn't... I had to get away and I couldn't think of anywhere else.' A sob cracks her voice.

Carl takes hold of her hand. It's freezing cold. 'I know. It's okay. You're safe now.' He smiles. 'You don't get rid of me that easily.'

'It was stupid, going back in the tunnel. It wasn't safe at all, was it? It was dangerous. You said it was.'

'Just a bit.' He smiles again, and cups her hand with his to warm it up. 'Don't talk any more now.'

She subsides gratefully against his shoulder, and for the rest of the journey he switches off his thoughts and watches the light trail that is London at night as it slides past.

By the time they reach Camberwell, Ellen has recovered sufficiently to walk into his flat unaided, carrying her rucksack. She even exclaims at what a nice place it is, and how lucky he is to live in such a quiet road. After all she's been through today, he's astonished to hear her acting out the role of polite guest. But then, Ellen's reactions have never been predictable – far from it – so perhaps he shouldn't be surprised.

He settles her on the sofa in his living room, switches on the fake coal fire, then goes to the kitchen to make tea and toast for them both. Tim pops his head around the kitchen door while he's doing this, nods towards the living room and asks if everything's all right. Carl says everything's fine, or it will be soon. Tim gives a thumbs-up and goes back to bed.

By the time he's back in the other room, Ellen's eyelids are drooping but he can't let her sleep yet. He hands her a mug of tea and watches her expression change to something approaching ecstasy as she sips it. He pushes the plate of toast towards her. She takes a piece and nibbles at it, mainly to please him, he thinks. Ellen is a people-pleaser; it's just occurred to him that this is what she is. If only she loved herself more.

After a while, they begin to talk, or rather Ellen does. She surprises him again by describing her visit to a woman called Georgie Smith, who works at Printabilly.

'That's why you left Owl Corner, to seek her out?'

'In the first place, it was, yes. And then I realised I couldn't take advantage of you any longer. You'd done everything you could, and it wasn't fair of me to stretch it out. My problems are mine to solve, not yours.' She gives a hollow laugh. 'And now, here we are again.'

Carl smiles, shakes his head. He needs to know where her head is before he breaks the news that will change everything.

'I don't like the sound of this Georgie woman,' he says. 'Even though you made a mistake and took the money, it didn't give her the right to make those threats.' He doesn't want to talk about that side of things, but it's a lead-in to what he really wants to ask.

Ellen shrugs. 'She's okay. A bit off-beam, I grant you.' She taps her temple. 'I'd say she's lonely. Loneliness makes people lose their grip, sometimes.'

'Yep, I imagine it does.' He remembers thinking Ellen was lonely. His opinion hasn't changed. He continues. 'The reason you went to see Georgie – was it because you were looking for some kind of backup? Proof that your version of what happened in the Tube was the right one?'

Ellen freezes, her eyes wide, and he can tell he's pushed her too far. He must remember how fragile she is and the terror she's suffered today, never mind the other times. But it's okay, because she relaxes almost immediately, and lowers her eyes, as if she's suddenly shy. 'When you put it like that, yes, that's exactly it.'

'Which means...' He pauses. 'You were having doubts yourself, about what you did. Am I right?'

She stands her empty mug on the floor. 'I couldn't *see* it any more. I could see myself following Matt and giving him a piece of my mind, but not the bit where I pushed him under the train. I saw myself leaving in a hurry, but not running. I don't remember the running part, only getting out of the station. It wasn't easy, with so many people. I couldn't have run even if I'd wanted to.' She looks at him. 'The memory changed. It was distorted, all wrong, somehow.' She shakes her head as if she's confused.

It's time. Carl feels she can handle the truth now, and believe it without a shadow of a doubt. He picks up his phone but before he can go any further, she throws him an appalled look, and he quakes inwardly at what might be coming next.

'Your face, Carl! What's happened to your face?'

He realises they've been sitting in the half-dark, with only a low-wattage lamp on. When he reached for his phone, he must have turned and given her a different view.

'Ah, that.' He touches a fingertip to the tender bruising, which now extends down the side of his nose and across the plane of his cheekbone. 'That's quite a story.'

And then he tells her every single thing, every little detail, of his movements since leaving Owl Corner. His first abortive visit to Matt's – Isaac's – office building, the building site where he'd wildly hoped to pick up some clue about Matt's existence, his return to the street where Matt worked, and ending with... *this*.

He pushes buttons on his phone and hands it silently to Ellen.

THIRTY-FIVE
ELLEN, FOUR WEEKS LATER

When I was ten and Rosanna twelve, I pushed her down the stairs. Or so I believed. It was all over something and nothing, although it wasn't nothing to me at the time.

My sister had arranged to go ice skating on Saturday morning with some girls from her class, having secured, after much wheedling and coaxing, our aunt and uncle's permission. I asked if she'd take me with her, and she'd rolled her eyes and said, 'If I must.'

Naturally, I'd taken this as a firm 'yes'.

We'd been glued to the TV for months, watching Torvill and Dean win championship after championship, and had even decided on the costumes we would wear if ever we were in Jane's place. Pink tulle for Rosanna – pink was always her favourite colour – and pale green velveteen for me, which my sister scathingly announced would make me look even more colourless than I apparently already was. I didn't care what she thought. I knew I would look, and feel, spectacular as I delighted the audience with my prowess on the ice.

The fact that neither of us could skate ever came into it, though Rosanna was one stage ahead of me, as she had been to our local rink once before and managed to complete several circuits without falling over. I hadn't been there to witness this feat, so I had to take her word for that.

On the Saturday morning in question, I'd run along the road to the shops on an errand for Aunt Margaret and arrived back at the house in time to see my sister in the back of a friend's father's car, gaily waving to me out of the window as she was swept away.

No amount weeping and wailing was ever going to inveigle Uncle Derek to drive me to the ice rink to catch up with them – my aunt and uncle were firmly in the 'chin up and get over it' camp – and I spent the next hour in my bedroom, thumping seven bells out of the pillow which was soaked with my tears.

It wasn't so much the skating itself, though I'd dearly wanted to go – it was more that I'd been cruelly deceived by my sister, who had obviously lied about the time we were being picked up.

I had calmed down by the time Rosanna came home, her face glowing from exertion and excitement. But as the two of us converged at the top of the stairs on our way down to tea, the full force of her treachery hit me afresh and something snapped inside me. My ears roared, my eyeballs were seared by a lightning flash, and I launched myself forward and pushed her with both hands.

Rosanna lay motionless at the bottom of the stairs, her hair across her face, one arm flung out across the parquet flooring.

I remembered seeing her lying there, and seeing myself staring at her from the top of the stairs.

As my brain replayed the incident, which it did, many times, I felt again the wool of her jumper on my palms, heard her scream. Or was it my scream? I was never sure of that. I couldn't recall scrambling down the stairs, or anything else that occurred directly afterwards, until my visual memory lifted me to the dining room where my sister sat at the table – with Aunt

Margaret and Uncle Derek – the epitome of the perfectly behaved child, not a hair out of place.

I remember feeling the weight of fright lift from me as if it were a physical thing, and that I accepted Rosanna's kicking of my shins beneath the table as my due.

I was never punished for my wickedness, which was unexpected and mysterious, if I knew my sister at all.

This, if anything, added to my guilt, which mushroomed appallingly until it filled my every waking moment. Two weeks later, unable to bear it any longer, I bought Rosanna a bar of her favourite white chocolate and handed it to her with a meek apology for having pushed her down the stairs.

She was incredulous. 'What're you talking about? You didn't push me down the stairs!'

Undeterred, I ran the film again in my brain with a detailed Technicolour commentary for my sister's benefit, even describing the shape her body made on the hall floor as she landed.

She just laughed.

'Oh, that,' she said, unwrapping the chocolate. 'Yeah, you were dead narked I didn't take you ice-skating but I didn't want my kid sister trailing along, did I? You pushed past me at the top of the stairs as we were going down for tea. You were quite rough, actually. I never fell down the stairs, though. I don't know where you got that from.' She paused, a shard of chocolate halfway to her mouth. 'You glared at me all through tea. I do remember that.'

'Is that why you kicked me?'

'S'pect so.' She handed me the chocolate. 'Want a bit?'

If only I'd remembered this evidence of my faulty memory before, it might have saved an awful lot of heartache and several lorry-loads of guilt, not to mention near-disaster. Instead, my brain decided to travel its own perverse route and bypass it altogether, until Carl showed me the photos of Matthew Leyton –

Isaac Malone, as I know now – and the stairs incident came flooding back.

I thought about it some more after Carl had seen me settled in his bed, switched off the light and gone to sleep on the sofa. I might tell him about it at some point, although I'm sure he's had more than enough of my craziness.

I stand at the window now and gaze at the farrago of rooftops, bridges, arches and cranes; the distant, uncompromising finger of the St George Wharf Tower pointing skywards, and feel a warmth running through me, an incomparable sensation that reminds me I'm home, and safe. A musky, sweet scent rises, pulling my attention from the view to a glass vase of daffodils on the sill. Golden and glorious, yet homely, they make me smile. Which, no doubt, was Carl's intention when he brought them for me. They remind me of Owl Corner, and I wonder how the garden is looking after Carl – and myself, after a fashion – gave it so much attention.

He said I could go back there if I wanted to. Not with him because he's working at the shop, putting in extra hours to make up for his absence, but on my own, to relax and enjoy the peace. It is a tempting offer, and I thanked him, but told him it would be better if I made inroads into getting back to normal which means Brixton, and some kind of job, although I haven't yet made any serious moves in that direction. I've paid Carl back for what he spent in Sussex – well, as much as he would accept, anyway – he was sweetly reluctant to accept anything – and I can manage on the money I have for now. There are more important things, namely my sister, whom I've neglected shamefully.

I call her an hour or so later. She answers straight away.

'Ell! Great, I was going to ring you. How are you? How's

Sussex? Oh, that was a while ago, wasn't it? Don't s'pose you're still there. Did you have a nice time, though?'

I'm momentarily wrong-footed by this bright welcome and the chain of questions. Especially the one about Sussex; I'd forgotten I told her about that. From Rosanna's over-effusiveness I deduce that ringing me wasn't top of her agenda, and I feel a dip of sadness that we seem to have drifted apart.

'Yes, it was good, thanks. Bit quiet, you know – all fields and woods and stuff, but that was kind of the point. Getting away from it all.' *Shut up, Ellen.* 'I'm home now, back in the flat. Well, of course I am. Where else would I be?'

'I bet it's not the same without me.'

I swallow, hard. 'No, it's tidier.' She laughs. 'I've even got flowers. Daffodils, on the windowsill.'

'You should have Facetimed,' Rosanna says. 'Then I could have seen.'

'I know. I will, another time.'

'Not that there's anything to see this end except my beautiful face. I'm in the stockroom surrounded by cardboard boxes. If the signal goes in a minute, you'll know why.'

'Oh.' I'd forgotten about Rosanna's job. 'Sorry, not a good time?'

'It's cool. Lowena shuts the shop on Wednesday afternoons. She's just about to lock up. I can't wait till I get home for my lunch, so I'm having it now.'

I wonder at this. 'It must be all that sea air.'

A pause, then: 'Yep, that'll be it.'

We chat about Cornwall, and Rosanna talks about the farmhouse, and Sarah and Jay, and relates some of the funny things little Chloe's done. 'She's so sweet, Ell!'

I wonder at this too. My sister has never been one to make a fuss over little kids.

Rosanna asks about Brixton and our mutual friends from the pub. I keep my answers vague and partly fictitious. I've only been to the pub once since I came home, and then I didn't stay long because I felt overwhelmed, as well as out of the loop. But my sister wants to hear I've been out enjoying myself, so this is what I give her.

She tells me she sent a postcard of Mevagissey to Aunt Margaret and Uncle Derek, and how surprised she was to receive one back of Ambleside, with a humorous message. I immediately feel guilty that I've not been in touch with our aunt and uncle in a while.

'I'll ring them soon,' I say, meaning it. 'I might even go and stay for a few days.' I've only just thought of this, but it's an idea. Or would that be running away again? Well, why not? I've become quite the expert.

It's while I'm thinking this that Rosanna reminds me she's still there.

'Sorry. I was just thinking.'

'You know what thought did. So, what about work, then? You getting another job, or what?'

I reply, truthfully, that of course I'll be looking, and I'm considering my options. My sister leaps in, happy to be of service, and tells me she will have a word with one of her contacts at the Bond Street recruitment agency where she used to work. They, apparently, will 'sort me out'.

'Because you don't want to land yourself with any boring old job, do you?'

I assure her that's the last thing I want, although at this moment I haven't a clue what I want, except not to wake up every morning filled with left-over gut-wrenching anxiety. Boring, in this context, actually sounds quite appealing.

We chat a bit more about nothing in particular, then Rosie says she has to go as Lowena is leaving, but we will talk again soon. I'm almost ready to cut the call, when I realise I haven't asked when she might be coming home, and she hasn't said. I ask now.

'Not yet, Ell. I'm kind of settled here, now I've got used to it.' She gives a nervous laugh. 'There are worse places. It'll be beach weather soon. You should come down. Sarah and Jay would be pleased to have you. They've got tons of room.'

'That would be good. I'll come in the summer. If you're still there.'

'I'll be here,' Rosie says, and there's something in her tone I can't identify – a note of defiance, perhaps. 'I'm staying put for the time being. It's... well, it's kind of complicated.'

Now I'm on the alert. What can be complicated about my sister spending some time with friends in Cornwall? Unexpected, yes, considering her declared attachment for all things London. But everything changes eventually. And everyone.

'Okay,' I say slowly. 'Are you going to elaborate on that or am I meant to keep guessing?'

Another pause, longer this time, and heavy with meaning. 'The thing is, Ell, I seem to be just a little bit pregnant.'

My heart stops. '*Pregnant?* Oh, Rosie...'

'Don't, Ell. Don't tell me how stupid I've been because I already know.'

I'm silent for a moment as I struggle to take in Rosanna's news.

'I wasn't going to say that. I'm just shocked, that's all.' This is true. If there's anything these past months have taught me, it's how precarious life is, and how easy it is to make the biggest mistakes. 'How far along are you?'

'Four months, going on five.'

'*Four...?* God, Rosie, didn't you suspect, like, before?'

I can almost see her shrug. 'You know what I'm like in that department. About as unreliable as our old school bus.'

And not that efficient at writing things down. I roll my eyes as if she can see.

'Nearly five months,' I say, thoughtfully. 'Matt, then?' I already know the answer.

'Yes, Matt! What do you think I am?'

'Okay, just checking.' I wait, then: 'I don't suppose he's been in touch?'

Of course he hasn't, considering he dumped her back in December, but I have to ask. I need to know where this is going. I can feel my next dilemma stealing the air from around me.

Rosanna confirms the total absence of Matt from her life and assures me that is how it's going to stay. 'He's an arse. He doesn't deserve me, and he doesn't deserve to know about the baby.'

Rosanna's flagrant declaration is so true to her personality, I can almost see the challenge in her eyes, the toss of her head. I smile.

I've missed you, Rosie.

'Matt's got his family,' Rosanna is saying. 'He's got two children already. He won't miss this one. There are probably others all over London.'

Her laughter is steel-edged. The crass remarks are her way of coping, and I don't respond. I feel inordinately sad for her.

We end the call with promises on both sides to talk again soon, I'm back at the window, gazing at the panorama beyond, whilst no longer seeing it.

My sister's ex-lover will always be 'Matt' to her, and I can't put her straight on that. Not without admitting I've been stalking him – well, not me personally, but Carl acted on my behalf, and it amounts to the same thing. Rosanna would want to know why we did that, and rightly so. I could pretend that investigating that man was for her sake, but it would be an outright lie – Carl did it to save me from myself, and only that. In any case, it's all behind me now. I can't put my mental well-being at risk by raking it all up again.

I feel a stab of pain and regret on behalf of Isaac's child, who will never know its father. But what else can I do?

THIRTY-SIX
ROSANNA

Rosanna sits on a wooden bench, the remains of her lunch on her lap. Behind her looms the grey stone sea wall, warmed by the sun; above it, pastel-painted cottages, like dolls' houses, climb the hill. Before her, fishing boats and small pleasure craft rock gently in the azure waters of the harbour. As she watches the mesmeric movement of the brightly coloured boats she thinks about how her life has changed in such a short space of time. How *she* has changed.

And it's not just her. Ellen didn't exactly shout out with joy at the news about the baby, but neither did she give her grief. She didn't even go on about how the father has the right to know. But then she'd always detested Matt, even though she didn't know him, so no surprise there. It's good to know they're on the same side for once.

She'd been right not to tell Ellen she'd tried to contact Matt through Trubridge and Jensen – that was still a mystery, but would have to stay that way. She wanted no more to do with him now. If, at some unforeseeable point in the future, they ran into one another in London, she'd deal with it then.

Rosanna has missed her sister more than she'd realised until they spoke just now. Ellen sounded fine, though, so she doesn't need to worry about her. The break in Sussex probably did her good.

A shadow falls across her lap as the space on the bench is filled. It's that guy again, the one who came into the shop last week. She'd helped him choose a birthday present for his mum. They'd run into one another a few times since, once in the bakery when she was buying Cornish pasties to take back to the farmhouse – never her kind of food before, but the baby insists on the carbs – and once down here, by the harbour.

'Hello,' Rosanna says. 'You surprised me. I didn't see you coming.'

'Sorry.' He grins, not meaning 'sorry' at all. 'I spotted you from round there.' He points across to where the long arm of the harbour wall juts out to sea, a white lighthouse on its tip. 'I was watching the catch come in.'

'You must have good eyesight if you saw me from there.'

'Ah, well, there you have me. I saw you before from the street, when you were walking down.' He smiles, and she glimpses a shyness that hasn't been apparent before. He must hide it well. 'Anyway, I'm David.'

The offer of the name makes Rosanna wary, she's not sure why. If this is a chat-up rather than one of the locals just being friendly, she doesn't want to know. That part of her life has been packed away, placed under lock and key. She's happy as she is, free of ties, apart from the strengthening bond she feels with her child.

She tells him her name anyway – it would be rude not to. She also tells him she lives in London, and has come here to spend some time with friends.

'You wanted a break from the Smoke, then?'

Rosanna smiles. She hasn't heard that term in a long time. 'Something like that.'

David is local, he tells her. He doesn't have a Cornish

accent, or maybe there's just a touch of West Country and she's so used to it now she doesn't notice.

'I live with my mother. Up there, on top of the hill. A big old white house with palm trees in the garden.' He points vaguely behind them. 'You can see it from the end of the harbour wall.'

He makes no apology for living at home, as most men of his age – late twenties or thereabouts – probably would. Rosanna likes that. There's no pretence about him, no attempt to impress. He does something in property, he says, though she doesn't catch exactly what. She's been too busy taking in his mussed-up blond hair, deep-set blue eyes, and the way he uses his hands expressively as he talks.

She tells him a little about herself. Virtually nothing of any weight. It feels better that way.

'Have you been out on a boat trip yet?' he asks. 'The scenery looks even more spectacular from the sea.'

Automatically, her hand goes to her stomach. She's been fine, really well, during these first months, but the idea of bobbing about on the waves makes her feel faintly queasy. She looks at David, at his honest face, his open gaze. Okay, she doesn't have the greatest track record when it comes to knowing who to trust, but what's the harm? It's not as if she's ashamed or anything.

'I'm pregnant. Going out on a boat might make me wobbly. Actually, I'm sure it would.'

There's the merest touch of awkwardness, and a slight reddening of David's face. Either that, or he's caught the sun.

She laughs. 'You don't know what to say, do you? It's cool. You don't have to say anything.'

He drops forward, leaning his elbows on his knees. 'A baby? Well, that's... that's just great. Good for you. So, is your... Are you...?' The question hangs mid-air.

'Nope. I'm not with anyone. I'm single, completely.' She speaks lightly, trying to save him any further embarrassment.

'Okay. Well, that's cool, too. When is...?'

'End of July. I'm staying here until the birth, at least. Then I'll consider my options.' She looks up at the sun, squinting against the brightness. 'I must go. Sarah – that's the friend I'm staying with – will be wondering where I've got to.'

This isn't strictly true – Ellen texted her earlier to say she was going down to the harbour – but she's had enough now. Easy though this David guy is to talk to, she's shared enough of her personal life for one day. She stands up, lifting her bag onto her shoulder. She wonders if he'll suggest walking with her. He doesn't; he stays sitting on the bench, and she feels grateful that he seems to be reading her correctly.

He looks up at her, shading his eyes. 'You should come up to the house and have tea one day. Only if you'd like to, of course. My mother loves meeting new people.' His eyes crinkle, as if he thinks he's said something funny.

'I might just do that,' Rosanna says.

THIRTY-SEVEN
ROSANNA

Rosanna isn't working at the shop today. She's in the farmhouse kitchen, making scones, something she hasn't done for so long it's a miracle they actually look like scones when she starts stamping them out from the dough with the metal cutter.

She and Ellen cooked and baked all the time when they first moved into the flat, until the novelty wore off. Now it's mostly Ellen who cooks, or rather, as Ellen describes it, puts things together. 'Shall we have baked beans with this, or peas?' It doesn't get more complicated than that. Now, Nigella and Jamie sit side by side on the high shelf above the kitchen counter, gathering dust and goodness knows what else.

Rosanna realises that she lets Ellen do too much of the cooking, too many of the household chores altogether. She never complains at doing more than her fair share, which makes Rosanna feel all the more guilty. She thumps out another round scone and levers it onto the baking tray. Well, so what? Ellen only has to say if she's unhappy about the way things work, doesn't she? Which must mean she's okay about it.

Another flash of guilt. Rosanna is making excuses for herself again; she tends to do that. At least she recognises this fault of hers – one of many. She wonders how many of her flaws the baby will inherit, along with the good bits. And how much of Matt will there be? If it's a boy, will he be drop-dead handsome, like his father, and then spoil it by being a complete dick? Given the parentage, a girl will have a better chance of turning out to be a decent human being, Rosanna thinks. Her next scan is scheduled for two weeks' time, but she won't let them tell her the baby's gender. Everything would be known in advance, then. No surprises left except the colour of its hair. Sarah didn't find out when she was expecting Chloe. She described her daughter as the most wonderful gift she'd waited so long to unwrap.

It does feel a bit weird, knowing there are other children – half-siblings to her child – out there in the world, unaware of the other's existence. It will stay that way – no danger of Matthew Leyton figuring on the birth certificate. She definitely won't change her mind about that, which is one little problem ticked off – not that it ever was a problem. And in a twisted sort of way, she's protecting Laura, Matt's wife, by leaving him out of it. She can't think about what will happen when the child is old enough to ask who its father is; it's too far in the future to worry about that now. But she's confident enough to know that when the time comes, she'll know how to deal with it.

Thinking about Matt's children reminds Rosanna of something that niggled at her, right at the start of their relationship. Boys, he told her. He and Laura had two boys. And then, a fortnight later, when she asked him some innocuous question about his home-life because it kind of came up in conversation, he'd mentioned a girl. 'You've got one of each, then?' she'd said slyly. Matt had just nodded, and moved the conversation on to something else. Rosanna was prepared to accept that she'd misheard, or misremembered, the first time. It wasn't a big deal. Maybe it should have been.

The tray of scones is in the oven when the kitchen door is

flung wide open and Chloe, fresh from playgroup, charges in, Sarah following, her arms full of coats, boots and finger-paintings.

'Mm, those smell good.' Sarah peers through the glass door of the oven. 'We can have some for lunch.' She turns to Rosanna. 'What time are you going out?'

Rosanna's mind immediately catapults away from Matt to what is happening this afternoon. 'Not till three.'

Having accepted David's invitation on a what-the-hell-why-not basis rather than any real wish to go, she's having tea at his house, where she'll meet his mother; his father died two years ago.

Unusually for Rosanna, she feels quite nervous at the prospect, which is silly because David is a friend, not a boyfriend. How could he be when she's in this condition? He's just a dead friendly guy she happened to hit it off with. Since their chat by the harbour, they've met twice, by arrangement: once at the ice-cream place after she left work one afternoon, and once for morning coffee on her day off. Rosanna thinks she's never felt so at ease with anyone in such a short space of time. It's as if she's known him forever – she forgives herself the cliché because it's undoubtedly the truth.

She cradles her little bump and wonders what to wear. Not that it matters what she wears as long as she's clean and tidy.

David picks her up in his black Mini Cooper – he insisted, as it's a long, uphill walk to his house from the village. She's wearing a loose cotton dress in a red ditsy flower print over leggings, and a cream furry Teddy jacket Sarah lent her. Her hair is swept into a ponytail. Seeing David's jeans, ripped at the knee, and fisherman's sweater, she's glad she hasn't dressed up too much.

They chat easily on the way and by the time they reach the

pretty, double-fronted white house with green window shutters – Edwardian, David says – her nerves have gone.

The slight-figured, attractive woman who holds her hand out to Rosanna as they enter is wearing a grey, loose-fitting sweater, narrow pink trousers and white sneakers. She looks incredibly young to be David's mother. Or perhaps it's just that Rosanna has lost touch with mothers and how they look.

'Call me Angela,' David's mother says, brightly.

She ushers Rosanna straight through the house and out onto a wide terrace enclosed by a stone balustrade, leaving David to follow, and waves towards a cluster of mismatched chairs. 'I thought we'd sit out. It's such a beautiful day. But if it's too chilly for you, Rosanna, do say.'

Rosanna chooses an orange canvas director's chair. 'It's fine. Fantastic view.'

Angela sits down opposite Rosanna. 'Isn't it. I never get tired of looking at it.' Angela smiles. It's David's smile. They share the same deep-blue, almond-shaped eyes, too, but Angela's wavy, shoulder-length hair is dark.

David takes the seat next to Rosanna. 'Okay?' he whispers when Angela's attention is diverted by a gull landing on the balustrade.

She nods in reply. A rush of emotion makes her eyes fill. Hormones, probably. Or actually, no. She'd forgotten what true kindness feels like, that's what it is. Matt never really cared about her. She's surprised she's thinking this now. She'd thought she was over him completely. But somewhere, deep down, the hurt still festers. *Damn you, Matt Leyton!*

She stands up and goes to the balustrade to hide her face and take in the view properly. David comes and stands by her, pointing out interesting features. It's all interesting, and totally gorgeous, with the sea, the harbour, the village and surrounding countryside bathed in soft sunshine, spread out before them. Below the balustrade, the garden slopes down, the three palm trees she saw from the harbour standing proud above a lawn that dips into shrubs and borders. Nothing is immaculate or too tidy. It's the way a garden should be, Rosanna thinks, as she sits down again. The ways hers will be when she has one.

Angela is as easy to talk to as her son. She knows the shop where Rosanna works, and knows Lowena, too. This isn't surprising – Lowena seems to know just about everyone in Mevagissey. David sits back, his long legs stretched in front of him, saying little, letting the women get on with it. Judging by his posture and the sideways slant of his head, Rosanna can tell he's not missing a single word of what she says.

After a while, a cool breeze wafts across the terrace. At Angela's suggestion, they go indoors for tea. There are little triangular sandwiches, cheese straws and a selection of cakes set out on a huge limed-oak coffee table. The tea has been poured in the kitchen and brought through in bone china mugs with seaside themes, like the ones Lowena sells in the shop.

'The cheesy things and the cakes are from the bakery,' Angela says, licking a blob of cream from her lower lip. 'My baking's a bit hit and miss.'

'Mostly miss,' David jokes.

He's sitting next to Rosanna on a floral-covered sofa that sags in the middle, so that they keep rolling into one another. The airy room that stretches the depth of the house and opens onto the terrace is comfortable, colourful and a little untidy, like the garden.

'I love your dress,' Angela says. 'I like a print.'

Rosanna automatically smooths the dress over her stomach. 'Thanks. It hides a multitude of sins.' She feels herself colour up as a giggle rises and escapes. 'Well, okay, just the one.'

Angela and David burst out laughing. 'Sorry, sorry,' Angela says. 'I couldn't help it. David, you were right about this girl. She's definitely a breath of fresh air.'

Rosanna's laughing too. At least the subject of the pregnancy is out in the open. It would have felt odd not to have it mentioned at all. Angela asks when the baby's due and praises the hospital where the birth will be. No doubt she has a dozen other questions on her tongue, but they don't get an airing.

Rosanna decides she loves Angela. If she had a mother, she'd like her to be just like David's. If she couldn't have her own, of course.

She wonders if David has told his mother her parents are dead. If so, she doesn't bring it up. They talk about plenty of other things, but not that. It's such a relief. Rosanna doesn't talk about her parents and the crash. She never has, because she can't. And nobody has forced her to talk about them – there might have been some gentle prodding at the beginning, when she and Ellen first went to live with their aunt and uncle, but she can't remember now.

Most people, when they find out her parents are dead, feel they have to refer to it in some way. If they don't know what else to say, they tell her how sorry they are, like it happened last week. She never knows how to answer. Her sister is much better at handling that sort of thing. Ellen is the stronger and braver of the two of them; Rosanna has always thought so.

She casts her mind back to a day, long ago, when they were sunbathing in the garden in Bexleyheath and, right out of the blue, Ellen suddenly asked: 'Do you remember them dying?' or something like that.

Rosanna knew straight away she meant Mum and Dad – her sister had been in a funny mood all day, sort of scratchy, like she wanted to kick something, hard. Or somebody.

She had no intention of being coerced into talking about their parents; Ellen should have known that. So she faked it, looking across to the spot in the garden where their pet hamsters were buried, pretending she thought Ellen was talking about Fudge and Flake.

'Yes, them,' Ellen said, with a small sigh. The moment passed. She never tried it again.

Matt never asked about her family tragedy. David, she suspects, won't ask either, but for entirely different reasons.

By the time David runs Rosanna home, she knows she has two more friends in Mevagissey: David and Angela. People she can count on, people who care. People like Ellen.

That's all that matters, isn't it?

THIRTY-EIGHT
ISAAC

Isaac thought he had put that strangely surreal incident to the back of his mind – which wouldn't normally have been a problem. Men are supposed to be good at compartmentalising, he knows, and Isaac wasn't just good, he was an expert. But his skills in that area seem to have deserted him.

That bloke, the fair-haired twenty-something who accosted him in the street, keeps springing up in his mind when he's not aware he's been thinking about him at all.

He picks up a Rotring pen and strengthens the lines on some brickwork detail, pretending to work rather than doing anything useful. That's another thing; his work doesn't seem to do it for him any more. This anomaly dates back almost to the day Rosanna Randall sent her henchman to do her dirty work. She *had* to be behind that confrontation outside the office – it resonated too closely with the lambasting her sister dished out on Victoria Tube station.

It's a mystery why Rosanna wanted photos of him, though, if that was her idea. She already had some as far as he was aware. Used to raise her phone and snap him without even asking. Love them, leave them, and move on, leaving no trail, had been his philosophy, right from the start. But he used to try to hide his annoyance so as not to turn the evening sour and spoil the pleasures to come.

It had crossed his mind that she intended to use the pictures as blackmail: post them online, or threaten to email them to Laura. But photos of him alone wouldn't carry any weight, and nothing of that sort has happened so far.

Email photos to Laura? That would be some kind of miracle, wouldn't it?

Isaac's gaze slides past his drawing board and through the floor-to-ceiling windows that overlook the back of the building. There's not a lot to look at. A pocket of green space studded with trees, an inadequate car park serving this and the adjacent office buildings, the tall slab of the building backing onto it – flats, not offices. A nondescript 1970s block with pointless Juliet balconies. He once dated a girl who lived there. Anna? Hannah? Something like that. When he realised where she lived, he was glad he'd never told her where he worked, and that she hadn't sussed it out for herself. He cut the relationship short a few months before its natural end. The set-up was just too close for comfort. He never saw her in the area after that, so maybe she moved out.

Rosanna knew where he worked. She asked him outright, and almost a bottle of wine in and his mind not fully on the job, he gave the game away without thinking. Or maybe he just became too blasé for his own good.

Isaac looks up at the oversized clock on the wall: 3.40 p.m. He would have given up pretending to work and taken himself off home before now if there hadn't been a meeting scheduled for five o'clock. He's only sitting here, doodling. Not achieving anything. If he didn't feel so sluggish, he might have panicked at this loss of motivation. His work means everything, gives him reason to get up in the morning. If he loses that now, he doesn't know what he'll do.

He worked his socks off to get to where he is today. Most people assume he's a nicely brought up, diligent bloke from a solid middle-class background, the product of an old-style grammar, or a minor public school. He doesn't correct them. Diligent fits. The rest? Nowhere close. Jason Malone, his father, was a builder's labourer, when it suited; his mother, Kelly, a barmaid at the local pub. Home was a poky terraced house on the Isle of Sheppey where you dared not open the windows for fear of letting in the sulphurous pong from the steelworks.

The teachers at the comprehensive school did their best but they were swimming against the tide; the place was always destined to produce more villains and general social rejects than professionals. But Isaac had been far-thinking enough to realise that education was his only means of escape, and he made sure he passed every exam until, finally, he landed a place at university to study architecture and design – a university 300 miles from home.

He'd achieved his goal, and felt rightly proud. But the years leading up to this pinnacle of endeavour were fraught with uncertainty, anxiety and often sheer terror. It was hard to put it all behind him. He'd never quite succeeded.

Jason was prone to frightening outbursts of violence. He only ever hit Isaac once – taking his belt to him when Isaac came home from school in tears, having suffered taunting from a kid who reckoned he'd seen Isaac's mother in a clinch with some bloke who was clearly not Isaac's dad. He hadn't meant to pass this information on, but his dad somehow got it out of him, then blamed Isaac for not standing up for himself.

The belting was never repeated – Kelly was the prime target. Why she didn't get better at covering her tracks, Isaac didn't know. But, sooner or later, the name of the man she was currently sleeping with would become known to his father, and off they'd go again, yelling and shouting insults and accusations, on both sides. Each round of this ended up in the same way: his mother, a new bruise fast developing, would make grovelling apologies, promising faithfully – *Faithfully?* That was a joke – that she'd never look at another man again.

Who could blame his father for lashing out? She drove him to it, he would say to Isaac. Even when he was a young boy, his father would include him in the narratives of these chilling domestic dramas.

'She drove me to it.' Words Isaac has never forgotten. In his own twisted way, his father loved his mother – he must have done not to have kicked her out or left himself. He loved her, and she broke him. That was the truth of it.

After each sordid little affair was over – over, if his mother was to be believed – life would settle down for a while, and their dreary little lives carried on as before. Isaac knew he should not have blamed his mother for finding her own way of escape. And yet, the way she went about it brought her so low in Isaac's estimation that the good in her – and there was plenty of that if you looked hard enough – didn't make up for her behaviour. That was a battle lost before it was begun.

Books, and studying, became Isaac's salvation. And later, when he'd changed his life around so radically as to be unrecognisable, he reinvented himself again, and became the attractive rogue who had no problem in charming any girl he set his sights on.

Amazing, really, how so many of them saw no disadvantage in his being married. These were girls who simply wanted fun and adventure, with a dash of danger to spice things up. They wanted to be wined and dined and bought expensive gifts. No strings? That was fine by them – most of them, anyway. Those who felt differently went along with it until their romantic ideals inevitably burst out of hiding. Girls like Rosanna Randall, who craved the whole 'in love' thing and made no secret of it. Isaac was happy to oblige, but only up to the point when it all got too heavy, and then he'd end it, sharpish.

Pretending to be married, with kids thrown into the mix as a useful little bonus, was a master stroke. He could enjoy all the benefits of a 'secret' love affair, while at the same time dictating its terms. That way, he kept complete control, which was something his father had certainly never done.

Landing that punch, and the kick in the ribs that followed, was as much a shock to Isaac as it was to his erstwhile stalker. He could have walked away, crossed the road and disappeared into the office building, and the guy couldn't have done a thing about it. Instead, he turned the unfortunate business into a public brawl.

Perhaps he is more like his father than he'd realised. Is he, in fact, turning into him? Is this why his mind keeps returning to the street incident? Because it resonates with what he has left behind, or tried to?

Isaac leaves his desk, heads for the water cooler, then changes his mind and walks to the next floor down where the coffee machine is. Back in front of his drawing board, his mind wanders again, this time to his old university mate, Alfie. Alfie dropped out of the architecture degree after the second year, having failed his exams, and transferred to the hospitality course. He now owns a hotel on the seafront in Torquay, bought with the aid of funds from his well-heeled father-in-law. There's a suite permanently available to Isaac whenever he wants it. He goes there at Christmas, and a couple of times during the year. He and Alfie stay up drinking till the small hours, reminiscing and putting the world to rights.

Alfie always greets Isaac with the same words: 'You've not been caught yet, I see. Nobody special, still? No finger you fancy putting a ring on?'

And when Isaac laughs, Alfie rolls his eyes and says, 'Don't blame you, mate. You stay exactly as you are. Free as a fucking seagull.'

In truth, Alfie, as well as Kath, his wife, are convinced that the time will come when Isaac will meet the woman he wants to spend the rest of his life with. But he doesn't have to look further than his memories of the terraced house on the Isle of Sheppey to know it's never going to happen.

Apart from the nightly sessions with Alfie, Torquay has another attraction. A shapely little blonde waitress called Greta is always very obliging, second-guessing his food orders, slipping him little extras when nobody's looking, and generally taking care of his every need, especially when she's off-duty. She takes pleasure in passing him little notes when she's waiting at table, letting him know when her shift finishes. Isaac waits in his room for the double knock at the door, and silently hands her the *Do Not Disturb* notice to hang outside as she enters.

Perhaps a break is what he needs now to lift him out of his downward-spiralling mood. He has some time owing; he could head west for a week or so. Sun, sea, sand, Greta. He tries to summon up some enthusiasm for the hypothetical trip but there's nothing. No feeling of lightness at the thought of lazing around with nothing to do except walk, read and watch the boats in the bay. No frisson of anticipation for the afternoon delights on offer, the vodka-fuelled nights of passion. Nothing moves him; nothing stirs in his brain.

Isaac finishes his coffee, crushes the paper cup in his fist with such force that the new architectural technician several feet away looks up from her desk and raises her eyebrows. He stands up, rips the sketch from the drawing board and stuffs it in the bin. Then, hooking his jacket from the back of the chair, he picks up his bag and heads for the door.

THIRTY-NINE
CARL

Tucked away amongst the fields and woods, Owl Corner slumbers peacefully, as Carl himself did last night. No traffic, no sirens, no shouts from the street, only the sighing of the trees as the wind passes through, and the mournful cries of the owls. The best night's sleep he's had in a while.

As soon as he finished work yesterday, he picked up a red Honda from the hire place and drove down to Sussex, paint and decorating equipment in the boot. He has all of today – Sunday – and most of tomorrow before he heads home on Monday evening. Enough time to make a good start on his refurbishment project. But there's no rush. He makes a second coffee and sits at the kitchen table, enjoying the warmth of the sun flooding through the window and listening to the birdsong. His thoughts, unsurprisingly, turn to Ellen.

Some of her things were still in the bedroom she used. They're packed up now and stowed on the back seat of the car. He'll drop them over to her in a day or two. He had imagined a gradual unpicking of their relationship, that once she was settled back in the Brixton flat they would meet a couple of times then drift apart. But it's early May now, six weeks since the tunnel rescue, and he can't seem to keep away. Ellen feels the same, apparently. If he leaves it several days without getting in touch, she sends a light-hearted text, and they'll chat until it's arranged when and where they'll next get together.

Despite what Tim says, always with comically raised eyebrows and knowing looks, they're not dating. Ellen prefers to meet at either of their homes – for some reason she's scared of going out properly – and they're never together for long. Just long enough for a coffee or a drink, and a catch-up chat. It seems as if she still needs him, on some level. After all she's been through, she's probably finding it hard to let go completely.

He thinks about Rosanna being pregnant – by Matt/Isaac, of course, who else? Ellen told him when he called by her flat in the week. Rosanna is happy about the baby now she's over the shock, Ellen says, and plans to stay in Cornwall for the birth. All well and good, Carl thought when he heard this, but what about the father? Is he to be named? Is Rosanna planning to try and contact him? That would be a task and a half, for any number of reasons. Ellen's eyes clouded with uncertainty when he asked her, and she began twisting her silver cuff bracelet round and round.

'I can't do it,' she said. 'I can't tell her who Matthew Leyton really is without telling her what we've been up to, can I? She'll never trust me again. Anyway, she's made up her mind to keep him out of the picture. It's her decision.'

'And if she changes her mind?' Carl asked, carefully. 'What do we say then?' It would be *we* in that case. He wouldn't let Ellen deal with it on her own.

'She won't,' Ellen said. 'So there's nothing to worry about.' Her voice held conviction, but her face creased into a frown. 'We know for certain he won't try and contact her. As certain as we can be, anyway.'

Carl really hopes she's right, and there will be no reason to put Rosanna in the picture.

He rinses his coffee mug in the sink and goes through to the living room. He needs to stop worrying about Ellen. She's doing pretty well as it is: settling into the flat, getting herself back into work – she's temping somewhere in central London. She was talking about going to visit her aunt and uncle in the Lake District, too, and to Cornwall to see Rosanna. She's looking forward to the future, and nobody can ask more than that.

He unpins Ellen from his thoughts, fetches the stepladder and begins unhooking the living room curtains. A cloud of dust makes him cough. The fabric is faded and virtually falling to pieces in places. He bundles up the curtains, takes them to the front door and drops them in a heap outside. A small, scratched mahogany table, two worn Axminster rugs and the pictures from the wall suffer the same fate. All this old stuff has to go – Ellen would agree with that. The sofa and chairs and other serviceable items he moves to the centre of the room and covers with plastic dust sheets. He lays more dust sheets and layers of newspaper over the varnished parquet wood floor, closest to the wall opposite the inglenook where he intends to begin painting.

The ceiling could do with a coat of paint but it's not dirty, and he's decided to leave that for now and concentrate on the walls. The paint goes on smoothly, a cheerful primrose yellow that Ellen helped him choose.

As yellow covers grubby magnolia, Carl reruns the phone conversation with his father he had two nights ago. Never effusive at the best of times, Fraser had nevertheless sounded so pleased to hear from him that he immediately felt guilty for having left it so long. They chatted for a while before Carl reached the main purpose of his call.

'Owl Corner? You've been back to the old place?' Fraser sounded surprised, but only mildly so.

Carl, anxious that he'd stirred up mud from the bottom of an otherwise calm pond, had apologised for not checking with his father before he'd made the first trip to Sussex. As if there could have been anything on his mind at the time apart from getting Ellen to safety.

'It's your house, too,' Fraser said. 'You have every right to be there. You don't need my say-so.' Then, after a meaningful pause, 'How was it?'

He wasn't asking about the house itself. He was remembering, as Carl had, that last weekend they'd spent at Owl Corner as a family; a whole family, before their worlds changed completely.

Carl was eleven at the time his mother left, and about to move up to secondary school. Fraser simply took up the parental reins and kept mostly silent on the subject of Linnie's departure. As far as Carl understood it when he thought about it later, his mother had decided she no longer wanted to be a wife and mother. Not a mother to him, anyway. The last contact he'd had was a card on his eighteenth birthday, with a German postmark.

The strange thing was – he'd not thought it strange at the time – that he'd always sensed something about his mother, a kind of aura of impermanence, as if at any moment she might stop what she was doing and just not be there any more. Which, as it turned out, was exactly how it was.

'Okay, actually,' Carl said, as if he was surprised himself, 'the house has stood up pretty well. You should come over some time.'

'I should have done something about it years ago. But if you say it's all right, then let's let sleeping dogs lie, shall we?' Fraser gave a little chuckle. Again, he wasn't really talking about the house.

Carl told him he might give the place a facelift.

'Good idea,' Fraser said. 'I expect it could do with a lick of paint by now. Anyway, you should come over to me for a holiday. The beaches are cracking. I'll send you the air fare.'

'You don't need to do that. But, yes, I will come, as soon as I get the chance.'

Perhaps he'll ask Ellen if she wants to go to Guernsey with him, Carl thinks now. He stops the inappropriate thought in its tracks before it takes hold.

An hour later, Carl's arm aches like it's about to drop off, but the first wall is finished. Balancing the brush across the paint pot, he sits crossed-legged on the floor, stretching his arms and rolling his shoulders. He sits there for a while, picking stray blobs of paint off the parquet with his fingernail, and thinks about Fraser locking away the painful memories to protect his son. He thinks about Ellen, and Rosanna, and Isaac, and Isaac's wife and children, and the coming baby.

When did life become so full of secrets, half-truths and downright lies?

FORTY

EMILY

'Who's it for?' Emily stops flicking through *Grazia* and drops the magazine onto the stool beside her.

The tall, totally gorgeous bloke wearing dark jeans and a T-shirt, with an expensive-looking jacket worn open on top, gives her a smile that sends heatwaves all the way up the backs of her legs.

'My grandmother. Her birthday.' He looks down at the card he's holding in its cellophane wrapper, then slips it back in the rack. 'Too much choice, that's the problem.'

His grandmother. When he came in, he made straight for the rack with the humorous and semi-pornographic cards: not at all suitable for any kind of grandmother she knew.

'Only a problem if you're in a hurry,' she says.

Which he obviously isn't. He's been in here a good five minutes already, most of which have been spent looking at her, not at the cards. This is the most exciting thing that has happened in Caroline's Cards all week. Correct that. *Ever*. And to think she came to London in search of adventure!

Could things be looking up at last?

Emily slips out from behind the counter, wishing she'd

reapplied her lipstick after that last cup of tea. 'What sort of thing does your gran like?'

He looks puzzled for a second. 'My... oh, yes. Landscapes, flowers – anything like that.'

'These won't do, then.' Emily nods at the rack.

He laughs softly, and looks right into her eyes, making her blush. 'Do you like working here?'

'It's okay as a stop gap, until I decide what I really want to do. I only moved to London six weeks ago. I like Angel. It's cool.'

'I suppose it is,' he says, blue-grey eyes capturing her gaze.

'Do you live near here, then?'

'Not far.'

Emily leads the way to the other side of the shop, where the more traditional cards are displayed. She stands quietly, arms by her sides, while he selects a card with a view of fields and cattle, then picks out two more cards at random, both with floral designs.

'I'll take these as well, then I can decide later.'

She takes the cards from him and goes behind the counter to put them through the till. He begins pulling a credit card from his wallet, changes his mind, and brings out cash from his pocket. She notices his hands. Nice hands, well shaped. Emily likes nice hands on a bloke. She notices, too, the faint woody, citrusy scent of aftershave or cologne.

'Thank you. You've been very helpful.' He reaches the door, turns back to her. 'What's your name, by the way, if you don't mind me asking?'

'It's Emily.'

He smiles. 'Pretty name. I'm Mark. Mark Hammersmith.'

FORTY-ONE
ELLEN

Carl messaged to say the paint colour looks great. I find it comforting, knowing he's in Sussex this weekend. I do want to go there again, and I will, some time, if that's still okay with him. I'd want him to be there with me, though. Owl Corner wouldn't be the same on my own.

Next time we speak, I must remember to tell him I went out last night. I think he'll be pleased. Socialising with lots of people, especially in the evening, is something I've avoided these past weeks. Whenever the Maystone Road ghost station springs to mind, I experience a weird sensation, as if I've been sealed off from the real world for a very long time. It doesn't take much for me to feel overwhelmed, though I'm trying to fight it.

My days consist of going to work – on the underground, which is fine now, if I don't think too hard about it – shopping for essentials, and going over to Carl's flat in Camberwell. These things use up all my mental resources. So when Rob, who lives in the flat downstairs, knocked on the door and invited me to his birthday bash at the pub, I said yes to end the conversation, with no intention of turning up. And then I decided to go anyway, because I could always leave if it got too much.

So I went, and I stayed nearly to the end, and I enjoyed myself, in a quiet sort of way. Rob was one of the neighbours who came to our Christmas Eve party. He obviously fancied Rosanna like crazy and hardly left her alone all evening, which of course did him no good at all as she was pining for Matt at the time and didn't even notice.

I can smile about that now – I must be making progress.

I still have nightmares about being trapped in my subterranean prison, and wake up in a sweat with the feel of cold tiles against my back, and my eyes skimming the rails, following the rats as they race silently by. My kind of hell. The one I made for myself. I haven't told Carl about the nightmares – he would only worry. They will stop, in time.

I've just been to the petrol station for milk, bread and a bottle of wine. I shan't go out any more today. I'm quite content here, catching up on chores, watching TV and imagining Carl refurbishing the house where he spent happy childhood holidays with both parents, until the idyll ended.

How can any mother abandon a child? Simply walk away and disappear out of their life? I feel so sad for him, but he never complains, never shows the slightest sign of feeling sorry for himself. Carl is an inspiration; he can teach me a thing or two about letting go and moving on.

'How are you now, really?' Carl looks across the table at me.

He has that intense look about him I know so well, as if he's trying to see into my soul. He does this with the best of intentions because, for some reason, he cares. I reckon he's got quite good at guessing what's going on in my stupid head.

It's Tuesday; Carl came back from Sussex yesterday. We've been to the cinema in Brixton, the first time we've done anything like that. He suggested a drink afterwards, but I said I'd rather go somewhere quiet for a coffee, if that was okay with him. Which, of course, it was.

The coffee shop is busy, but the atmosphere is low-key and we've found a corner where we can talk. Not that I want to talk, particularly. At least, not the kind of talking that Carl clearly has in mind. But it's sweet that he's so concerned about me, and I answer his questions as best I can.

'I'm good, mostly. Still working through a few things but I'm getting there.'

Carl sips his coffee and waits. I take a long breath and continue.

'After you showed me the photos of Matt – Isaac, I mean – even with the evidence in front of me, it was a while before I could let myself truly believe it. D'you know what I mean?'

Carl waits.

'I ran it all through in my mind, everything that happened that night, from when I came out of work until I got to the Tube station, and... *he* was there. I know you asked me to do that, when we were at Owl Corner, but I pushed against it. I knew what I knew and that was that.' I give a little smile. Carl smiles back, encouragingly. 'So, after I'd thought about it some more and tried to reconnect with what happened, I started to see it all for what it was, as if I was remembering it for the first time. Does that make sense?'

Carl nods. The relief on his face is plain to see.

'He stopped me from falling under the train. That was why he grabbed hold of me and pushed me back, because I was too near the edge of the platform. I didn't notice. I was too busy laying into him for treating my sister like she was nothing. His poor wife, too, come to that. Oh, I'm not saying he was a hero or anything. I'll never be sorry for those things I said. He deserved that. Even more, now I know he wasn't even using his real name.'

'And after that?' Carl prompts. 'After you'd moved back from the edge? What happened then?'

'After? Well, the train came and he got on with everybody else. I couldn't have seen him board the train. I was running away by then, or trying to – there were so many people on the platform. I know he did, though. He got on the train. What else would he have done? It's obvious, isn't it?'

Carl nods again, slowly. He sits back in his seat, satisfied that the story in my head is the real one. 'It wasn't your fault, Ellen. None of it. Never think that.'

'Well...' I'm not so sure I believe this.

Carl leans forward, resting his arms on the table. 'When you clapped eyes on Matt that day, you were at your lowest point. You were worried for your sister because you could see she was about to have her heart broken. Yet at the same time you were anxious in case you'd got it wrong and that man was about to steal Rosanna away from you. You were confused, and upset, and you wanted him out of both your lives so desperately that your imagination took over and filled in the rest. That's a rather simplistic explanation, I know, but I believe that's what happened.'

Carl is right, of course. He's also right in thinking there's more to it than that. I've been carrying my grief for my parents around with me, never moving on from it, letting it colour who I am, and how I think and behave. I'd been so lost, felt so alone, for the greater part of my life. My parents were gone, and the thought of being without my sister, too, scared the life out of me. By the time I'd spotted her lover on the station platform, my grief had compounded into something so dark and deep that it filled every part of me, and I would have done anything to keep Rosanna with me, even for just a little longer. *Anything*. It's taken me until now to fully understand what was going on in my mind; I know it's something I have to deal with, and I will.

But I don't want to talk about it now. I don't want to talk any more.

'Thank you,' I say, my voice small, choked with emotion.

Carl grins and shrugs, flinging his arms out theatrically. 'Any time, kiddo.'

FORTY-TWO

ISAAC

Sunday morning. Isaac stands on Westminster Bridge, a cortege of red buses and black cabs passing along behind him. Tourists hold phones to the skyline, the meandering river, and the ornate limestone façade of the Houses of Parliament.

He may be standing on Westminster Bridge, but the last thing he feels is poetic. He doesn't even know how he got here, or why.

But here he is, and the least he can do is take in the iconic view of the city while the light breeze folds itself around him, and try to feel positive about something. About anything.

But what is there?

He should be looking forward to his date with the red-haired girl – Emily, is it? – tomorrow night. But looking forward to a date and the fleeting pleasures it might lead to feels almost like duty, something to be ticked off a list of the things he does, day in, day out: as trivial as brushing his teeth. Why did he even bother? He'd noticed her a few times, through the window of the card shop, and then he'd caught a close-up as she came out of the shop one evening as he was on his way home. The decision to follow up these sightings happened almost on automatic pilot, as if it wasn't a decision at all.

His Monday night date isn't his usual type. Perhaps he doesn't have a type, not in the physical sense, anyway. Willingness to take a chance on him, 'complicated' though he claims to be, is the only criterion. That, and attractiveness, of course. Girls who've had enough of being cautious and behaving sensibly all the time; they have this in common, too.

She's really cute, gorgeous figure, this Emily with the big grey eyes. He pictures her as he says this in his head. But the words are weightless, his image of her unclear, as if he sees her through a mist or from behind frosted glass. If it wasn't for the crazy tumble of curls the colour of autumn leaves, he might not even recognise her again.

What will it be tomorrow night? Or the next date or two down the line, if she's playing that game, fooling neither him nor herself. A back-street hotel? A Premier Inn? A sleazy shag in an alleyway? Some of them go for that in a big way. Nice girls, too. Girls who ride the Tube the morning after in Joseph trousers and sharp jackets or carefully curated smart-casual ensembles, on their way to the office. Legs primly crossed. Glaring at any bloke who dares to give them the eye. As if butter wouldn't melt.

Isaac stands close to the cast-iron balustrade. He watches as a police launch glides by below, the river-bus not far behind. The ripples widen in their wake, silken folds of ochre on khaki, then vanish beneath the shadow of the bridge. He narrows his eyes and stares at the river until he's mesmerised by its movement. He visualises the water flowing, cold and dark, through his brain, cleansing it of everything and everyone. Of girls like Emily, and Rosanna Randall. Especially her.

His brain refuses to co-operate.

He talks to girls about love, if it's required. But it's just words. He has never been in love; he isn't capable. This is one thing he is sure of amongst so many unknowns; or rather, amongst so many things he doesn't care about, has no feeling for, one way or the other. His capacity for forming meaningful, loving relationships, if it ever existed in him in the first place, got left behind on the Isle of Sheppey. Bundled up, shoved in a bin liner, and floated out to sea to be washed up on the estuary.

His father loved his mother, in a brusque, inept kind of way – it had taken Isaac a long time to understand that. But Jason Malone was either too blind or too stupid to realise that the kind of life he gave her wasn't what any woman wanted. Their lives were dull, uncertain, tainted with poverty and brutality, and very, very small. Maybe it wasn't his father's fault; maybe it was. But he did love Kelly, and look what she did to him. Look what *he* did to *her*. What they did to each other. At least Isaac had the sense to break free and make a different life for himself.

It did him no good.

It's still inside him. He can feel it, a bitter poison in his gut. He's a mixture of the two of them. Luck, and nature, have dictated his genetic pattern, dished out the worst of his father, the worst of his mother. A disastrous combination if ever there was one. And you can't beat nature.

The girls he dates so easily don't need him, don't really want him, no matter what they think or say. In the short-term, maybe. Other than that, no. And it's fine. He doesn't *want* to be wanted. Doesn't *need* to be needed. He doesn't hide what he is. All they have to do is open their eyes. Yet on they go, sprinkling their fairy dust, pretending they're swinging along a two-way street instead of one with a great big *No Entry* sign and a brick wall at the end.

Nothing is going to change, ever, because it can't. And this is why the future is impossible.

This is the only truth. The only thing that matters.

Isaac leans on the balustrade and stares deep down into the water at his reflection, which is so far below the bridge that he only imagines he sees it. He pulls his gaze upwards and lets his eyes skim the sullen surface of the river, its determined, relentless flow. The barrier before him is little more than waist-high, so not insurmountable. That's been proved a thousand times. But how do you know the survival instinct won't kick in and you swim, and keep on swimming? How do you *know*?

A Chinese girl wearing a back-to-front baseball cap nudges his arm accidentally as she backs up with her phone in order to capture the perfect picture of the Eye. She smiles an apology and goes on snapping. Pulled out of his contemplations, Isaac straightens up and moves back from the balustrade. A minute later, he turns and walks quickly away. He has things to do.

FORTY-THREE

EMILY

Emily looks at her phone to check the time: 7.50, ten minutes early. She'd thought she was going to be late. There are only two bathrooms in the big old house she shares with five other tenants, and Sod's Law dictates there'll be a queue for both when she's in a hurry. Typically, her hair went all wrong, too. Curls springing up in places where they had no right to be. By then it was too late to start with the straighteners again.

Mark has booked a table at a cute little restaurant she's been dying to try. Apparently, it's easier to get a booking on a Monday night. They've arranged to meet in the coffee shop opposite. Their first date! At last, something to get excited about. She orders a fizzy water at the counter and sits down with it, right in the window, so he'll see her as soon as he arrives. She'd hoped he'd get here first, but he'd said 8 p.m. so it won't be long now.

Emily's stomach swerves with a bout of nerves. She's never usually this nervous about a first date, but this one, she senses, is a bit special. Mark Hammersmith doesn't wear a ring, but that doesn't mean anything – she's not that naïve. He didn't exactly say he was married when he came back to the card shop to ask her out. What he did say was that his situation was 'complicated' and if she could run with that, he'd love to take her to dinner, especially as she was new to the area.

For 'complicated' read 'married' or 'in a relationship', Emily thinks, ruefully. Or it could be something else, like a child rather than a partner – anything really. Well, no doubt she'll find out before long. She may be in the dark about his status but there's one thing she does know about Mark Hammersmith: he's dangerous. She only had to look at him, that first day he came into the shop, to suss that out.

He's a fair bit older than her, but that's cool. Older, fantastically good-looking, probably worth a penny or two, and dangerous to know. Right now, with the expanse of her new life in London stretching before her with all its unknowns, these are qualities Emily embraces. What's the point of a fresh start if you don't take a few risks?

Emily sips her fizzy water and surreptitiously checks the time again, not wanting to give the impression she's bothered. It's 8.12. Okay, he's been held up. It's only twelve minutes. He hasn't texted her, which means he'll be here any second now.

She turns her phone into a mirror and tweaks ineffectually at a curly tendril escaping from her otherwise smooth fringe. It's damp out, misty, which hasn't helped. Any more of this and she could be mistaken for a grown-up version of Annie.

She sighs, lays her phone down on the table and gazes onto the street, checking the knots of people passing by, appearing around the corners. But there's no sign of her date. She's finished her water, but holds on to the plastic glass in case it's swept away and she has to leave.

8.25. She'll give him another five minutes, then that's it, she's done. Mark Hammersmith has missed his chance with her, good and proper.

At 8.40, Emily leaves the coffee shop and goes home to cheese on toast and another night in front of the box.

FORTY-FOUR

ELLEN, TWO MONTHS LATER

I'm beginning to feel more settled; it's taken a while, but I knew it would. I'm enjoying being back at work, preferring to temp for now rather than looking for something permanent. The flexibility of it suits me, and three weeks ago, I found the time to take the train to the Lake District and stay for a few days with Aunt Margaret and Uncle Derek. They seemed pleased to see me, and I was definitely happy to see them. They may be miles away, but they're still an important part of my life, and I'm looking forward to visiting again before long.

As it transpired, Sussex was also on my travel agenda.

'You should come for the weekend,' Carl says, when he last rang. 'See the house at its summer best.'

So here I am, back at Owl Corner. The house slumbers in the summer heat like a contented cat. The garden is an untamed riot of colour, the wrap-around lawn – misnamed now – has been left to its own devices. A wildflower meadow, Carl calls it, with a touch of humorous pride, before he laughingly admits the old mower doesn't cut any more and he hasn't bothered to buy a new one.

'It's gorgeous. I love it,' I say.

The long grass feathers my sandal-clad feet as I walk around, examining everything. The fruit trees are heavy with embryonic fruit. Clouds of cerulean-blue love-in-the-mist hover above the beds, the edges overflowing with self-seeded sweet alyssum and marigolds. Alongside the house walls, tall daisies flourish against warmed brickwork alongside spindly stalks bearing pink and cream and wine-red bell-shaped flowers.

'Are those hollyhocks?' I ask.

'Foxgloves, I think.'

Carl's been here all week, painting and generally fixing things that need fixing. Apart from the pale yellow in the living room, which looks wonderful, he's painted the walls white, which is cheaper than colour, and we both agree the pared-down look suits the house. He has begun to sand the doors and woodwork, but it's a long job, and he needs a break. But I have to say he looks well on it: lightly tanned, fit and healthy.

I feel a familiar stab of guilt at the effort Carl put in on my behalf. I had become used to seeing him drawn and worried-looking. All that has gone now. My instinct, when I arrived at Owl Corner and Carl opened the door, was to hug him. I didn't; I wasn't sure how it would be received. So I fiddled and faffed and talked a lot to cover my awkwardness.

I seem to have lost sight of how to behave normally with Carl. There is no such awkwardness on his side, unless he's hiding it well. We have been seeing a fair bit of each other in London, so why would there be? It's just that, being back here, everything feels different.

I mention this as we're eating dinner at the kitchen table.

Carl spears another prawn from the foil container – we've ordered in a Chinese to save the bother of cooking. 'I know. I thought it might feel strange for you, being here, after... well, after all that. I'm glad you came, though. It can get lonely with just the owls for company.'

I doubt Carl has been lonely here, but it's typical of him to say so to make me feel even more welcome.

'It was a bit intense, the last time,' I say. 'Sorry about that.'

'Not your fault. We were here for a purpose, not for a holiday.'

I help myself to more rice. 'It's good, being here. No bad vibes.' I wave my fork towards the open window through which we can hear a thrush's song and watch the sun melt below the treetops. 'How could there be?' I have a thought. 'How do *you* feel about being here?'

'Fine, as it goes. Dad asked me that, though not in so many words.'

'It shows he cares,' I say, wondering what on earth qualifies me to make such a statement, ignorant as I am about the dynamics of Carl's relationship with his father.

But Carl just nods again. 'I know. I'm heading over to Guernsey in the autumn. September. It's a good time to be there. I'll take a bit of time off, between the jobs.'

'Good plan,' I say.

Carl has a new job, managing a fashion store in Carnaby Street. He went for the interview a couple of weeks back, and I couldn't be more pleased for him.

I snap the caps off two more Tiger beers, pass one to Carl, then sit back and watch the sky turning pink and apricot. It's so peaceful here, and I'm looking forward to having all day tomorrow – Sunday – to enjoy it.

Carl reads my mind. 'What would you like to do tomorrow? We could go for a walk—? Explore the woods like kids? Or we could just put the deckchairs up and stay put.'

I sigh with pleasure. 'Any of that. All of it.' I smile.

Carl smiles back.

.   .   .

In the morning, however, all plans fly away when my sister rings at the unearthly hour of 7 a.m.

Scrabbling for my phone that I've managed to drop onto the floor beside the bed, I answer sleepily. 'Rosie? What is it?'

'I'm in labour! It's ten days early. My water's have broken and I'm scared, Ell! Please come. I need you here. I can't do it without you.' Rosanna's words fall over themselves. I've never heard such panic in her voice. Never.

'Okay, calm down.' I lever myself upright in bed. 'You'll be *fine*, Rosie. You've got Sarah. She's your birthing partner, isn't she?'

'Yes, yes, I know. But I *need* you. Say you'll come!'

I'm halfway out of bed. Carl's head appears around the door. 'Everything all right?' he mouths.

I point at the phone and raise my eyes. 'Rosanna. Baby.'

'Born?' He grins.

I shake my head, then turn back to the phone. 'Rosie, I'm two hundred and fifty miles away...' Then I realise I'm talking to Sarah. As expected, she's calm and practical, tells me my sister is fine and everything's under control. 'She does seem to want you here, though, Ellen. She really does. So, if there's the slightest chance...'

Half an hour later, we're in the car heading west, and Carl is once again my saviour. He must be fed up with this by now.

FORTY-FIVE
ELLEN

I spend the hot, sweaty journey with my phone clutched in my hand, snatching up each call from Sarah with a swish of nerves to my insides. I realise I haven't thought about the actual birth, or if I have, it was only to tell myself that Rosanna is strong and fit, and will sail through it as she does everything else.

Apart from the Matt thing, of course, but broken hearts are a law unto themselves, even my sister's.

Happily, every update is a positive one and I listen with relief to Sarah assuring me that Rosanna is fine, medically speaking, although making a lot of fuss and noise otherwise – I can actually hear her yelling at one stage, even though Sarah is apparently standing in the corridor outside the hospital birthing suite.

'This baby's in a hurry,' Sarah adds. 'Everything's moving pretty fast, and a good job, too, for all our sakes.' I hear her chuckle as she ends the call.

Now it's obvious there's no way we're going to make it in time for the birth, I graciously allow Carl to stop for a quick breakfast, and we fall into a motorway services restaurant with rumbling stomachs and stupid grins on our faces at the unexpected novelty of this expedition, although quite what Carl is finding to smile about is beyond me.

By the time we've negotiated the weekend traffic around St Austell, it's after 1 p.m. and the air in the maze of hospital corridors is soupy with the smell of institutional dinners and pine disinfectant.

We take a few wrong turns but eventually find the right room. I smooth my hair, take a deep breath but as I'm about to tap on the door, it opens and Sarah comes out. She tells me to hang on while she checks that it's all right to go in, but already my sister is waving me in from the high, white-covered bed. In the corner of the room, a midwife tidies equipment. She turns and smiles at me. It's only as I tiptoe inside – it feels right to be as quiet as possible – that I realise Carl has followed me in. Does nothing faze this man? I almost giggle.

Too late, Rosanna is already peering round me, straight at Carl, and her face breaks into the widest smile that gives away every bit of what she's thinking. I ignore it and throw my arms around my sister.

'You got here, then,' she observes, drily. 'Better late than never.'

'Rosie, it took, like, forever...'

'I *know*. I'm only joshing. This one wasn't up for hanging about.' She nods towards the cot on the stand on the other side of the bed. But I'm already there.

As I stand, speechless with wonder and emotion, at the sight of the tiniest, most perfect baby, Rosanna says casually, 'You can hold her if you want.'

I find my voice. 'A girl?' Tentatively, I lift the little bundle in the white blanket and hold her to me. Blue eyes open momentarily and she blinks at me before they close again.

'Pass her over here, will you?' Rosanna says, sounding for all the world as if she's talking about a parcel.

She takes her daughter in her arms, exuding her special brand of devil-may-care confidence that even Matt – Isaac – hasn't managed to destroy. The midwife bustles from the room, telling Rosanna a nurse will be in shortly.

I hear a voice from behind me. 'Congratulations, Rosanna! I'm Carl, by the way.' He jerks a thumb towards me and smiles. 'Her chauffeur.'

I'd forgotten he was there. I feel my face redden inexplicably. But this is a weird situation – Carl's first introduction to Rosanna taking place in a birthing suite. My sister hasn't missed my embarrassment, and fixes me with an enquiring look.

'Carl's the friend I went to Sussex with,' I say.

It's a woefully inadequate explanation but all I can manage at this stage. Luckily, it's all that is called for. Rosanna says hello to Carl, her thoughts again written all over her face, and he takes his leave and slips out of the room.

I turn my attention back to the baby to forestall any questioning from my sister. 'Have you named her, yet?'

'She's called Elizabeth.' Rosanna meets my gaze, and I see in her eyes the emotion she's been hiding since I arrived.

'Oh, Rosie,' I say. 'You gave her Mum's name. That's...' My voice slides away from me.

'And yours. She's Elizabeth Ellen Randall.'

I smile through my tears, and a look of pure understanding passes between us.

Sarah and Jay put us up at the farmhouse overnight, which is kind of them as we'd not thought that far ahead, apart from flinging a few things in a bag before we left Sussex.

There's a tricky moment when Sarah shows us to a bedroom on the first floor containing a double bed. By not meeting Carl's eye, I manage to keep my cool. 'Thanks, I'll be fine in here,' I say, emphasising the *I* bit.

Sarah doesn't miss a beat. 'Carl, if you'd like to nip up to the attic floor, you'll find a little room with a sofa-bed, next door to Rosanna's room,' she says briskly. 'As long as you don't mind sloping ceilings.'

Carl assures her he doesn't, and all is well.

Little Chloe is as cute and as rumbustious as Rosanna said, Carl and Jay strike up an instant rapport, and we're made very welcome. The plan is to stay until mid-morning the following day, by which time my sister and the baby should be home from hospital. That should give us a couple of hours with them before we set out on the journey to London. Carl had planned to stay in Sussex for another couple of days, but I've got work on Tuesday and, typically of him, he insists on driving me right the way home.

As it turns out, Rosanna and Elizabeth are not discharged until midday the next day and, concerned about the traffic, Carl and I only stay long enough to welcome them before we have to leave.

But before we do, something interesting happens.

Carl and I have just got into the car when a black Mini Cooper sweeps into the yard, and a blond, athletically built guy gets out and marches up to the door of the farmhouse. He's carrying a large bouquet of pink roses and cream carnations.

'*No*,' Carl says, grinning, as I glance at him. 'You're dying to know who he is but we are leaving, right this minute.'

'I never said...'

'You didn't have to.'

And so we bump across the yard, and Carl chuckles as I last only until we reach the end of the lane and turn onto the road before I take out my phone.

'His name's David,' I announce with satisfaction, after a fast turnaround text exchange with my sister. 'He's a friend, she hasn't known him long, he lives in Mevagissey, he's in something to do with property, and she's been to tea with his mother.'

'Inside leg measurement?'

'Shut up and drive.'

Carl obliges, stamps on the gas and we're away.

Apart from one short stop at the motorway services for coffee and the loo, we keep going. I don't talk much on the journey, not wanting to distract Carl from driving. I glance surreptitiously at him occasionally, and what I see puzzles me slightly. His lips are folded in a tight line, his forehead furrowed, and I have the impression it's something other than concentration on the road. Is he regretting becoming entangled with me and my life, wondering how he can peel himself away without leaving a scar? If this is true, I must make it easy for him.

We make Brixton before 5 p.m. When we arrive at the flats, Carl says he won't come in when I invite him. We're both tired – him more than me, because of the driving – and he knows I'm only asking out of politeness. He gets out of the car, then comes round and opens my door before I've gathered myself in time to do it. I climb out shakily, not only from the long journey but from the emotional toll of the last twenty-four hours, and retrieve my bag from the back seat.

I want to thank Carl for driving me to Cornwall on a mercy mission that was, in effect, nothing to do with him, and then let him go. But somehow I can't find the right words, so I stand there in silence, looking down at the bag at my feet. When I look up, Carl is standing close to me, really close. He rests his hands lightly on my shoulders, drawing my eyes to his, and I can't look away, I just can't.

When we kiss, it's not Carl kissing me, or me kissing Carl, but both of us kissing one another equally, without awkwardness or shyness or surprise, or any of that. And that is when I understand how close we've become over the past months, how connected we are, and this is a natural extension of a friendship that began in the most extraordinary way you could think of.

Some things happen in the proper order. Other things happen entirely the wrong way round. Well, I guess there's always a reason.

FORTY-SIX

JASON

In the dismal hallway of a terraced house on the Isle of Sheppey, Jason Malone stoops to pick up a flurry of post that has just been poked through the letter box. 'Junk. Junk. Junk.' He discards one item after another, dropping them back on the floor, and rubbing his aching back.

The last item, a thick brown padded envelope, he carries through to the kitchen. It's addressed to Mr and Mrs J Malone. The handwriting looks vaguely familiar. He examines the envelope back and front before peeling it open. He tips it up, gives it a shake, and two keys on a metal ring rattle onto the countertop.

Sliding his fingers inside the envelope, he extracts a single sheet of white paper with a few lines of writing and a wad of pristine bank notes in a rubber band. There must be, what, a couple of grand? More? *What the devil...?*

Breathing heavily, he puts the money next to the keys and drops onto a stool to read the note.

'Kell? Would you come and look at this?' Silence, no sign of movement. '*Kelly!* Get yourself out here, will you?'

A minute or two, and his wife pads barefoot into the kitchen from the living room. She's wearing a red fleece dressing gown and her hair's all over the place. Sooty smudges of last night's mascara ring her eyes.

She stands with her arms folded. 'What?'

Jason passes Kelly the sheet of paper, but her eyes have already landed on the cash. 'Where's that come from?'

'Just read it, will you?' Jason feels a bit funny, like he's going to pass out or something.

Kelly's lips move as she reads silently. Her face drains of what little colour there was before. She looks at Jason. 'Christ.'

She gives the note back to him and leans against the edge of the sink. An overexcited voice announcing a competition on breakfast telly drifts from the living room. Jason scans the note again.

There's an address at the top, a London address. Something in the back of his mind tells him he knows it. Then:

Mum and Dad, here are the keys to my flat and £3,000 to be going on with. There will be more money, and the flat and every-thing in it is yours now, but you'll have to see the solicitor about that. His address, all instructions and a letter explaining every-thing are in the drawer by the bed. Take care of yourselves. Sorry. My best wishes, Isaac.

Jason's hands are shaking. He stares up at Kelly.

Kelly stares back. 'Bloody hell,' she whispers.

A polite but forceful tap sounds from the front door, knuckles on wood. Jason and Kelly look towards the sound. Eventually, Jason gets off the stool, walks along the hall and opens the door to two uniformed police officers: one male, one female. Kicking the junk mail to one side, he silently holds the door open for them to enter.

FORTY-SEVEN
GEORGIE

What was it they said? TGIF? Yes, that's it. One of the boys said it in the lunch queue today. His mate had been having a moan about some computer shutdown that had wasted half the morning, and the other one – handsome lad, bit on the short side, but that wasn't his fault – said, 'Never mind, me old son. TGIF!'

Georgie asked Alika, who was serving next to her, what it meant. 'Thank God it's Friday,' Alika said, rolling her eyes. 'Don't tell me you've not heard that before.'

Georgie had, of course. She hadn't wondered about it before, that was all. Like all these expressions, the spoken ones and the texty ones, it was pointless. Anyway, if it had to be used at all, she would have preferred, 'Thank goodness it's Friday.' If her dad heard her or Charlotte taking the Lord's name in vain, a sharp clip around the ear would have surely followed. And the rest.

Georgie stops musing over her day – a hectic one, her feet are killing her – and unwraps the parcel of cod and chips. Her Friday treat from the best chippy in the area, two streets away.

Family business, Greek-Cypriots. Always ready with a smile and a friendly word.

TGIF indeed! The phrase is still on Georgie's mind as she takes the beanbag tray through to the living room and aims the remote at the TV, setting it to the right channel ready for *Emmerdale*, then *Coronation Street*. Before that, it's the news. Georgie only half listens while she eats.

As each white flake of fish and golden chip vanishes, the weekend creeps closer. Should it be M&S tomorrow? Bit of a browse through the rails to see what's new, then up the escalator to the café, as usual? No reason why not, except... There's that woman, the peculiar one with the orange-tinted hair who made a beeline for Georgie last week. Reckoned she knew her from somewhere. Which, of course, she didn't. It was only an excuse to plonk herself down at Georgie's table, uninvited.

Georgie enjoys a chinwag as much as the next person, but boy, that woman could talk the hind leg off a donkey! She wouldn't mind, but it was all such nonsense. Most of it was about her daughter, and how she had gone and married some awful bloke who'd stolen money from her purse to fund his gambling habits. Georgie had muttered a few words of sympathy – it would have been impolite, otherwise. But as soon as she'd finished her tuna panini and pot of tea for one, she looked at the clock above the counter and made a big thing of gasping at the time.

'I'll look out for you next week, then,' her ginger-haired companion had said, as Georgie rose to leave.

The poor old dear's probably lonely, Georgie thinks now. The daughter with the problems might not even exist. She might have made it all up for effect. She did have that look in her eye. *Away with the fairies.* Georgie's seen it before.

She pops the last chip into her mouth and chews thoughtfully. Whatever, it's not her worry, is it? This is the trouble when you start talking to strangers – or they talk to you. You never know what's coming, and before you know where you are, you're playing agony aunt to some lost soul.

So, not Marks tomorrow. She could try John Lewis. She likes their café, even if it's a bit pricey. You meet a nice class of person there.

Georgie pauses the TV – it's almost time for *Emmerdale* – and takes her tray to the kitchen. She's running hot water to soak the plate when the doorbell rings. *What the...?* It's a funny time for visitors, not that she's expecting any, and it's too late for the Jehovah's. She trundles along the hall and opens the door.

At first she doesn't recognise the petite blonde woman standing there, although she thinks she may know her from somewhere. Then it dawns. It's Sonny's mother. She's wearing tight white jeans and an oversized navy-and-white striped sweatshirt which has slipped sideways to reveal part of one shoulder. No bra strap, Georgie notices. Now she's up close, she reminds Georgie of that Australian singer. What's her name? Kylie. That's it. Kylie Minogue.

'Carrie, from next door.' The woman holds out a hand and Georgie takes it. She feels all of a dither. 'It's Georgie, isn't it? I don't think we've met properly before.' Then, before Georgie can answer, she glances towards the hallway. 'I'm sorry, I'm disturbing your meal.'

She can obviously smell the fish and chips. Georgie hopes Carrie doesn't think she exists on takeaway meals. Well, so what if she does?

'No, no, I'm quite finished.' She stands a little to one side, hesitating as she remembers the clothes airer standing in the kitchen with her smalls drying on it. 'Did you want to come in?'

Georgie's memory fastens on Sonny and his virtual explorations on her behalf, using his father's computer. Has his mother found out and come to take Georgie to task over it? She looks friendly but that could change any minute now.

'No, I won't stop. It's just that Greg and I – Greg's my

husband – are holding a little get-together, next Saturday evening. Just nibbles and drinks, that sort of thing, and we wondered if you'd like to come round?'

Georgie's hand flies to her chest. 'Me? Really? Why?'

'Well...' Carrie glances at her feet then back at Georgie. 'We were saying we hardly know anyone in this street, and that's our fault. We shout "Good morning" as we rush by and that's about it.' She laughs, a bit awkwardly. 'Sonny said you live alone, and I didn't even realise that. So, will you come? We'd like it if you would.'

This is so unexpected, Georgie's face has forgotten how to arrange itself.

'I know exactly what you mean,' she says, gathering herself. 'I hardly know the neighbours either.' *Not that they'd want anything to do with me.* 'Your Sonny's a nice lad, though. Always passes the time of day.' If his mother knows he's been in her flat, she's not letting on. This is not the time to mention it.

'He's done better than me, then.' Carrie smiles. 'So, shall we see you next Saturday? About seven?'

Georgie nods, and smiles. 'Yes, thank you. I'll put it on my calendar, right away.'

Georgie doesn't take in much of *Emmerdale*, or *Corrie*. She's too busy thinking how strange life is, and how it can turn on a sixpence.

FORTY-EIGHT

THE LONDON EVENING STANDARD
Thursday 17th September 2020

The inquest on Isaac Jason Malone was held on Tuesday 1st
September 2020 at St Pancras Coroner's Court, Camley Street,
Kings Cross, London N1C 4PP.
Mr Malone, 40, single, late of Angel, London Borough of Isling-
ton, was a talented architect, well-respected in his field, and a
key player in a number of award-winning building designs. Mr
Malone died on Sunday 28th July 2019 after being hit by a
Tube train at Blackfriars station on the London Underground.
The circumstances of the death were unclear. An open verdict
was recorded.

Carl holds the two-day-old paper closer and reads the item
again. He'd been flicking idly through the previously unread

paper before throwing it in the recycling bin when the small announcement in the corner of a page caught his eye.

It has to be him. Has to be. *God.* Carl drops into a chair. Poor bloke. What a way to go, however it happened. An open verdict, though? He takes several deep breaths. He feels hot, then chilled, right through. The word 'suicide' writes itself across his mind's eye. But there was no proof of that, apparently.

Now what? Does he tell Ellen, risk pitching her headlong into a chasm of guilt and torment? How would she cope with the knowledge that Matt – Isaac – was, in the end, killed by a Tube train? Who knows what mental damage this sinister link to her former troubles might inflict? And besides, once Ellen knows her sister's former boyfriend is dead, the dilemma as to whether to confess all to Rosanna will surely resurface.

So, no. He can't tell her. Perhaps he will, some time in the future. Just not now.

Another secret. Another lie – but only by omission. Is that better or worse? He has no idea.

FORTY-NINE
ELLEN, THREE MONTHS LATER

My sister and I are sitting side by side on the window seat in the living room of her new home. Elizabeth sleeps in her baby nest on the sofa nearby. She makes tiny whimpering sounds as she sleeps. We twist sideways, the better to watch the ever-changing colour of the sea and the boats in the harbour being buffeted by the autumn winds.

Rosanna is renting the cottage from Lowena, the owner of the shop where Rosanna used to work. Along with a couple of other properties she owns, this one was a holiday let, until Lowena decided it would be perfect for Rosanna and her daughter.

My sister couldn't believe her luck. She could have stayed at the farmhouse for as long as she liked; Sarah and Jay said they'd love to have her and the baby – Chloe especially would be thrilled – and they have plenty of space. But having her own place was always the plan, and it's right for her.

The pink-painted cottage is tucked in amongst similar dwellings on a narrow, twisty street that rises with perilous steepness from the main street. The room where we are now is on the first floor, having been set up that way to take advantage of the view. Behind it is a kitchen/dining room. On the floor below are two small bedrooms and a bathroom, and there's a walled garden at the back, big enough for a toddler to play in. Perfect, as Lowena said.

Rosanna still sees Sarah and Jay all the time, as the glamping idea is back on the agenda and she's working with them to get the business on its feet. Once the season begins, she'll handle the marketing side and generally help to run things.

So, my sister has a home and a job, as well as a gorgeous baby girl. She also has a boyfriend – okay, that might be me getting ahead of myself as, according to her, David is just a mate. *That old chestnut*, as Carl would say. But after Matt, it's not surprising Rosanna is being circumspect where her love life is concerned. Or maybe it is – this is not like my sister at all, or it never was before. But I guess being a parent gives you a different perspective.

A self-declared city girl through and through, Rosanna has apparently chucked all that out of the window to settle in a Cornish fishing village. For some reason, I find this funny.

I give a little laugh as I think of it now.

'What?' Rosanna looks at me curiously.

'Oh, nothing.'

'You're mad, you are.'

'I know. You said that once before. A long while back.'

Rosanna grins. 'Just goes to show, then.'

'Goes to show what?'

'That I was right.'

'Which obviously you always are.'

'Yep.'

This little exchange whisks me back to our Bexleyheath days, the way we bantered and joshed and bickered with one another constantly. I like the reminder. It sends a smile all the way through me, like drinking hot chocolate on a cold winter's day.

Rosanna slides off the window seat to tuck the baby's blanket over her toes where she's wriggled free, then sits down on the sofa beside Elizabeth, keeping one hand on top of the blanket.

'I like your Carl,' she says. 'He's a sweet guy. Thinks the world of you, that's obvious.'

A smile spreads across my face at the sudden mention of Carl. He's in Guernsey this week, visiting his father, and already I'm missing him like crazy. That's why I came to Cornwall, to help take the edge off.

'I know. He is pretty special.'

'Where did you say you met him?'

I didn't say, as Rosanna well knows. 'At a Tube station, if you must know.'

'Where? Which station?'

Trust my sister to want chapter and verse. Well, it was only a matter of time. A series of names runs through my brain. And then, because nothing else is possible, I say, 'Maystone Road.'

Rosanna looks at me in disbelief. 'Maystone Road? Are you sure? I've never heard of it.'

'No, I don't suppose you have.'

Rosanna gives me a funny look. Thankfully, she doesn't pursue the subject.

I happened to be in the Maystone Road area a couple of weeks back, and walked along, past the rust-coloured door. Okay, that's a lie. It was no accident I was in the area. I went on purpose to see if the place existed, in case I'd imagined the whole thing. I didn't tell Carl, though. It was real enough, of course. Somebody – from the underground authorities, obviously – had fixed a metal grill across the door, a small version of the big one across the old entrance to the main station. Sealed it off forever. *Best thing*, I thought.

The sky darkens. The wind picks up and hurls raindrops at the window like a handful of gravel.

'Shall we have tea and crumpets?' Rosanna says. 'I could just fancy something toasty.'

'Ooh, yes. It's definitely crumpet weather.'

We giggle at this. Rosanna stands up, then seems to change her mind and sits down again, her face suddenly serious.

'Ell, if ever you want to talk, like, properly, it's cool. We can do that. Any time.'

She doesn't elaborate – she doesn't need to. My heart hitches as I realise we know each other that well, despite our differences.

'You mean talk about Mum and Dad,' I say. It isn't a question.

'Yes, them. I can handle it, so you don't need to worry.'

These are brave words from Rosanna. She doesn't really want to talk about our parents and the tragic accident that ripped them from us. She may have changed in other ways but not about this.

But she will do it, for me.

'Ell?'

'I don't think so. One day, maybe.' I pause. 'As it happens, Aunt Margaret asked me the same thing when I was up there. She was dead relieved when I said no, I could tell.' I give a little laugh. 'She never was one for raking over the past.'

'And you're okay with that?'

'Totally.' I smile.

Rosanna studies me closely to see if I'm telling the truth. Her eyes soften as she sees that I am.

'Talking's overrated anyway, if you ask me,' she says.

'It wouldn't change anything.'

'No.'

We let the silence fall. Rosanna examines her nails, frowns, and picks up an emery board from amongst the clutter on the coffee table, applying it rigorously, with great concentration.

'Remembering the old days, though,' I say, sounding as if I'm seventy or something. 'That's different. Sharing the memories, the happy ones, keeping them alive. That's okay, isn't it?'

'Yep, that's okay.' She looks up from her filing. 'Except...'

'Except what?'

'Well, you know when you think you remember something from way back when you were a kid, and then next time you think about it, you remember it all wrong. Or you could have remembered it wrong the first time, of course, in which case—'

'—you go back to the beginning and start again. Simple.' *As if calling up a memory was ever simple.*

Rosanna's face lights up. 'Exactly.'

'We should remember together,' I say. 'Your version and my version, and see who gets it right.'

'How we will we know which of us is right?'

'We won't.'

'It won't matter, though, will it?'

My heartbeat picks up speed, my nerves take flight. I wait until the feeling passes. Then I smile. 'No, I don't suppose it will.'

A LETTER FROM THE AUTHOR

Dear reader,

Thank you so much for reading *The Girl in the Dark*. I hope you enjoyed Ellen's story, along with Rosanna's and Carl's. If you want to join other readers in hearing all about my new releases and bonus content, you can sign up for my newsletter.

www.stormpublishing.co/deirdre-palmer

If you enjoyed this book and could spare a few moments to leave a review that would be hugely appreciated. Even a short review can make all the difference in encouraging a reader to discover my books for the first time. Thank you so much!

My initial idea for the book began, as it often does, with a place. Ever since I heard about the 'ghost stations' of the London Underground, I've been intrigued by this hidden world below the city streets and thought it would make a suitably creepy setting for the right story.

In case you didn't know, there are around forty abandoned underground stations, all with a story to tell. These spooky stations with their bricked-up tunnels came about because they weren't successful as part of the Tube network, and were either relocated or abandoned altogether. One of the best-known is Down Street, in between Hyde Park Corner and what is now Green Park, which was closed in 1932 due to low passenger numbers. Down Street briefly came back into its own in 1939 when Winston Churchill and his War Cabinet met in its forgotten chambers.

Strand Station, later renamed Aldwych, ended up as the only station on a useless spur of the Piccadilly line. Its only real usefulness was to house the Elgin Marbles during the Blitz.

The traces of all these stations remain if you know where to look, the architecture of the underground forever imprinted on the streets in which they stand. Some are open to the public and you can book tours, or you can take a virtual tour, as I did for the purpose of writing *The Girl in the Dark*. Or you can become an urban explorer like Carl, and simply hack your way in – but I didn't tell you that, right?

Maystone Road station is not a real place. It exists only in my imagination and hopefully now in yours. Any mistakes in the book about Tube stations, past or present, are entirely my own, or the facts have been altered to suit the story.

Do stay in touch through the links below – I'd love to hear from you.

Deirdre

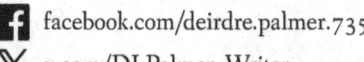 facebook.com/deirdre.palmer.735

x.com/DLPalmer_Writer

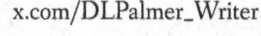 amazon.com/author/3cxx8bE

ACKNOWLEDGMENTS

With thanks to Kathryn Taussig and the rest of the wonderful team at Storm for their superb guidance and attention to detail.

I'd also like to thank the many friends who take such a keen interest in my writing and keep me going all the way.

Above all, thanks to my nearest and dearest – Michael, Christopher and Luke – for their unfailing support and postings on Facebook, complete with slogans such as 'This is my mum's book!'